T0319126

Books by Dane McCaslin

The Proverbial Crime Mysteries
A Bird in the Hand
When the Cat's Away
You Can Lead a Horse to Water

The Two Sisters Pet Valet Mysteries
Doggone Dead*
Cat's Meow*

Coming in 2021
Playing Possum*

*Published by Kensington Publishing Corp.

Cat's Meow

Dane McCaslin

LYRICAL UNDERGROUND
Kensington Publishing Corp.
www.kensingtonbooks.com

LYRICAL PRESS BOOKS are published by

Kensington Publishing Corp.
119 West 40th Street
New York, NY 10018

All Kensington titles, imprints, and distributed lines are available at special quantity discounts for bulk purchases for sales promotion, premiums, fund-raising, educational, or institutional use.

Special book excerpts or customized printings can also be created to fit specific needs. For details, write or phone the office of the Kensington Sales Manager: Kensington Publishing Corp., 119 West 40th Street, New York, NY 10018. Attn. Sales Department. Phone: 1-800-221-2647.

Lyrical Press and Lyrical Press logo Reg. U.S. Pat. & TM Off.

First Electronic Edition: March 2021
ISBN-13: 978-1-5161-1015-5 (ebook)
ISBN-10: 1-5161-1015-3 (ebook)

First Print Edition: March 2021
ISBN-13: 978-1-5161-1018-6
ISBN-10: 1-5161-1018-1

Printed in the United States of America

This book is dedicated to the many volunteers at pet shelters across our country. Thank you all for the wonderful service and love you provide to the animals you serve.

Chapter 1

"Run it by me one more time, Sis. Who's been invited to this get-together?" Nora Goldstein, my best friend since kindergarten and the closest thing I had to a real sister, was sitting cross-legged on one of her overstuffed sofas, working on one nail (fake, of course) as though her life depended on it. I watched as she held up the nail tip for inspection and then began sawing at it again in earnest. I'd never worn anything false in my entire life, unless you counted the time I stuffed wadded-up tissues in my bra for the eighth-grade dance.

"Hang on a minute and I'll double-check."

As co-owners of Two Sisters Pet Valet Services, we'd received an invitation to the annual Clear the Shelter fundraiser, a really big deal in our town. Picking up my newish smartphone, I opened the Google search engine and carefully tapped in with one finger: Greater Portland Shelter Association. A colorful banner featuring adorable dogs and cats floated across the top of the page, their cute little faces making me smile.

"What's making you grin like the Cheshire cat?" Nora glanced up from her nails, a tiny pucker between her carefully shaped eyebrows. "See any good-lookin' men on that page?"

I ignored the comment and tapped on the menu icon. The event's list of participants was there, and I spotted our names in the lower third.

"Looks like Miss Oregon will be there, along with the mayor, a few television personalities, and a handful of minor Portland celebrities." I held up my phone for her to see the screen. "And us, of course."

It felt like a dream to see my name there alongside those of well-known Portlandians. Gwen Franklin, retired teacher, mingling with local celebrities!

Nora snorted as she leaned in closer to inspect her nail, but I could tell that she was pleased. Our pet-care business was small but thriving, thanks to word-of-mouth advertising and the fact Nora lived directly across the street from Portland Pooch Park. Being included in this annual fundraiser was proof that we were making a mark in the local pet scene.

"I think I remember hearing something about the glorious Babs Prescott doing some of the presentations, but that could be wishful thinking." Nora shot me an amused glance as she said this, and it was my turn to snort. Babs was only glorious to those who mattered, namely herself.

Babs Prescott, one half of the evening news team on the local station, had the requisite big hair and big teeth, plus a big personality to boot. The problem with her, though, was she was a legend in her own mind. Whenever she appeared on television or out in public, I did my best to avoid her. I tended to break out in hives around folks like her.

"So, you gonna try to sit at her table?" Nora glanced at me as she tucked the emery board back into her clear makeup bag. "Or is that a definite 'no' I hear?"

"What do you think, smarty-pants?" I crossed both arms over my chest and scowled at the image on my phone's small screen. Even in miniature, Babs managed to appear colossal, filling the display with her big, toothy smile. Of course, it could have simply been the way she'd turned to face the camera. With big hair and even bigger, uh, female assets, she made sure she was the center of attention whenever an opportunity presented itself.

Like the time she'd come to the school I taught at to raise awareness about the pitfalls of social media. Needless to say, by the time she'd finished her speech at the assembly, I was *not* her biggest fan.

Of course, it might have had something to do with the way she managed to turn the presentation into a slide show starring none other than a certain blond news anchor, and some of the images were, in my opinion, not appropriate for the younger crowd. Judging by the frequent outbursts of whistles and catcalls, I'd say I was right. When the principal decided to shut the whole thing down and send the students back to class, I was relieved the show was over.

I was also very irritated because she'd pre-empted a great lesson on rhetorical devices I had worked on for days.

"Sure you're not jealous?"

Nora's voice was teasing, but I wasn't in the mood. Just thinking about Babs Prescott was enough to turn me into a grump the size of Mount Hood.

"Positive," I said firmly. "Now, what's up with next week's schedule?"

"It's on my iPad." Nora unwound herself from the sofa and stood up, lifting both arms over her head and arching her back in a feline stretch. "By the way, is Brent back from his trip down south?"

Brent Mayfair, one of my many ex-students and our official dog walker, had taken a road trip down through California with his girlfriend, Rachel, and precious dog, Aggie, in tow. I missed him horribly, but only because I'd been stuck with most of the dog-walking duties while Nora took on the various pet-sitting assignments. Too much of Brent on any given day was grounds for sainthood.

"The last text I got from Rachel said they should be back in town sometime late tomorrow." I glanced at my phone and opened the message. "Says here they're staying at Mount Shasta tonight."

"Nice." Nora nodded in approval as she walked over to her desk and retrieved the tablet. "I'm glad to see them having fun together."

I laughed. "And I'd love to have been a fly on the wall when Rachel told her folks she was going on vacation with Brent."

"Right? Especially that tough cop dad of hers." Nora curled back up on the sofa, reaching up to pat her blond curls. After a disastrous escapade with a perm-happy hairdresser last year, she was finally able to go out in public without a scarf or a hat.

"Speaking of tough, what's the latest on Marcus?"

Nora tossed her head, losing one hoop earring in the process. "If I never see him again, it won't be too soon for me."

Same song, second verse. Or perhaps it was verse five. Nora and Marcus Avery, her on-again, off-again beau, were the talk of the luxury apartment building where she resided. I made sure to drop a few juicy tidbits now and then for the new concierge to share with the other residents. I saw it as my duty to liven up the place, especially since the average age of those who lived there was well over sixty-five. I saw it as my contribution to the collective heart and circulation health of Nora's neighbors.

"Well, you'll have to see him tomorrow." I scooted closer to her so I could see the iPad's screen. "Isn't he coming by to drive us to the fundraiser?"

"We could Uber it."

Taking an Uber was something of a private joke between us, thanks to Brent and his one and only attempt at being an Uber driver. We liked to say we'd single-handedly saved the good folks of Portland when we hired him and got him off the road.

"Or I could drive. Of course," I added doubtfully, "I'm not sure my car will start. It's been in the garage since I retired last year."

"That's all right. I'll handle Marcus."

Smiling, I read over the upcoming pet-walking and -sitting jobs. It was clear our business was growing, and it was probably time to hire another walker. I wasn't fond of the end result of a walk—having to clean up after the little darlings. My own dog, Hercule, was another matter. He was home at the moment, enjoying the good weather and barking at the squirrels.

"Have you thought about taking on another employee to help Brent with all the dog-walking jobs?" I glanced up from the tablet and swiveled around to face her. "Maybe Rachel?"

"Maybe. Isn't she still in junior college?"

"Yes, but only two days a week. And the dog-walking job she had last year ended a few months ago, so she might consider joining us."

"I'm sure Brent would love that, but it's tough enough keeping the kid focused on his duties as it is."

"Rachel wouldn't mess around." I sounded more confident than I felt, but I was determined to get myself free of the walking end of our business. "That girl has more common sense than most folks twice her age."

Nora nodded. "True. Particularly one certain private investigator I know. He's such a nitwit, Gwen." She shook her head in disgust. "Why I even bother with that man, I have no idea."

Marcus Avery was a private detective whose business had been bankrolled by her. I hadn't liked that arrangement then, and I didn't like it now. The less my pal was connected to him, the better off she'd be. Of course, she listened to me about as well as Hercule did whenever he spotted a cat in our yard. The difference was that my dog was probably trainable. Nora definitely wasn't.

"Amen to that," I muttered as I looked at my phone. I'd received another text, this time from Brent. "Hang on a sec. I need to check this message from the boy wonder himself."

Hey Miss F We're having a good time except maybe Aggie since she got stung by a bee. OK see you tomorrow.

Dear goodness. Had the boy been absent the day I taught punctuation? How he'd managed to graduate was a puzzle, but he had, and now he and I were coworkers in one of those weird universal flips.

"Well? What'd our resident genius have to say?" Nora's words might have been sardonic, but her tone was soft. She'd really taken to Brent, something that never ceased to amaze me, especially since I'd never known her to suffer fools gladly. That might have had something to do with her five (or was it six?) marriages.

"They're enjoying themselves, but it sounds like Aggie might be under the weather a bit. Blame it on a bee."

"Oh, poor baby." Nora grabbed the tablet and began scrolling. "Can dogs die from bee stings?"

I shrugged. "If she has an allergy, she probably could. Brent didn't seem too upset about it, though."

"Wonder if Marcus has any allergies?"

I stared at her, one hand on my chest. I'd love to say "on my bosom," but that part of my anatomy had recently begun its own trip south and hadn't returned. "I hope you're kidding."

"About what? I only said—"

"Oh, forget it. You'd better play nice tomorrow, though. We might need a ride home as well."

She wrinkled her nose at me but turned her attention back to the tablet.

I absentmindedly reached down to pat Hercule and then remembered I'd left him at the small bungalow he shared with me. I'd finally gotten brave enough to have a doggy door installed after a couple of break-ins last year. Of course, one was perpetrated by my best friend, trying to prove a point, but I still hadn't wanted to give anyone else carte blanche to enter my house. Waking up to Nora skulking in my dark living room had been more than enough to turn my gray hair white.

Hercule was something special, though, and well worth a doggy door. He'd come into my life one rainy night and had never left. With a sleek black coat and a white front and paws, he looked as dapper as the fictional detective Hercule Poirot, hence the name. Having a dog could be a chore at times, but I wouldn't have traded Herc for anything in the world.

"Earth to Gwen—come in, space cadet." Nora snapped her fingers in front of my face, and I jumped. "I asked if you wanted to take a walk to The Friendly Bean."

"The Friendly Bean?" My mind was still on break-ins and bee stings. "Right now?"

"Yes, Gwen. Now." Nora mimed drinking a cup of coffee. "We need caffeine, and lots of it."

"Sure. I guess." I pointed to the iPad. "Shouldn't we make up our minds about another employee?"

"We can do that on the way." Nora jumped up and headed down the hallway toward her bedroom. "Give me a sec, all right?"

I sighed and settled back on the sofa. A Nora "sec" could be anywhere from two minutes to thirty, depending on how dolled-up she was getting. My friend loved heels, the higher the better, and any clothing made from stretchy material. Her typical outfit of black, yoga-type leggings and neon-colored tight tops was in direct contrast to my preference for cotton capris and loose, flowy shirts.

And Birkenstocks. I did love my sandals, no matter the weather. Rain in the forecast? Add thick socks. Snow? Even thicker socks. Going by the number of similarly shod feet I saw around town, I wasn't the only one who felt this way.

"Hurry up," I called out. "You've got me craving a latte. And a croissant."

Or three. I loved my food as well, that was for sure, and our local coffee hangout made the best croissants this side of the Columbia River: buttery, flakey, and absolutely delicious.

As I waited for her, I idly thumbed through my social media accounts. I'd only recently joined Instagram and Facebook; those seemed to be the common platforms my ex-students used. Call me nosy or unable to let go, but I loved being included in their postings and commentary. Seeing the pictures of their own sweet kiddos made me feel nostalgic.

And old.

I was about to close my Instagram account when something in the feed caught my eye: a picture of none other than Miss Babs Prescott herself, one tanned arm slung over the shoulders of a sullen-looking Shelby Tucker. Shelby, also a former student, was a journalist with the *Portland Tribune* and my go-to for help with all things digital.

"Catching flies, are we?"

Nora, dressed in all-black Lycra, came teetering into the front room in the highest pair of heels I'd ever seen.

I snapped my mouth shut and silently held out my phone to her. Taking it, she peered at the screen, and her own mouth gaped open in shock.

"Holy guacamole, Sis. What in the world was Shelby doing with that piece of work?"

I shrugged. "No idea. I'm thinking we need to give the girl a call."

"Indeed we do. And there's no time like the present." Reaching into the front of her top, Nora pulled out a slim cell phone and began scrolling through her contacts.

I had to shake my head. Why a woman of fifty-something would carry a cell phone in her bra was beyond me, especially since her clothing was usually tight enough to reveal even the smallest freckle.

"Shelby, this is Nora Goldstein." Nora gave me a thumbs-up, perching on the edge of the sofa as she spoke. "Listen, Miss Franklin saw something on Instagram that has us both a tad curious." She paused, listening, one eyebrow lifted slightly. "That's right. Any idea why she would post that?" Nora's eyebrows rose and her eyes widened as she listened to Shelby's response. "I see. Well, isn't *that* a hoot, considering the source. I wouldn't give any credence to a word that woman says." Another pause.

I could hear Shelby's voice clearly, although I couldn't make out anything she said. Maybe I needed to have my prized supersonic teacher's ears checked.

"Well, keep your chin up, girlie. Karma can be a powerful you know what in the you know where."

By the time Nora had ended the conversation and replaced the cell in her secret carrying case, I was wound up tighter than an eight-day clock.

"And? What did she have to say?"

"You're not gonna believe it."

"Until I know what it is, I have no idea whether I will or not." I gestured impatiently. "Spit it out already, slowpoke."

"Don't get your panties in a wad, woman. I'll tell you on the way to get coffee."

"Fine," I grumbled. "And don't forget we still need to discuss hiring another dog walker, so get busy talking."

Nora, much to my chagrin, chattered about insignificant topics until we exited the lobby of the luxury apartment building.

When I was beginning to think I couldn't stand it any longer, she reached over and clutched my arm, stopping me in mid-shuffle. I was wearing Birkenstocks, after all, and that required a slight toe curl to keep them in place as I walked.

"Okay, Sis, listen to this. The Wonderbra Woman of television has dissed our sweet Shelby so badly she's considering murder."

"Who is? Wonderbra or Shelby?" I couldn't picture Shelby killing anyone, not really, and I certainly could not picture Babs Prescott doing so either. It might wrinkle her Botoxed face and designer dresses.

Nora poked me in the side irritably. "Shelby, silly. Babs had the nerve to suggest Shelby needed to book herself into a spa for a makeover. She even suggested one, some place called the Fabulous Fattie Farm."

I had to hand it to her: Babs certainly had some nerve. Knowing her, she'd probably flashed her teeth and wiggled all the way through the conversation. No wonder Shelby had been glaring in the Instagram post.

"Well, I don't blame her for being upset." I nodded a greeting to a pair of whispering women and pulled my arm from Nora's grasp. "And let's start walking. People are beginning to stare."

Shelby, in my opinion, was far from overweight. Sure, she'd never be found on a catwalk or wear a size triple zero, but she definitely wasn't in need of a makeover. What had possessed Babs to make such an idiotic suggestion?

As if reading my mind, Nora said, "Apparently, Shelby was at the state capitol at the same time Babs and her cronies were, covering a new bill about food labeling. Isn't that the craziest thing you've ever heard?"

"I'm not sure I'd call it crazy. More like commonsensical." We'd reached the corner across from the coffee shop, and a light breeze coming in from the river ruffled my hair. "Don't you want to know what's in the food you're eating?"

"Of course I do." Nora spoke impatiently, jabbing one finger on the button to activate the WALK signal. "What I'm talking about is why those two were sharing the same oxygen, Babs and Shelby. I call that crazy."

"Probably because both of them are in the news business. You know, television and newspaper?"

"I know that, goofy. I meant I've never heard of the Great One actually speaking with other reporters before. Something must've happened to cause that. Or not happened. Maybe she didn't get her daily dose of public admiration or something."

The light turned green, and the sign lit up, allowing us to cross safely. I trudged along as I normally did, but Nora was giving every driver an eyeful of undulating black Lycra and strutting heels. I ignored her, hoping no one could tell we were together. She could be an entire headline herself, and I wanted no part of it. Retired teachers didn't cavort with people like that.

"Hey, you," she called out loudly, and I groaned, turning around to watch her prance the last few steps. "Mind waiting up for me?"

"Trust me, there are times I wish I didn't have to." I headed for The Friendly Bean's entrance, stepping aside to let a giggling gaggle of teens exit. "Do you always have to walk that way when we're in public?"

Nora preened, patting her curls and putting one hand on an outthrust hip. I held back an eye roll, pushing her inside ahead of me. Apparently, Babs Prescott wasn't the only publicity hound in these parts.

"And deprive the good folks of Portland? I think not." She grinned over her shoulder, dropping one eyelid in a playful wink. "Now, how 'bout that coffee?"

I snagged an empty table near the rear of the café while Nora placed our orders. In our town, coffee was almost a religion, one I tended to follow with unwavering devotion. I liked my coffee dark and black and hot, although I'd recently ventured into the froufrou land of cappuccinos and mochas. By the time Nora had swayed back to the table, carefully balancing a pair of steaming lattes, I was ready for my daily dose of caffeine.

"The barista says she'll bring our croissants over when they're heated." Nora took a sip from her coffee cup and closed her eyes. "Ah. That hits the spot. Nothing like a latte made with almond milk."

I paused, holding my mug in midair. "Please don't tell me you put that stuff in my drink."

Nora merely smiled.

"Fine. I'll handle it this time." I glared at her over the rim of my cup. "Next time I'll order my own coffee, thank you very much."

"It's much better for you, Gwennie. You know, healthy and all that jazz. Don't you want to live to be a hundred?"

I snorted. "Not if it means drinking milk made from nuts. If God meant us to drink almond milk, he'd have given them little almond boobs."

"Here're your croissants." The barista slid a thick white plate between Nora and me, her eyes wide as she stared at me. "Miss Franklin? Is that you?"

I could have kicked myself for that last comment about almonds and body parts. Forcing a smile onto my mortified face, I looked at the young woman, trying to recall her name. "Yes, it is. And it's Kate—Katelyn, right?"

She beamed at me, and I gave a small sigh of relief. I'd had well over one hundred students per year throughout my twenty-plus years of teaching, and it was almost impossible to remember each and every name. Unless, of course, they'd done something to stand out, like plagiarizing a paper or leaving tacks on my chair.

"I'm getting ready to graduate from college." She leaned one hip against the table and smiled proudly. "And guess what? I'm going to be an English teacher like you."

"Oh, honey, you're a brave soul." Nora reached over and patted Katelyn's arm. "Look at Miss Franklin here. That's what happens after being in high school for fifty years."

"It was twenty." I spoke through gritted teeth, my lips curled up in what I hoped would pass for a smile. "And ignore my friend here. She doesn't get out that often. Issues, you know." I tapped the side of my head.

Katelyn flashed a look of sympathy at Nora. "That's all right. My grandma's got that too, the disease that makes you forget your name and say all kinds of crazy things." She glanced over her shoulder at the front counter. "Whoops, I'd better get back. It was great talking to you, Miss Franklin."

"Well, thanks a bunch, best friend." Nora leaned over and snagged a steaming croissant, juggling it between her hands. "You made me sound like a raving imbecile."

"And you made me sound like a drooling old hag, so we're even." I held up my coffee cup. "Here's to another fifty years of friendship."

We clinked our mugs together, smiling at one another with real affection. We'd been inseparable since kindergarten, and nothing as petty as name-calling would ever break us apart. At least it hadn't yet.

We were in the midst of discussing Rachel as a possible employee when the television hanging on the wall behind us flashed the latest news bulletin from around the greater Portland area. Channel 12's "News at Hand" was the best way to find out what was happening in our part of the city and usually focused on local farmer's markets and craft fairs. I glanced causally at the screen, waiting to see what they'd say about the Clear the Shelter event.

The first item, however, caused me to gasp and Nora to sputter around a mouthful of croissant, sending a shower of crumbs across the table.

"We begin this broadcast with sad news." The earnest young man seated at the news desk looked appropriately solemn, and I sipped my latte as I waited to hear the bulletin. "Shortly after a press conference at the state capitol today, the body of news anchor Babs Prescott was discovered in a nearby parking garage. This is a breaking story, and we'll bring you all the details as soon as they come in. In other news, members of the local garden club . . ."

We looked at each other and said in one voice, "Shelby."

Chapter 2

I stared across at Nora, my voice filled with horror. "You don't think she actually did it, do you?"

Nora's face was grim as she extracted her cell phone and hit REDIAL. "I wouldn't blame her one bit, but I sincerely doubt it. She's too smart to throw her life away on someone like that." She waited for Shelby to answer, her mouth a thin line of unease. "Shelby, it's Nora Goldstein again."

My heart began to race as I watched Nora's expression change from concern to shock as she listened.

Finally, she said, "Don't you worry, girlie. I'll call Marcus, and we'll get right on it, okay? You hang in there. And give me a call if you need something."

She slowly slipped the cell back into her top and looked across at me, her expression somber.

I was absolutely dumbstruck: Shelby Tucker a killer?

"She found the body." Nora's tone was as dark as her words. "And you know what that means."

I nodded soberly. "The person closest to the crime scene is usually the suspect." I paused for a moment, thinking. "Do you think someone overheard that conversation about the fat farm?"

"I'd say that was likely." Nora tore off a piece from the last croissant and chewed it slowly, a thoughtful expression on her face. "And obviously they told the cops about it as well." She shook her head, sending her curls bouncing like deranged corkscrews. "It must have been one doozy of a discussion."

"So you think Marcus will be able to help?"

"Possibly. He helped me last year, right?" Nora took a sip of her latte and made a face. "This is cold." She inclined her head at my cup. "How about yours?"

I took a small drink. "It's cooled down, but it's still drinkable. Do you want me to ask Katelyn to heat yours up?"

"No thanks. I'll leave it. Besides," she grinned across at me, "it was the croissants I really wanted."

I looked at the empty plate. "Obviously." I used one finger to pick up a few of the crumbs, popping them into my mouth. "What's not so clear from the report is how Babs was killed. That's the first thing we need to find out."

"Text Rachel."

Rachel's father was a homicide investigator with the Portland Police Department. We'd first met him during an earlier investigation that involved Nora and, to some extent, Marcus, Brent, and me.

"If I do, I'm going to offer her the job before I ask her to start digging for information."

"Of course." Nora's expression was pure innocence. "That's exactly what I was going to suggest."

"Uh huh." I shot her a sardonic look and then glanced back at the television screen, where a smiling troop of Girls Scouts held up boxes of cookies for the camera. "It looks like there's nothing else about Babs. Let's head back to your place so we can make a battle plan to help poor Shelby." I shook my head. "I'd be barking at the walls if someone was blaming me for something I hadn't done."

"Don't forget we've got a business to run as well." Nora stacked our cups and plate in the tub near the door. "Hopefully, we'll be able to get everything taken care of between the two of us."

After I'd taken early retirement from my teaching career, Nora had decided I needed something else to fill my time. Taking care of pets seemed as good as any place to begin, and so we'd started Two Sisters Pet Valet Services. I'd been hesitant at first, especially since I'd always suffered from allergies, but between Benadryl and Hercule, I'd developed a tolerance of sorts. Cats still did a number on my eyes, though, so Nora or Brent handled those jobs. For the most part, though, I was fine.

"And the Clear the Shelter event tomorrow evening as well."

The temperature had dropped while we'd sat inside The Friendly Bean, and I wished I had worn a heavier jacket instead of my favorite long cardigan. Some climates might let folks collect a variety of light clothing or swimsuits to wear, but here in the great northwest we were all about our coats and boots. And Birkenstocks.

"I wonder who they'll get to replace Babs at the event."

Good question. There would undoubtedly be no shortage of those who'd want their fifteen minutes in the spotlight. It wasn't for me, though. I'd always been fine with an audience of thirty or so teens in various stages of wakefulness, but speaking to a crowd of adults was definitely not my thing.

"You should volunteer," I said.

Beside me, Nora gave a distinctively sarcastic snort.

"I'm serious. You'd be great with a crowd. Besides, they'd be so busy gawking at your outfit they wouldn't pay attention to a word you said."

Nora could still run, even in heels. Flopping sandals, unfortunately, weren't conducive to a speedy getaway.

* * * *

Back at my bungalow, with Herc sprawled cozily across my feet, I thought about what had happened that day. No one deserved to be killed, not even a showboat like Babs Prescott, but no one deserved to be falsely accused of the crime either. Poor Shelby. The last thing we'd heard, she'd been let go with a warning not to leave the Portland city limits.

"I have no idea how I'm going to do my job," she'd wailed over the phone. "The paper sends me all over the place to cover the news."

Nora had called her after we'd returned to her apartment, out of breath from running like a pair of loons, but definitely warmed up.

"Maybe they'll let you take some vacation days," Nora had suggested. "Only until this mess gets sorted out." She'd slid a glance at me before adding, "Or I can call Marcus. I'm sure he'd be more than happy to help you."

I'd rolled my eyes at her words. Shelby needed someone who could dig through information for answers, not a plaid-wearing wannabe Sam Spade.

Shelby's reply had burst from the phone, causing Nora to hold it away from her ear, grimacing as she did. I wouldn't have been in Shelby's shoes for all the gold in the world, and it certainly looked like it was going to cost some gold—or at least a few thousand dollars—to straighten out this debacle.

Sighing, I reached over and gave Herc's ears a quick pat. At least I had him in my corner. As long as I kept him in kibble and treats, he'd back me up from here to the moon. Shelby had no one. Picking up the top volume from a towering pile of "to be read" books, I forgot about reality for a while and followed the canny Miss Marple around St. Mary Mead as she solved yet another baffling mystery.

It was while Herc and I were on our way home from our evening walk that I heard someone calling my name. Turning, I spotted a tall, well-built man, one hand wrapped in two leashes and the other lifted in greeting. My cheeks grew warm in spite of the cooling breeze as I waggled my fingers in return.

What *was* the man's name? My pulse began to pick up as I wracked my brains for a hint. I'd met him briefly during a walk last year and had admired the two golden retrievers that had exchanged sniffs and tail wags with Herc, not to mention the handsome man holding their leashes. Maybe I could get around it by falling back on my fail-safe greeting of "Hey, you."

I paused on the sidewalk, holding Herc's leash tightly as I waited for the man to catch up. Could there be anything more awkward than watching someone approach whom you barely know? Thank goodness for the dogs. At least they gave me something on which to focus my gaze.

"It's nice to see you again." I reached out with my free hand and gave each of the retrievers a quick scratch on their ears, buying time before I had to confess that I had no idea what his name was. "Hasn't the weather been nice? It's so nice to be out walking without getting soaked."

"It certainly is *nice*." He gave the inane word a slight inflection, and his eyes twinkled. "Although I might call it 'serendipitous' or 'fabulous.'"

So much for showing off my extensive vocabulary. Heat inched its way up from my neck to my cheeks as a smile played in the corners of his mouth. A rather sensual mouth. A *nice* mouth.

"It's been somewhat of a crazy day so far."

"Really? How so?" Roger—oh, thank the memory gods above—switched the leashes to his other hand as the retrievers and Herc began their ritual circling and sniffing.

"Someone I know, a former student, has been accused of killing Babs Prescott."

There. Once it was out in the open air, it almost sounded ridiculous. Who stood around discussing murder, for Pete's sake?

"Babs Prescott? Is that someone I should know?"

I should have bought a lottery ticket. I'd met the only man in Portland who didn't know who the blond goddess of the airwaves was.

"She's one of the prime-time news anchors—or was—on Channel Thirteen." Seeing he still had no idea who I meant, I added, "You know, the one who's always on those huge bulletin boards around town. Has that big hair and those big, uh, teeth. You might have noticed."

My face was getting warm again. I'd almost said "boobs" but stopped myself in time. Nora was really beginning to rub off on me.

He shook his head almost regretfully. "No, I can't say that I have. And I'd have liked to have seen her big teeth." He flashed a grin at me, displaying his own set of pearly whites. "I'm a retired dentist."

One of the golden retrievers tired of the circling ceremony and flopped on the sidewalk with a loud sigh.

"Well, I'd better get going before I end up carrying these two fellas home. I'd like to know how it turns out for your friend, though. Maybe we could find a spot and talk while these gents run around."

"She's a student, not a friend," I corrected automatically, and my face heated again. "And yes, I'd like that. We could meet up at the Portland Pooch Park."

"Then it's a date." Roger's charming smile was back, and so was my racing pulse. Had he used the "d" word? "Let's say the day after tomorrow around ten. I'll bring the coffee."

"That sounds . . . nice," I replied lamely, and my cheeks burned even hotter.

Herc gave an impatient tug on the leash. Even he was beginning to disapprove of my word choices. Or maybe he was anxious to get home and to his food bowl. With a quick goodbye for Roger and another ear rub for the two dogs, we were off. As flustered as I was feeling at the moment, it was a wonder I hadn't waved a farewell to the dogs and rubbed Roger's ears.

Apparently, Portland had recently installed padded sidewalks. I felt as though I was walking on air the rest of the way home.

* * * *

I'd gone to sleep thinking about Roger and his invitation, wondering if I'd imagined the entire thing, and I was wide awake before the sun came up, thanks to an impatient bladder and an even more impatient dog who wanted his breakfast. At least I didn't have to get up to let Herc outside to do his business anymore, thanks to the doggy door.

Groaning as I felt for my slippers, I tried to think what could have made my legs so sore. It came back to me as I shuffled first to the bathroom and then to the kitchen. Running from Nora might not count as exercise to most people, but it was all I'd had in goodness knew when. Maybe I needed to add some yoga to my daily dog saunter.

I flipped on the radio to the local news station, then filled Herc's food bowl and checked his water. All I needed at the moment was a cup of coffee. I grabbed my favorite coffee mug from the cabinet, ready to enjoy that first cup of the day, when my ears caught Babs's name in the morning report.

Moving as quickly as my sore muscles would allow, I turned up the volume and stood listening, empty mug dangling precariously from one finger.

"Investigators have been working all night on what they're calling 'the suspicious death' of local news anchor Babs Prescott. According to our source, only one person of interest has been identified. While no one has been officially arrested yet, the police department's source has assured the public this will be happening shortly. Earlier this morning, police issued a statement saying, 'We found additional evidence that points us to a motive and means, and we hope to have a person of interest in custody later today.' We'll keep our listeners posted on the latest in this ongoing case. In other news . . ."

I sagged into a kitchen chair, coffee and radio chatter forgotten. Had the police found something that tied Shelby to the killing? I still couldn't believe it. Yes, Babs had been snarky to her, but that was Babs's modus operandi in general. If that was the Portland PD's idea of a motive, they'd need to look at the entire population of Portland. Okay, maybe that was a slight exaggeration, but only slight. Even I hadn't cared for the woman, and I was only a public viewer.

I pulled my cell phone from my worn bathrobe's pocket and thumbed open my contacts list. Shelby's name was at the top of my "favorites" list, put there when I'd experienced the break-ins at my house. She lived not too far from my own neighborhood, and she'd told me to call her whenever I needed help. It seemed to me, though, that she was the one who could use help now. Without another thought, I pressed the icon beside her name and waited for her to answer.

"Shelby Tucker." Her voice was rough in my ear, and I heard the radio news show playing in the background. She'd probably heard the same report I had.

"Shelby? It's Miss Franklin calling." I kept my voice low and soft, something that William Shakespeare referred to as "an excellent thing in women" and that I called my "I'm here to help" voice. "I know it's probably too early to ask how you're doing, but would you like to come over for coffee? I've got a fresh pot made. And I could probably wrangle up a cinnamon roll or two."

There was a moment of silence that made me think she'd either hung up or I'd lost the signal. Finally, I heard her sigh. "Sure. Might as well. It'll most likely be my last cup of coffee as a free woman."

"Now, don't think that way. You know Nora and I, and even Marcus, are working to clear this thing up." I found myself sitting up straight, as if I was behind my desk and Shelby was a student needing comfort. "I'll tell you what. Take a shower, and get some clean clothes on, and get down here pronto. I'll have the coffee ready and waiting."

Was that a sob I heard?

"Yes, ma'am," came the muffled reply, and then the call was disconnected.

Smiling to myself, I scurried back to the bathroom for my own ablutions. If it was war they wanted, then war was what they'd get. Gwen Franklin never backed down from anyone, not even the Portland Police Department.

* * * *

Shelby looked as rough as her voice had sounded. Despite a shower and reasonably clean clothes, she looked as though she'd slept very little, if at all.

I'd decided to hold my consultation in the kitchen. Between the homey scent of coffee and the frozen cinnamon rolls I'd popped into the oven, I hoped Shelby would relax enough to spill every last bean. I'd just poured coffee for both of us when the front door seemed to rattle and then open under its own volition. Nora stood there, framed in morning sunlight that turned her frizzy curls into a blond Brillo pad.

"I see the party's started without me. Well, pour another cup, Sis, and tell me what's going on." She leaned over and gave Herc's ears a friendly rub as he sniffed her feet and wriggled against her legs. "Glad someone's happy to see me."

I looked over at Shelby and rolled my eyes. "Ignore her. I do."

"That's a fine way to speak to your best friend." With a broad grin aimed somewhere between Shelby and me, she sank into a chair with a groan. "I think I'm getting too old for scooters, you know?"

I paused mid-pour, staring at her in shocked silence. "Please don't tell me you rode one of those electric things dressed liked that!" I stared pointedly at her stilettos, a rather lovely black pair with a sassy white bow on top. "One of these days, Nora Goldstein, you're going to trip or fall or something equally disastrous. Why don't you wear flats like the rest of us?"

"Easy." Nora reached out and took her coffee from me. "I can't get a good wiggle going in shoes that look like they'd be right at home in the Dark Ages." It was her turn to stare at my feet, comfortably resting in my favorite Birkenstocks.

"Um, should I go so you two can maybe hash things out?"

I'd almost forgotten Shelby in my surprise at seeing Nora.

"Oh, ignore us." Nora reached over and laid one ringed hand on Shelby's arm. "We've been doing this for half a century." She gave Shelby a firm pat and turned back to me. "So, I take it we're here for a strategy session?"

I nodded. "Absolutely. And I think it might be time to give Rachel a call as well."

"Let's get some particulars written down first. Shelby, you're a journalist. How would you go about taking notes?"

Shelby gave a half smile and pointed to her cell. "I use this baby for nearly everything. It's got an awesome recorder that can pick up the tiniest sound as well as an app that lets me take notes with a stylus."

"Then I nominate you for secretary." Nora gave a brisk nod. "Gwen, you can take care of contacting Rachel, and I'll sit here and think of things for Shelby to write down."

"Absolutely. But, first, cinnamon rolls." I spoke firmly, handing each of my visitors a paper napkin. "I can't think on an empty stomach and besides, I *did* invite Shelby over for coffee."

My veiled comment sailed right over Nora's head. The woman could be as thick as a stack of bricks at times.

"Perfect." Nora beamed at no one in particular. "You'll love Miss Franklin's cinnamon rolls, Shelby. I always say that if she's nothing else, at least she's a great cook." She gave her head a small shake. "Still can't figure out why the woman's never been married."

"Thanks, pal," I said dryly as I donned a pair of quilted oven mitts. "And for your information, I've got a date tomorrow."

My cheeks heated as I slipped the tray of rolls out of the oven. I could have bitten my tongue as soon as the words flew out. A fatal case of shutting the barn door after the horses had left, plain and simple. Trust Nora to get that out of me, though, one way or another.

"Aha! Do tell, and quickly." Nora sat with her chin propped in one hand, a bevy of gold bracelets clanging together as she moved. "I'm dying to hear about your new Romeo."

"He's not my Romeo." I spoke more sharply than I meant to, but I was thoroughly embarrassed. "And maybe we should choose our words more carefully," I added with a slight nod in Shelby's direction.

"That's okay, Miss Franklin." Shelby held out her hand for the plate of steaming cinnamon rolls. "It's not like I'm going to put it in the paper or anything."

"What did I say?" Nora snagged a roll and tore off a large piece, popping it into her mouth. "I only meant—"

"Forget it." I waved her comment off, peering into each coffee mug before I sat. "Anyone need a coffee refill yet?"

We ate in companionable silence for a few minutes as Herc circled the floor underneath the table, hoping for a few crumbs. My mind was divided between a solution for Shelby and my upcoming date (a date!) with Roger, making me feel almost dizzy with the effort.

"You'd think that they'd be looking at folks closest to her." Nora's voice jarred my thoughts and pulled me back to the present. "From what I've heard, Babs Prescott didn't have too many friends in the business. In television, I mean." She gave a quick glance at Shelby.

"I don't think too many people actually liked her," I said. "Dealt with her, yes, but liked her? No." I looked from Nora to Shelby, emphasizing my comments with a decided nod of my head.

Beside me, Shelby gave a grunt of agreement. She certainly didn't seem to have any respect for the newscaster. I took a bite of roll and chewed slowly as I thought over who might have had the most reason to want Babs dead. Judging from what others had said about her, I had a feeling the list was going to be longer than we'd anticipated.

Chapter 3

The three of us sat in silence for a few moments, my last comments hanging in the air between us.

Finally, Nora spoke up, articulating my thoughts exactly. "It makes you wonder if she'd finally done or said something that made her killer mad enough to do her in. By the way, how *did* she die? Shelby, do you know?"

Shelby's cheeks flushed a bright red as she gave a quick shake of her head. I glared at Nora. She'd practically accused Shelby of being on the scene at the time of Babs's murder.

"That was tactful." I reached over and patted Shelby's hand. "And just ignore her, all right? Mrs. Goldstein is used to eating crow."

"Well, she *was* the one who found her." Nora's chin jutted out as she returned my scowl. "I'm only trying to figure out how the woman kicked the bucket, capiche?"

"It's all right," Shelby said. "I knew what you meant. And yes, I think I do. Her face was a funny color and looked all twisted. I'm leaning toward a bad allergic reaction or something, I don't know, like poisoning." She gave a tiny shrug and reached for another cinnamon roll.

"Did you get a good whiff?"

Shelby and I both stared at Nora, baffled.

"Whiff? Of what, pray tell? Her perfume?" I just managed to stop an eye roll. It wouldn't do to let a former student see just how juvenile I could be at times.

"Oh, come on, you two. Doesn't poison leave a certain odor behind, like almonds or something like that? Gwen, you should know this since it's in those goofy books you like to read."

"Agatha Christie did *not* write goofy books, thank you very much. And the scent of almonds is tied to arsenic poisoning, something that went out of fashion long ago."

"Aha! I told you she'd know," crowed Nora, a triumphant expression on her face. "Miss Franklin is one dangerous gal, Shelby."

I decided to ignore her. With my best friend, sometimes it was definitely a case of "least said, soonest mended." Turning back to Shelby, who'd managed to eat two rolls, despite her lack of appetite, I smiled. "I'm glad you got away from that scene without touching anything. Whatever killed her might have been on something she was carrying."

Shelby nodded soberly. "I thought the same thing. I mean, she'd been perfectly fine ten minutes before I found her, and I don't remember her eating or drinking anything at the presser. She was more concerned with how she'd appear in front of the camera." She gave a contemptuous snort. "Not that they'd ever give out anything to nibble on anyways. They always act like it's a huge imposition to make a statement to anyone, much less the lowly press."

I sat quietly, tapping my chin and running my mind back through the different types of poisons I'd read about. The color and state of her face was a dead giveaway. And wasn't there one type that was transdermal? Babs Prescott might have touched something accidently, causing the poison to get into her system. If that was the case, then no one was to blame for her death except herself. The issue would be to find what she'd touched before another person died from whatever it was.

Of course, if it was a fatal allergic reaction, she should have carried an EpiPen at all times. I posed the question to Shelby.

"I'm thinking about anaphylaxis, something that might require an EpiPen. Would you know if she had any allergies?"

Shelby thought a moment, her bottom lip caught between her teeth. "I think she *did* have some pretty scary allergies, now that you mention it. I remember one time at a presser when they had bowls of peanuts sitting around, and she raised holy h-e-double-hockey-sticks about it."

"We need to find out if they found an EpiPen in her purse. And we need to find out what her toxicology report says." I sat up straighter, lifting my coffee mug to my lips.

"And how, smarty-pants, will we do that?" Nora's finely drawn eyebrows lifted slightly. "I don't think even Rachel can get hold of that."

"But I can," Shelby said suddenly. "It'll be part of the information pack released to the press, once it's completed."

"Really? You mean the state medical examiner's office will hand that stuff out for the asking?" Now Nora's brows were hovering around her hairline, or at least where it would be once it all grew back in. "That's crazy."

"Takes one to know one," I muttered under my breath. I looked across at Shelby. "How soon do you think you'll be able to get a copy?"

Shelby shrugged, her fingers tapping restlessly against the table. "Maybe in a week or so. Most likely longer. It really depends on how quickly the ME gets the toxicology tests completed. I know they can rush these things, but . . ." She lifted her shoulders again and let them fall. "First, I've got to convince my editor I can do my job while this whole fiasco plays out."

"I'm sure they'll let you back. Who else can they find to cover all those nutty political rallies?" Nora wrinkled her nose as if she'd just smelled something unpleasant.

Shelby laughed, a spontaneous reaction, and I was pleased to see her expression relax. She'd looked absolutely dreadful only a few minutes before, but now it appeared the coffee and conversation, not to mention *moi*, were working their magic on her.

"Isn't that the truth? I tell you, Mrs. Goldstein, I had no idea grownups could act so—so juvenile! In my opinion, if you don't agree with someone, you can at least be civil about it." Shelby's tone was as wry as her expression, and I nodded. There were too many overgrown babies in today's society, in my not so humble opinion.

"Or disregard them. That's the way I do it, right, Sis?" Nora poked my arm with one false nail and let out a cackle of laughter that sent Herc scrambling for the safety of the backyard.

"And I return the favor, so we're even." I stood and reached over for the still-warm coffee carafe. "Anyone want a top-up?"

* * * *

After Shelby and Nora left, I changed back into my comfy bathrobe and curled up on my favorite end of the sofa, eyes closed. Playing counselor and host so early in the morning had zapped my batteries, and I needed a few minutes to recharge.

I awoke to my bathrobe pocket buzzing and vibrating.

"Hello," I croaked as I struggled to sit up. "Who's calling, please?"

"Miss Franklin? Is that you?"

I could hear Aggie's excited barking in the background and someone trying to quiet her down.

"Brent? Where are you?"

"Actually, I'm sitting in my car right outside your house. Is it all right if me and Rachel come in? And Aggie too."

A cacophony of enthusiastic yips echoed in my ear.

I winced at the noise. I needed to let them in quickly before the neighbors began complaining.

"Of course." I managed to get my feet on the floor, flinching as I did. My legs were either still asleep or reacting to Brent's horrible grammar. "I'll unlock the door. Give me a minute to get decent."

Herc, who had been snoozing on the floor beside the sofa, rose to follow me, giving himself a quick shake.

"Your buddy's here." I leaned over and gave his ears a fond rub. "Maybe the two of you can go play in the backyard while the grownups talk."

Of course, I was referring to myself and Rachel. Brent, in my mind, was still a kid. I could hear him and Rachel approaching my front door, Aggie's excited yelps adding chaotic punctuations. Herc barked in reply, and by the time I made it to my room, it sounded as though someone had opened a petting zoo in my little house.

"Hey, Miss F., wanna see where Aggie got stung?"

I'd gotten dressed as quickly as I could, my legs still buzzing with sleep, and joined them in the living room. Rachel had curled up in my only armchair and was busy tapping away on her cell phone. Brent was on the floor, both dogs vying for his attention.

"Sure." I leaned over to call Aggie to me. "Were you able to get the stinger out?"

"Yeah. Some old guy was at the campground and showed us how."

Rachel lifted her head briefly, wrinkling her nose. "He used half of an onion, Miss Franklin. I thought I'd never get the smell out of her fur."

I had the sneaking suspicion this "old guy" was probably my age, but I kept my mouth shut. Instead, I looked closely at the spot Brent was pointing at. I could barely see a tiny red bump.

"Looks like the old man was right." I smiled as I patted Aggie's side. "There's something to be said for wisdom of the ages."

"I guess." Brent's tone seemed doubtful as he glanced at Rachel. "I mean, he only stuck an onion on there and got the stinger out. Anyone coulda done that."

Oh, for the innocence (or ignorance) of youth. Sighing inwardly, I settled back on the sofa. Conversations with Brent usually made my head spin.

"I'm not sure too many people actually carry onions around with them, Brent." Before he could dissect that remark and reply, I turned to Rachel. "Have you two been following the local news?"

"Oh, you mean about that dead chick? The one with the big—"

I held up both hands at Brent's comment, his attention already shifting from onions to, well, other things.

"Thank you, Brent. I think we get the idea." I gave a small shake of my head as I looked from him to Rachel.

"What'd I say? I was only talking about her hair."

To his credit, the kid really *did* appear to be honestly baffled. I decided to leave well enough alone.

"That's the one. And I'm pretty sure your dad is the lead investigator, Rachel."

She gave a tiny shrug as she reached over and scratched Herc behind his ears. My dog almost melted, oozing down beside her in a virtual doggy rug. Some loyalty there.

"Most likely. I mean, he was just promoted to head of his department, so he gets first dibs on any case that comes in. And with a victim as well-known as this one, well, I'd say it's a good chance he's the one investigating."

I couldn't have asked for a better segue. Leaning forward, I looked her directly in the eyes. "You know I wouldn't ask if it wasn't necessary, but . . ."

I let my request hang there, waiting for Rachel to fill in the blanks.

"Oh, that's no problemo, Miss F. Rachel's really good at snagging things from her dad, aren't you?"

He turned to give his girlfriend a proud smile, and I sighed. Only Brent would think that "snagging things" from one's parents would constitute a talent.

"Sure thing. I'll take as many pictures as I can of his reports and text them to you and Mrs. G." This time it was Rachel's turn to smile impishly. "I'm assuming both of you are interested."

I nodded, not bothering to excuse myself or Nora. This was Shelby's future we were talking about, not some nutty treasure-hunt party game.

"That'd be great." I paused a moment, considering how much to say in front of Brent. Throwing caution to the wind, I added in as casual a manner as I could muster, "It's really for Shelby Tucker. You remember her, don't you?"

They both nodded, Brent's head moving like an oversized dashboard figurine. Before my imagination could add a hula skirt to the mental image, Herc rose and tottered over to me, clearly expecting another massage. Aggie, her stumpy tail wagging, followed him, and I gave both dogs a quick rub before settling back on the sofa. I needed to explain the how's and why's of the case, preferably in terms Brent could understand.

"I'm sure you'll find this hard to fathom, but Shelby's been accused of the murder." Before he could ask, I added, "Fathom in this context means 'comprehend' or 'understand,' Brent."

"Why didn't you just say so in the first place?" He scrunched up his face like a little child, his lips thrust out in a pout.

Rachel and I ignored him.

"Shelby's the journalist, right?" Rachel sounded concerned, and I could see her mind scrambling to make a connection. "What happened, Miss Franklin? Did they have a fight or something?"

I started to shake my head and then stopped. After all, there had been some bad blood between them, thanks to Babs's "fat farm" comment. Maybe Shelby had snapped.

"Actually, it all started at the press conference held by the governor's office." I closed my eyes, trying to recall the order of things. "Babs Prescott made a rude comment to Shelby concerning her, uh, physique, and things went downhill from there. Of course, I've only heard Shelby's side of things, so maybe I'm biased."

Or being led by the nose, as my dad would say. In my experience, anyone could do anything at any given time, me included. While I would have assumed Shelby could never have done something so heinous, much less have access to poison, stranger things had happened.

"Wait a sec." Rachel shifted in her seat, tucking one foot underneath her as the other leg began a slow swing. "So what you're saying is a put-down from Ms. Fabulous could have prompted Shelby to kill her? You'd think she was smarter than that, considering the amount of firsthand witnesses there are at a press conference, right?"

"Correct. After that comment and then the Instagram post—"

Rachel and Brent began talking at once, demanding to see the post.

"Slow down, all right? I'll show you two in a minute, not because I think it's a nice picture but because it might be germane to the case."

Brent's forehead wrinkled.

"That means 'important.'" I fished my cell phone from my pocket and opened my Instagram app. "In my mind, the worst thing that happened was Shelby was the one who spotted Babs in the parking garage. And I'm sorry to say this, but you know how most murder investigations go. The one with the biggest motive gets the spotlight."

"I can't believe that an Instagram picture is enough to give someone a reason to kill." Rachel moved next to me to see my phone.

"I can." Brent moved closer so he could also see the picture I'd pulled up. "Remember that time your old boyfriend put all those pictures of you—"

"Aaaaand that's enough, thank you very much." Rachel's cheeks were bright red, a visible stop sign for any question I might have asked. "Let's just say I get it, all right?"

After I'd finally seen them off with a promise to share the latest news, whenever I got it, I flopped back on the sofa and attempted to get my thoughts organized for the day. The only dog-walking job had already been taken care of (Nora had done that before crashing my early-morning meeting with Shelby), and the only item left on the day's list was the Clear the Shelter event. Curious about the change in presentations since Babs Prescott obviously wouldn't be there as the presenter, I opened the Google app on my phone, hoping that something would be in my news feed.

"'Clear the Shelter is an annual event designed to bring the public's attention to the need for more foster and adoptive families for the thousands of strays taken in every year.'"

I stopped reading for a moment and thumbed through a series of pictures guaranteed to break the heart of every pet lover in Portland. The only thing missing was a melancholy song about angels and love, and that was because my phone was on mute.

"'The Greater Portland Area Pet Shelters are pleased to be joining local dignitaries, celebrities, and donors in honoring the past year's star volunteers, George and Leticia Lafoe, for their unselfish donation of time and money to our cause.'"

I paused again, thinking. I'd taught with a Tim Lafoe at our high school a few years back. Maybe he was related somehow to the illustrious volunteers. I tucked that piece of information away in case I needed it at the event as an introduction to the honorees. Even those with grownup children still liked to talk about them.

"'With the sudden and unforeseen passing of this year's award presenter, Ms. Babs Prescott, we have asked her co-anchor, Matt Robb, to fill in.'"

Aha. So Babs's partner on the television program was taking her place. Had he also been behind the "unforeseen passing," as the website so eloquently noted? Clicking out of the site, I quickly dialed Nora's number.

"What now?" Nora's voice on the other end of the line was cranky. Probably something to do with Marcus.

"No need to jump down my throat and stomp on my liver," I said mildly. "I'm calling with a piece of information about tonight's shelter event."

"Sorry, Sis. I thought you were Marcus calling me back. He's really driving me insane."

"What's Portland's Lothario done now?"

Herc sidled up for a pat. I was happy to oblige.

"You don't want to know. Or maybe you do. I'll tell you later." I could hear paper crinkling as Nora opened something. "I guess if you're not doing anything else today, you probably should come on over. We can leave from here."

"I don't want to leave Herc by himself that long," I protested.

Herc looked up at me and seemed to nod in agreement.

"But I guess he'll be okay with the doggy door. I'll leave some food in his bowl and fill a couple of dishes with water."

"Sounds good. And wear something besides those horrible capris and sandals."

"There's nothing wrong with the way I dress." I held the cell phone out and stuck my tongue at it. "But don't worry, Miss Lycra. I'll figure something else out."

She began sputtering in my ear, and I disconnected the call, grinning as I headed into my room. I knew exactly what my partner in crime would be wearing: black pants so tight they might as well be leggings, a bright, neon-colored top in an equally skin-hugging material, and sky-high heels. Anything else and I'd need to check her temperature.

As I perused the meager contents of my closet for something that wouldn't give Nora fits, I thought about her relationship with Marcus Avery. They had to be the most on-again, off-again couple I'd ever known. At least with Nora's trail of ex-husbands, it had been a "wham bam, let's get married" kind of deal with each one. She was either becoming pickier in her advancing years or she'd developed a joy in playing yoyo with someone's heart.

Knowing my friend, it was most likely the latter. She was the oil to his pilot light, and the resulting arguments could make even me blush. I thought I'd heard it all as a high school teacher, but these two were something else entirely.

Holding out a linen skirt and an embroidered cotton blouse for closer inspection, I wondered who it was that Babs Prescott had made so angry. Maybe it was her co-anchor. I'd seen them together on the air several times and had noticed tenseness in the obligatory banter between them. I'd be sure and keep my eyes on Matt Robb at the shelter event. Maybe he'd do something or say something to give himself away. After all, it happened in Agatha Christie's books, so why not in real life?

Humming to myself, I began to change. This day was looking better and better.

* * * *

I was halfway to Nora's luxury apartment building when my phone began buzzing in my skirt pocket. I pulled it out, stopping to sit on a shaded bench. That was one thing I loved about Portland: shade could be found on nearly every street and alley in the city. From magnificent white oaks to Ponderosa pines to crepe myrtles, there was something for every budding arborist in town.

Miss F this is Brent I am at your house again where are you?

Drat the boy and his headache-inducing run-on sentences. And what in the world was he doing at my place? Showing up without prior warning really wasn't like Brent, especially when he was with Rachel. She was the soul of propriety and usually a good influence on Brent.

I carefully tapped out my properly punctuated message with one finger.

I'm on my way to Mrs. Goldstein's. What do you need?

Rechal has some info well meet you at Mrs. Gs.

I had to smile even as I was shaking my head. He couldn't even get Rachel's name spelled correctly.

Nora opened the door as soon as I knocked. She looked slightly flustered, her color high and her hair standing on end as though she'd been running her fingers through it or playing with a light socket.

"I'm so glad you're here." She gave my outfit a brief glance. "Where in heaven's name did you get those shoes? Inherit them from your great-grandma?"

I looked at my feet. True, I'd pulled the slip-on penny loafers from the back of my closet and dusted them off, but I really didn't think they were that bad. And they were almost as comfy as my Birkenstocks.

"I got a text from Brent a few minutes ago." I decided to overlook her fashion commentary. "He and Rachel on are their way."

"Oh, good." Nora headed for the kitchen, calling over her shoulder. "Check out what's on my iPad and let me know what you think."

I slipped my feet out of the offending shoes and sat on one of the overstuffed sofas. Nora's iPad was lying there in its purple cover, a cursor blinking brightly on its screen. Picking it up, I saw that Nora had started writing something. I scanned the contents quickly, my eyes growing wider with each word.

"Nora, you didn't tell me you were asked to be a presenter tonight."

She appeared around the kitchen doorway, smiling broadly.

"Yep. They called me right after I got home from your house this morning. Cool, isn't it?"

"Cool, indeed. Actually, it's rather inspiring." I lifted both hands and acted as though I were photographing her. "My best friend, the greatest small business owner in Portland."

"Co-owner, goofy. And whatever. It's probably because of all the donations I've made over the past year." She disappeared back into the kitchen, rubbing the fingers of her two hands together. "Money talks, baby."

No kidding. Money and looks were a currency that would never go out of vogue. I thought about Babs Prescott and her perma-tanned, sculpted, Botoxed body. Someone in her life didn't buy what she was offering, and that was the person we needed to focus on. The problem lay with figuring out who this person could be, and I had no idea where to begin.

Chapter 4

Brent and Rachel arrived as I was rereading Nora's speech, Aggie trotting in the doorway first. Patting my leg as I called her over, I looked at Rachel and saw her expression was serious.

"Hey, Miss F. Check out this picture." Brent strode over to the sofa, waving his cell phone in front of him like a shield. "I took it at Mount Shasta."

I held out my hand for the phone, trying to focus on his moving hand.

"Brent, I'd appreciate it if you'd keep that thing still." I grabbed it from his hand and held it in front of my face. "What exactly am I looking at here?"

Brent plopped down on the sofa, leaning over to point at the picture on the small screen. "That's the guy who put that onion on Aggie. Rachel said he looks familiar."

"Really?" I glanced over at Rachel and then back at the picture. "Is he someone your parents know? Or maybe someone from the college?"

Rachel shook her head, the serious expression still in place. "No, I'm pretty sure it's no one like that. I think it's that guy on television."

"On television? You mean like an actor?"

"No, I think he's that news anchor. The one who worked with the fake blonde."

I looked back at the picture, only seeing a blurred figure bending over Aggie. "I'm sorry. I can't see it."

"Told ya she'd say that." Brent looked over at Rachel with a triumphant look. "Old people can't see very good." He shot a devilish grin at me. "Sorry, Miss F."

"Depends on what you call old." Nora sashayed into the living room with a tray full of brownies. "Gwennie, I think these kids might be too young for this."

"Wait, Mrs. G." Brent held up both hands, palms outward. "I didn't mean *you* were old. And I like brownies, I really do."

Nora flashed an amused smile in my direction. It was amazing what chocolate could do to a perpetually hungry teen like Brent.

"He's referring to me," I said dryly as I reached for a still-warm square. "You know, the retired teacher. He probably thinks I'm nearing one hundred."

"Take it from me, kid. Retirement isn't all it's cracked up to be." Nora handed me a napkin, dropping one eyelid in a wink.

I glared at Nora as she held out the tray to Brent. "And what would you know, Miss I've Never Worked a Day in My Life."

"I did so." Nora shot an indignant look at me. "My parents made me mow the front lawn every week *and* weed the flower beds."

"Well, la dee dah." I found myself doing that head wiggle thing, eyes narrowed and mouth a tight line. "*I* had to watch four younger brothers and clean the whole house, and you wouldn't believe how messy boys can be."

We sat glaring at each other, the tray of brownies held between us like a barrier.

"Um, Miss Franklin? Mrs. Goldstein? Brent and I are going to leave now."

"It's all right," we said in unison and then laughed. Nora and I could always find something to restore the balance between us. That was how we'd managed to remain best friends since that long-ago day in kindergarten when two nervous little girls had gravitated toward one another, giving each other a feeling of security.

"If that's who it is," I said to Nora, "then he couldn't have been the one to murder Babs."

I glanced again at the fuzzy picture, trying to will the face into focus. "If this is her co-anchor, then he's off the suspect list."

"I never thought he was in on it." Nora set the tray down and leaned over the phone. "He's one good-looking man. Maybe those looks are covering something not so nice, if you get my drift."

I rolled my eyes. Trust Nora to equate killer looks with a killer personality. Literally.

"Nature shows us the best killers are the ones that have the best looks." I popped the last piece of my brownie in my mouth and reached for another. "Take the loris, for example." I looked at my audience to make sure they were listening. "It's got these huge eyes and is absolutely adorable. It may look like something from *Star Wars*, but it's one of the few venomous mammals in the world."

"Are you sure you weren't a science teacher?" Nora lifted one eyebrow in question.

"Not even in your wildest dreams." I wrinkled my nose. "The science department couldn't keep up with the English teachers."

"I'll say," Rachel murmured.

I glanced sharply at her, examining her face for a hint of sarcasm. I saw none. Maybe she was one of the few who actually enjoyed writing and reading.

"You should tell Miss F. about that creepy teacher you have, Rachel." Brent looked up from petting Aggie, a wet patch on his face from where she'd licked him. "You know—that one who taught that class about rocks and stuff."

"Maybe later." Rachel seemed flustered. "I'd rather hear about what's up with the Babs Prescott case."

I looked at her curiously, noting the high color in her cheeks. Had one of her teachers given her a bad grade or rejected a big paper? You never could tell what might set a student off, in my experience—or their parents.

"I want to know about the teacher." Nora's gaze darted between Rachel and me. "And I'm sure Miss Franklin wants to hear as well."

I nodded, leaning forward slightly in encouragement. "Nothing leaves this room, Rachel. Promise."

"Yeah, like that Las Vegas commercial, where everything stays there." Brent looked pleased with himself, but Rachel clearly wasn't.

She glanced over at Brent, annoyance on her face. Whatever it was, she didn't want to share it. I wasn't sure why I felt as though she should, but I did. Call it an instinct from decades of being in the classroom: you knew when one of your students had an issue.

Finally, with a great sigh, she began to speak. "Well, I had this one instructor last semester for geology, kind of a geeky-looking guy. You know, glasses, cardigans, the whole nine yards."

I nodded. I knew exactly what she meant. Why some educators felt they needed to perpetuate the stereotype, I had no idea, but then again . . . I glanced at my shoes and smiled wryly. I got it. Sometimes it was cheaper to look "geeky," as Rachel put it, than to update a wardrobe.

"So what did he do to make you uncomfortable?" Nora's expression was avid, her upcoming speech lying forgotten on the discarded iPad. "If you say he tried to feel you up or something, I'm siccing Marcus on him."

"Nora, do you have to sound so crude?" I shook my head in exasperation. "I'm sure if something such as Rachel being touched inappropriately has happened, her father can handle it."

Rachel was shaking her head as well, her face still flushed. "No, nothing like that. And yeah, my dad would've torn him limb from limb and then asked questions."

Brent nodded enthusiastically. "You betcha he would, Miss F. I practically had to take a lie detector test before our trip."

Beside him, Aggie whined for attention, digging her nose into his hand.

"It wasn't that bad." Rachel smiled fondly at Brent. "Besides, he gave me a can of pepper spray to carry. You know, in case you got out of line."

"Seriously? Wow, that's so cool." To my amusement, Brent looked more impressed than upset. "We coulda used it on that bee that stung Aggie."

"It's not bug spray." I exchanged a smile with Rachel. "It's meant to stop an attacker so you can get away."

"Yeah, like a bee. It attacked Aggie, right, Rachel?" He shook his head, looking disgusted. "And that guy used a stupid old onion. Pepper spray woulda been way cooler."

"I think this kid's mom must've dropped him on his head," Nora murmured, and I stifled a laugh. Brent was certainly one of a kind.

"At least Aggie's all right." Rachel leaned over and gave the small dog a fond pat on her head.

"Back to the teacher issue." I leaned against the sofa's plump cushions, wriggling my bottom to a more comfortable spot. "First of all, tell us what he's done."

Rachel gave Brent a quick glance and then lifted one shoulder in a small shrug. "Well, at first it wasn't anything really big, like maybe pausing near my desk while he was lecturing, or walking me through a lab while ignoring the rest of the class. After a few weeks with him acting like this, it started feeling weird." She looked at her hands, and I noticed the color was rising in her face again. "And then he started putting a hand on my arm or shoulder, and then . . ." She looked at me, a troubled expression on her face. "Then he started leaving me notes on my papers that had nothing to do with the grading or anything."

"Rachel, have you told anyone at the school about this? Maybe spoken to your counselor or another teacher?" I didn't like what she had to say and, more than that, I didn't like the way I could see it made her feel talking about it. "This sounds like someone who doesn't understand professional or personal boundaries."

"That's what I told her," Brent blurted out.

Rachel held out one hand as if to quiet him.

"Tell Miss F. what he did after your final."

To my surprise, Rachel's eyes filled with tears. Covering her face with her hands, she began to cry almost silently. Aggie padded softly over to her and pushed against her legs. I'd seen the little dog display almost bloodhound tendencies before, and now she was acting like a trained therapy pet.

"Rachel, I really think we need to let your parents know about this. You're clearly upset, and I can tell you that no teacher should act this way toward a student." I was beginning to feel angry at whoever it was that had made Rachel feel so badly. If I had my way, this teacher would be out on his nerdy behind before he bothered another student.

"He said he was going to fail me so I'd have to take his class again."

Nora and I stared at one another in shock. What planet was this man from, anyway? I stood and walked over to where Rachel sat and squatted in front of her. Aggie, thinking it was a game, let out an excited bark and licked my hand.

"Rachel," I began firmly, "this is a reportable incident."

She dropped her hands and began to protest, but I held up one hand.

"No, I'm serious. This doesn't sound like anything we should ignore."

"But it happened last semester." Her face was blotchy from crying. "And he didn't really fail me. I passed the class with a B."

"Be that as it may, he still sounds like someone who manipulates people. And that is *not* a good thing, believe me."

"I'll think about it." Rachel wiped both of her eyes with the edge of her shirt. "I really want to forget it ever happened."

"That's exactly what they want you to do," Nora said. "Trust me. I was married to some real pieces of work."

"Well, no one who sees Mr. Lafoe would think he's that way." Rachel gave a hiccupy laugh and reached down to ruffle Aggie's fur. "He's such a dweeb."

"Lafoe?" I said sharply, glancing at Nora. "I used to teach with a Tim Lafoe. And now that I think about it, he *was* in the science department."

"That's gotta be him." Nora picked up her iPad and tapped on the screen. "And according to the info for tonight's event, it's George and Letitia Lafoe who'll be getting the award for volunteering for shelters." She tossed the tablet on the sofa. "Maybe someone ought to tell them about this creep."

"Depending on how old they are, I'd guess he's their son, or at least a close relative. That's not a common last name." I straightened my legs and stood, both knees sending out a twenty-one-gun salute to age. "I think we ought to let her handle this, Nora." I looked straight at Rachel, my tone as somber as my expression. "And, Rachel, I *am* serious about this."

"And I think I want more brownies." Trust Brent to think about his stomach in the middle of a crisis.

And trust my own gut instincts to be kicked into overdrive. Something was bothering me about Tim Lafoe, and it wasn't only Rachel. Hopefully, it would come back to me. In the meantime, Nora and I had to focus on the Clear the Shelter event, and she had a speech to make.

* * * *

Once Brent and Rachel, along with a tail-wagging Aggie, were gone, Nora picked up her iPad. She stared at it for a few moments, brows drawn together and lipsticked mouth pursed.

"Do you know when you'll be making your speech?" I sat with the tray of brownies on the sofa between us, breaking off the crispier edges and popping them into my mouth. There was something about those pieces of dark chocolate that I loved, and the harder the edges were, the better I liked it.

"Would you stop with the crunching already? I can't think with all that noise in my ear." Nora glanced over at me, a scowl on her face.

I handed her the soft middle of the brownie. Chocolate and sugar were mood lifters, at least according to the many cozy mysteries I'd read over the years.

"You're going to be fine." I leaned across the tray and gave her arm a squeeze. "You've got more panache in your little finger than most folks do in their entire body."

"Yeah, whatever."

But I saw a smile beginning in the corner of her mouth. If I could keep her buoyed and happy between now and the shelter event, I'd have done my duty as her best friend.

And if I could figure out who had wanted Babs Prescott dead, besides nearly everyone she came across, I'd be a happy camper. Where to begin looking was my first task. Maybe Marcus had been able to find out something from one of his so-called "confidential informants." I'd have to ask him when I saw him later in the evening.

"You're not a television cop." Nora had laughed when he'd first told her about a CI he needed to interview. "Only detectives and real investigators have those, you ninny."

"I *am* a real investigator, thank you very much," he'd replied stiffly. "Marcus Avery, Detective at Large, remember?"

"And if you get any larger, you'll need a bigger office."

The only answer had been the slamming of the front door as he'd stomped away. And that was the last time she'd spoken with him, this person who was supposed to be our lift to the Clear the Shelter shindig.

Sighing inwardly as I recalled this, I turned back to Nora. She was sitting with her eyes squeezed tightly shut, her lips silently moving as if in prayer. Or maybe she was casting a spell. Knowing Nora as I did, I wouldn't have put it past her.

"You know you've got to see Marcus this evening." I earned a sour look from her. "And one of us needs to call him fairly soon."

"Already taken care of." Nora stood and headed for the kitchen. "I told you I'd handle it."

I got up and followed her. At the very least I could get some coffee out of this exchange. What I got was the shock of my life.

Sitting at the kitchen table in all his plaid and striped glory was Marcus Avery, Detective at Large.

"Marcus!" I stood with one hand clutching the front of my circa 1985 embroidered shirt, my mouth hanging open in a most unbecoming manner. "When in the world did you get here?"

He grinned at me and then across at Nora. To my amazement, she was grinning as well, a Cheshire cat smile that lingered even when she turned back to the coffee maker. I didn't know what was going on here, but I was sure going to find out.

"I've been here all along, my dear. Right down yonder hallway in this good lady's room." Marcus had a way of sounding both sincere and cheesy, something that usually made me smile.

Usually. At the moment, I was far from smiling. I'd spent the last few hours of my time listening to Nora grumble and complain, trying to make her feel better, letting me think she'd broken it off with him yet again. Trust me, I wasn't in the mood for sophomoric antics, especially those of the romantic kind.

"Look, you two." I stood with both hands on my hips, feeling irritated at the grinning twosome for pulling the wool over my eyes and at myself for the additional rolls of fat I could feel breaking out around my waist. "It's not any of my business how you choose to conduct your relationship, but I'd appreciate it if you'd leave me out of the drama."

"Drama? What drama?" Marcus could look as innocent as a newborn baby when he wanted to.

Nora didn't bother. Instead, she smirked at me as she thumped three mugs of coffee onto the kitchen table. I glared back at her. It was probably her fault I'd gained weight recently, what with all the fussing and brownies and Marcus.

I waved my hands wildly around the kitchen, taking in Marcus and Nora and even the coffee maker. "It's everything! Between Brent and his idiotic comments and you and your . . . your boy toy here, I can't take it anymore. And now I'm gaining weight, and Roger wants to see me tomorrow." I burst into tears, covering my face with my hands.

"There now, Gwennie. There now." I felt Nora's arms go around my shoulders and steer me toward a chair. "You sit right here. Marcus, get that box of tissues from the living room."

"I don't need tissues." I wiped my eyes on one sleeve, sniffing loudly. Thank goodness, I didn't wear makeup or I might have added a few black streaks to the embroidered pattern. "What I need is a month at a spa. And no more murders."

"Aha," said Nora softly. "It's that Babs Prescott reaching out from the great beyond or wherever she's ended up, doing her best to stir up trouble."

Marcus came back into the kitchen and tossed the box of tissues on the table, narrowly missing my coffee. "Babs Prescott was bad news when she was among the living."

He spoke with such feeling that Nora shot him a suspicious look. He met her gaze and gave a slight shrug, but I saw his cheeks reddening slightly. Well, he wasn't known as Portland's Lothario for nothing.

"It's everything at once." I took a deep breath, trying to preserve what little dignity I still had. "And, to be honest, Rachel's issues with that instructor really have me upset. I absolutely abhor it whenever an educator takes advantage of a student, planned or otherwise. Makes me wonder exactly why some folks bother going into teaching in the first place."

"I know, I know." Nora rubbed my back with one hand. "And now we're going to go celebrate his folks for being such wonderful volunteers."

"It's not their fault," I said quickly, my natural equanimity beginning to bounce back under my best friend's kindness. "We can't blame them for what their son has done, if he *is* their son."

"Well, he's gotta be something to them. Lafoe isn't a common last name."

I shrugged. "Maybe. But still, we aren't going to say anything to them, are we?" I craned my neck around to stare at her. "Are we?"

"Fine, we won't." She moved around to her own chair and slumped into it. "Does that include Romeo here?"

"Yes. Let's just get through this evening. Tomorrow we can start digging, but right now I need to keep it together." I gave an embarrassed laugh. "Sorry for that outburst. That wasn't like me."

"Maybe you've got what my mom called 'men's paws,' that time of life when you don't like men's paws on you anymore." Marcus's eyes twinkled as he looked at me.

Nora just rolled her eyes.

"Your mom sounds like a card." I managed a smile for the two of them. "Believe me, when that bit of nonsense starts up, I intend to fight it with chocolate, chocolate, and books. And chocolate."

There was only room in my life for one issue at a time, however, so I relegated Rachel's problem to the back of the line. Since she was safe at the moment, it would keep.

Tonight, I intended to keep the focus only on those attending the ceremony. Someone didn't want Babs around. And according to all the mystery books I'd read over the years, there was every chance this person would show up at the event.

We arrived at Coopers Hall in style, Marcus's lime-green van giving only one undignified belch as he turned off the engine. The outside of the building, a repurposed Quonset hut, was glowing with light, a bank of gleaming windows showcasing the combined winery and taproom inside.

I slid across the bench seat and out of the van, my pulse picking up the excitement of the evening. Nora, I saw to my amusement, was already in "slink mode," placing one high heel in front of the other, as if walking in a fashion show. Marcus, bless his heart, was having a difficult time keeping pace with us.

"Would you look at that," Nora murmured in my ear as she poked one bony elbow into my side. "I'd say he's got some nerve, showing up here tonight."

I craned my neck to see who she was staring at, amazed she'd managed to pinpoint only one person in the steadily moving stream of Portland's A-listers.

"Where?" I rose to my tiptoes, trying to get a glimpse of whoever it was. I spotted the well-dressed back of a familiar figure. "Do you mean the mayor? It's part of his job. He has to attend things like this."

Portland's mayor, a rather good-looking man with the rather unfortunate last name of Dinwitty, seemed to suffer from a chronic case of "open mouth, insert foot," and his latest spat with one particularly pushy city council member was currently making headlines. Suffice it to say the mayor's nickname, Ol' Dimwit, made for great copy.

"No, you nut, not the mayor, although I might like a few minutes alone with that cutie pie." Nora gave my ribs another jab, and I returned the favor, nearly knocking her off her four-inch high heels. "Tim Lafoe, the one Rachel told us about."

"Nora, don't be such an idiot. I'm sure he's here to support his parents and nothing else." I craned my neck, trying to spot him among the crowd of local luminaries. "I can't see him."

"Oh, never mind. You've already missed him. Let's get in there and get a seat before they're all taken." Grabbing my arm, she pulled me along behind her, using her arms to nudge others out of the way.

I played my usual role of minder, offering apologies as Marcus and I were swept along in Nora's ever-widening wake. I could only hope she wouldn't be greeted with boos when she made her speech. Knowing Nora as I did, she'd have no issue with returning the complaints with interest. Not my idea of advertising for our business, that was certain. Maybe I'd better find her some chocolate to nibble on beforehand.

Coopers Hall offered several areas for meeting and greeting. Nora made a beeline for the main room, a large space defined by a row of used wine barrels and a working bar. The light fixtures that shone from the high ceiling lent a glow to the people milling below and the etched silver taps behind the polished mahogany tasting bar.

"Grab those chairs, would you?" Nora directed her orders to Marcus, pushing me toward the line forming in front of the bar. "I'm gonna grab some of that wine before it's all gone."

"It's a winery," I reminded her, my tone as dry as the merlot being handed out to the attendees. "I'm sure there'll be plenty to go around."

She snorted loudly, causing a rather snooty-looking couple to turn and glare in our direction. Nora glared back. You could probably guess who won that little contest.

"For your information, smarty-pants, I'm referring to the vintage they're auctioning tonight. I want to get in a bid for at least one bottle."

Bless her heart. Even with her overgrown and over-greedy ex-stepchildren, Nora could be generous to a fault. Knowing the bids would be starting at a level too astronomical for a mere retired teacher, I leaned over and gave her a hug. Weird clothes and ankle-killer shoes aside, Nora was more philanthropic than anyone I knew.

And that included the "Lady of Portland," a self-important logging heiress named Louisa Lovejoy Turner, whose lifestyle boggled the mind. At least it boggled mine. I'd never seen anyone with so many diamonds and gems on wrists, neck, and ears. Maybe she'd gotten the event confused with an invitation to Buckingham Palace. She swept majestically through the crowd, her high nasal tones both filling the room and grating on my ears as she hailed a visibly cringing Mayor Cutie Pie.

"Oh, dear God and all that's holy," I heard Nora mutter, her tone decidedly not as generous as her checkbook. "Who invited that peacock here?"

"Peahen, not peacock," I said automatically. "Only the males have the brilliant colors and those large fanned tails."

Nora scowled at me for a moment and then smiled, a sign her wicked sense of humor was returning in full force. "No, I definitely meant 'peacock,' as in a—"

Sighing, I put my hand over her mouth before she could complete the rather uncouth comment. I'd have to resume my duties as Nora's minder since Marcus was still occupied with securing a place for us to sit.

"All right, all right. I get the picture." I paused as Nora's eyes began to twinkle with laughter over my hand. I dropped it to my side. "Okay, maybe I don't mean a picture exactly—and get your mind out of the gutter, goofball. You know exactly what I meant." I peeked curiously over at the woman, noting she'd managed to waylay the mayor by hooking his arm with one heavily ringed hand. "What is it about her that you don't like? Aside from the obvious, that is. I have to admit she *is* ostentatious. And gutsy."

Nora gave a contemptuous snort. "Where to begin? For starters, she managed to dodge death taxes, claiming some arcane loophole that allowed her to inherit without giving the state their due. Not to mention she claims to be a direct descendent of one of Portland's founders."

She gave another derisive snort, this time loud enough to draw the attention of several more folks. Maybe she needed a glass or three of pinot noir instead of sugar in order to reset her disposition. In the meantime, it would be up to me to talk her off her emotional ledge.

"Well, maybe she is. And as to the taxes, how does that affect you? I can see how it affects the state, but I'm not seeing anything that should concern you, to be honest." I kept my voice soft and the tone light.

This was how I spoke to students whose irrational classroom spats required me to don the metaphorical referee stripes. Nora, as much as I loved her, could wander into irrationality at the drop of a hat.

She didn't respond right away and then shrugged. "I guess it doesn't, not when you put it that way. But if you knew how high my taxes went after husband three, it'd make you rethink some of these laws we've got."

"At least she's not our problem." I tipped my head in the woman's direction, noting the expression of near-panic on the mayor's face. "He looks like he'd rather be anywhere except where he's at right now."

"I couldn't agree with you more." Nora looked around, rising on tiptoe to peer over the heads of the people standing beside us. "Where's that Marcus when I need him? I swear, he's about as useless as a chocolate coffeepot."

"I'm right here." An offended Marcus spoke up from behind us, his tone and expression miffed. "I'll have you know—"

"Save it, sweet pea." Nora broke across his complaint, grabbing his arm and pushing him in the direction of Louisa Lovejoy Turner. "Get over there and rescue Ol' Dimwit, Romeo."

With a final shove aimed at his well-padded backside, Nora sent Marcus careening into an upturned barrel that had been turned into a wine-tasting station.

The carefully arranged glasses already contained a deep burgundy wine that was practically guaranteed to permanently stain anything in its vicinity, and they toppled over in quick succession. Between Nora's screeching and Marcus's struggling efforts to right himself amid the vino carnage, I found myself playing the part of a human blockade, both arms thrown out to the sides in order to keep anyone from getting too close to the shards of crystal that littered the floor.

It reminded me of the time I'd had to react that way when a hapless student had taken a tumble down the bleacher stairs and busted his chin wide open. Keeping all the waving cell phones away from the scene had been a tough job.

My concern was centered on Marcus as he extracted himself from among the broken glasses. The floor had become a slippery stream of wine, and one false step might send the rather paunchy private detective flat on his behind. Carefully bending forward, while keeping one arm out to force onlookers back, I held out the other hand out to a very pale Marcus.

"Grab my hand, and I'll guide you around the mess, all right?"

I gave him an encouraging smile, keeping my gaze fastened on his. He was beginning to sweat profusely, and I could tell his breathing was becoming shallower as the moments passed. *Classic signs of a heart attack ready to kick off.* Panic began rising in my own chest, and I redoubled my efforts in helping him navigate the confusion. He needed to be seen by a paramedic and quickly.

Needless to say, our introduction to Portland's movers and shakers was one for the record books. Mayor Dinwitty had managed to disentangle himself from Louisa Lovejoy Turner during the fracas and was now nowhere in sight. She had stayed behind, a look of pleasurable shock on her round face. This was probably the most excitement she'd had in years.

Thankfully, Marcus's color began to return as he was being evaluated by the emergency team. Crisis not quite over, but on its way to being averted. Maybe this would be the wakeup call he needed to take better care of himself.

Once the ambulance had taken poor Marcus off to be assessed at the nearest hospital and the wine mess had been cleaned up, things began to settle down. Nora, however, did not. She'd become as jumpy as Herc whenever he had to do his business out in snow. I was beginning to think she should have gone with Marcus as well, except her stop might have included a comfy padded room.

"Look, pal, you've either got to get yourself under control, or we're going to have to bow out of here." I handed her another glass of sparkling water, careful to keep myself between her and a tableful of gawkers.

Of course, they might have been looking at her clothing ensemble, but I'd caught a few of the comments, and none of them were complimentary. Nora Goldstein's reputation as eccentric was rapidly gaining ground.

"I am under control," she said through gritted teeth. "If you want to see me really lose it, I can oblige, trust me. Ask any of my exes. Or ex-stepkids." She spat the final word out as if she'd tasted something very unpleasant.

I took a good look at her then. I was beginning to realize her current state wasn't Marcus-related at all. As I followed her line of sight, I saw precisely what, or *who*, it was that had her cage so rattled.

Seated at a table across the room, her low-cut dress exposing way too much of her freckled acreage, was Phoebe, one of Nora's brood of disreputable ex-stepchildren. Judging by her over-loud voice and crazed head tossing, she was well on her way to being as smashed as those unfortunate wineglasses. Classic Phoebe, from what I could recall. She was very fond of her booze, and the earlier the better. If it was seven-thirty now, she'd most likely been on the sauce for quite a few hours already.

It was her companion, however, who took me aback. Sitting beside Phoebe was none other than Matt Robb, the co-anchor of the not-so-dearly departed Babs Prescott. Their cozy closeness had alarm bells going off. I could tell Nora was hearing them as well.

At least she was focused on something else besides Marcus. As unsympathetic as it might sound, he was in the best possible place for this health scare. And maybe a doctor could convince him to lose some of that donut belly he carried in front of him like the wobbly prow of a weather-beaten ship.

The concern of the moment, though, was why Nora's nutty stepdaughter was hanging around with Babs's co-anchor. What, if anything, did it have to do with the murder? Were Phoebe and Matt acquainted before Babs's demise, or was this another development? I needed a place to begin my queries into her death, and Phoebe was probably my best bet, given her loose lips due to alcohol. Taking a deep breath, I smoothed my skirt over my hips, called up my internal Miss Marple, and headed for their table.

Chapter 5

"Well, looky what the cat dragged in." Phoebe's gaze met mine in an unfocused gaze, but I could still hear the mockery behind her comment. I was right. She'd already been indulging long before this evening. "Is my useless excuse for a stepmama with you?"

"If you're speaking of Mrs. Goldstein," I replied in my most glacial tone, "then yes. However, I wasn't aware she was still, as you say, your 'stepmama.'"

I gave the last word a disparaging emphasis. It went right over Phoebe's frowsy head, as I'd known it would. Her table companion, however, caught every last nuance, and his carefully shaped eyebrows lifted a fraction on his unnaturally smooth forehead. So, Babs wasn't the only Botoxed beauty at the television station. It made me wonder if this was down to contract or conceit. I'd bet both.

"Oh, blah blah blah," Phoebe giggled. "Matty Boo, be a dear and get me some more of that delicious red stuff. I can't talk to this frump without some help, if you get my drift."

One eyelid drooped in a drunken wink, and a loose strip of false eyelashes detached itself, hanging precariously over her eye like a dead centipede. Disregarding it, she gave Matt Robb a wide smile as she handed him her empty glass.

Matty Boo grabbed the glass and headed toward the bar. Not a wise move, in my opinion, but it gave me the opportunity to ask my questions. Phoebe, on the other hand, had other ideas. With an almost graceful movement, she began sliding downward in her chair, eyes closed and soft snores emitting from her slack mouth.

This event was rapidly morphing from bad to worse. Diving under the table, I managed to cushion her head before it hit the concrete floor. Believe me when I say that even cafeteria duty with a roomful of hormone-crazed adolescents had never been this stressful.

"Oh, good grief."

I looked up to see Nora's black patent stilettos and Lycra-encased legs standing near the table. Gently placing Phoebe's head on the floor, I left her snoring peacefully and struggled to my feet. My movements weren't even close to nimble, and I was glad no one else noticed my awkward position. I'd never been very agile, even as a child.

"My thoughts exactly." I panted slightly as I straightened my clothing. "How on earth she managed to connect with that clotheshorse, I'll never know."

"Clotheshorse?" Nora's carefully painted brows drew together in question, craning her neck as she looked around.

I gestured toward the bar. Matt Robb was leaning across it toward a very pretty bartender, a charming smile aimed at her ample cleavage.

"Matt, of course." Anyone who dressed better than Marcus Avery qualified as a clotheshorse, in my opinion. That man had no more sense of style than, well, than I did. "I wonder where Phoebe met him."

Nora gave an inelegant snort. She pulled out an empty chair and motioned me into the one next to her. Beneath the table, Phoebe snored on.

"Who knows what my ex-stepdaughter does? I'd say that anywhere she can drink for free, that's where you'll find her." Nora peered under the table with a distasteful expression. "The real question is who invited her to this shindig."

"You don't think she came here with him?" I motioned toward Matt with my chin. "They were looking mighty chummy when I first saw them."

"I think she saw a crowd, latched on to the first single man she saw, and invited herself in. Besides, Matt Robb is a married man, not that you'd know it by his current behavior."

I started at this pronouncement. Nora might be man crazy, but I knew she had standards when it came to the marital status of her beaus, at least some of the time. Apparently her ex-stepdaughter had no such scruples at any time.

Beneath the table, Phoebe made a gurgling noise and then resumed snoring. Nora lifted the edge of the tablecloth and gave Sleeping Beauty a cursory glance. "And I'm tempted to leave her here. At least she can't cause any more trouble."

"I wouldn't count on that," I said with a nod at the rapidly approaching Matt. "Here comes Prince Charming."

Nora watched Matt's approach with interest and an appraising look. I watched carefully, waiting for the inevitable charm attack.

"Well, hello there." Nora flashed a smile at him, the light catching on the large diamond studs in her ears. "You'll have to forgive my stepdaughter for being such a nuisance."

Matt hesitated a moment, looking around for the missing nuisance before resuming his seat.

"She really shouldn't mix her meds with alcohol. I'm always telling her that." Again that flash of charm. Leaning her chin on one hand, Nora leaned in, ready to make her move.

Matt Robb placed the refilled wineglass on the table.

"Maybe I shouldn't have gotten that for her." He looked over his shoulder as if expecting to find Phoebe there. "Did she leave?"

I glanced at Nora, hiding a smile behind a sip of wine. As long as Matt didn't stretch out his legs or lift the tablecloth, Phoebe could sleep peacefully on, drunken gurgles and all.

"In a manner of speaking, yes," replied Nora. "But enough about her. What I want to know is how you're holding up?"

"Holding up?" Matt sounded as confused as he looked before his face cleared and a sorrowful expression filled his eyes. "Oh, you mean Babs." He paused, looking at his well-manicured hands. I now saw that the ring finger on his left hand was bare, but a distinct white line could still be seen. Interesting.

And he's buying time, I thought with a wry glance in Nora's direction. He was either trying to think of a suitable response or was too upset for words. I voted for the first option. Nora, however, appeared to be genuinely touched by his apparent grief. The only thing missing in this little scene was the tears.

I wasn't disappointed.

Nora scooted her chair closer to the news anchor, offering him a hug and me a wink. Matt carefully dabbed at his eyes with a pristine white hankie, and I could have sworn I saw black smears. Did the man wear eyeliner? I was still contemplating that thought when a tousled blond head appeared above the tabletop, startling Matt and causing Nora to scowl.

"Did I mish anything?"

I had to hand it to her. Phoebe's timing was almost as good as Nora's.

"What in the world are you doing down there?" Matt's mouth hung open in the most unflattering manner as he stared at Phoebe, giving a handful of event attendees the perfect opportunity to snap a quick picture.

I ducked too late and groaned inwardly. I made a mental note to check Facebook and Instagram later. The last thing I wanted, or needed, was to be seen holding a wineglass next to a clearly snookered Phoebe and a gaping local news anchor. No wonder Shelby had been upset over that post.

Thinking of Shelby snapped me out of the mini-drama playing out before me. I turned to Nora, lowering my voice to barely above a whisper. "Shouldn't you be asking them a few questions?" I inclined my head at Phoebe as she struggled to regain her vacated chair, her giggles drawing even more attention than before. "You tackle him, and I'll speak with her. If I can get her to listen, that is." I saw a wary expression cross Matt's face as he tried to hear what I was saying but chose to ignore it. Nora could give him the lowdown. I needed to concentrate on the lush teetering on the edge of her chair.

Phoebe carefully navigated the refilled wineglass to her lips.

"That one certainly likes her drink." Matt's distaste was clear.

"Oh, never mind about her, Matt. Can I call you Matt?" Beside me, Nora grinned wickedly, pulling Matt by one arm closer toward her and away from the spectacle sitting on his other side.

I gave her the ol' eye roll and head shake combo. Maybe I shouldn't have used the word "tackle" when it came to Nora and a man. Turning back to Phoebe, I scooted as close to her as I dared, nearly asphyxiating myself when I got a whiff of her alcohol-drenched breath,

"Phoebe, how did you end up here tonight? Did you get an invitation? Or did someone invite you?" I angled my chair so I could see both Nora and Phoebe at the same time.

Nora, I noticed, was already deep into her act, and Matt appeared to be falling for it.

My conversation wasn't going as well. Phoebe was still staring at me as if trying to translate my questions into a language she could understand. When no answer was forthcoming, I tried again.

"You do know where you are, right?" I paused, giving her a chance to compute and slowly nod. "And do you know who invited you to be here?"

This time I managed to get through to her wine-soaked brain. She drew herself up straighter and nearly toppled sideways onto my lap. "I'm not an idiot, Miss What's-your-name."

"It's Miss Franklin." I gave her the benefit of my snootiest tone. "Who was it, Phoebe?"

To my amazement, she jabbed a finger in Matt's direction.

"Matty Boo did, of coursh." She giggled, swaying slightly in her chair. "He needed someone glam-glamourosh, he said. Not like his plain ol' wifey." This last pronouncement was followed by a hiccup and another giggle. "Oopsh. 'Scush me."

Well, Matt certainly misjudged this one, or his definition of "glamourous" was vastly different from mine and Noah Webster's.

Before I could think of a response, Nora leaned over and tapped my arm. "Gwen, Matt says he has no idea who might have wanted Babs dead. According to him, everyone loved her."

The sarcasm in that last sentence wasn't lost on me. Matt, on the other hand, had adopted a suitable expression of sorrow that seemed practiced. Phoebe, not wanting to be left out, leaned over and aimed her hand at his arm. Unfortunately, she managed to tumble out of her chair and onto the floor, her dress riding up to expose a pair of dimpled thighs and a flash of undies, which weren't much more than a few judiciously placed strips of lace.

"Oh, good grief." Nora reached over to haul a giggling Phoebe to her feet. "Can this evening get any worse?"

Behind us, someone applauded, and Phoebe attempted a bow before Nora pushed her back into her seat. My cheeks were hot as necks craned in our direction, the ubiquitous cell phones held aloft to catch the action. Matt gave one horrified glance over his shoulder and quickly stood up, knocking his chair over in his haste to escape the flashes and clicks of digital cameras pointed in his direction, muttering something about being needed at the front of the room.

At least it gave me a chance to yank Nora away from the table and head toward the ladies' room. Sinking onto the brocaded sofa just inside the door, I covered my face with my hands and groaned. "Can this entire fiasco just be over? Now?"

To my surprise, Nora chuckled. "Oh, it's not quite as bad as all that, Sis."

I dropped my hands and stared at her.

"Surely you jest." I gestured toward the bathroom door. "On the other side of that is a roomful of folks who now have a picture of us with a drunk." I shook my head in disgust. "That's not quite the image I want to give out, in case you hadn't noticed."

"Number one, it wasn't a 'roomful.'" Nora crooked her fingers in air quotes. "It was only a few, and they were focused on Matt, not us." She paused a moment, considering. "And maybe Phoebe as well. I'll give you that." Before I could add my two cents, she held her palm out. "Number two, I managed to get a few interesting tidbits from ol' Matty Boo while you were wrangling that nutcase."

"Did he admit to killing Babs?" I sounded petty, but I was in no mood for further games. I'd already had enough for the next year in one evening.

Nora shot me an injured look. "No need to get snarky with me. For your information, he said he'd overheard Babs arguing with someone on the phone a few days before she was killed."

Now we were getting somewhere. "Did he know who it was? On the phone, I mean."

The bathroom door crashed opened and a pair of tipsy young women staggered in, clutching each other as they made their way to the toilets. Fabulous. If this was an example of the general population, Nora's speech would be delivered to a roomful of pickled attendees.

Nora waited until they'd each disappeared inside a stall before leaning closer, lowering her voice to a whisper. "He said he thinks it was someone she'd interviewed. Apparently she was working on a story concerning excess spending in education or something to that effect."

My ears perked up at that.

"Excess? Really?" I paused for a moment, thinking. "I can't see how anyone would think there's excess anything in education. Of course, there's the current 'pay based on test scores' issue, as well as the problem behind increasing class sizes. Those issues have been around for the past few years." I paused again, taking in a deep breath to slow down my heart. Talking about these things always made me react inadvertently. That was something I didn't miss in my retirement. The students, yes. The politics? Not on your life.

"Seriously? You think someone killed her over that load of malarkey? If that's the case, the ground would be littered with dead journalists."

I sniffed, offended. "I'll have you know those are real issues. And real people are affected."

"Oh, get the twist out of those granny panties, Gwennie. I just meant there're bigger stories out there. No one in their right mind would bump off a two-bit Botox babe over something like that."

"Of course not, but what if they *weren't* in their right mind? Wouldn't that push the killer over the edge? And trust me when I say there're plenty of people in education who'd fit *that* description."

Nora stared at me for a moment, then leaned over and hugged me. "And that, dear Sis, is exactly why I keep you around."

I snorted as I pushed her away, but I was smiling. "And I thought you kept me around to balance out that crazy life of yours."

"We balance each other out," Nora corrected me. "But back to the whole crazy issue. That *has* to be the reason behind this. I've got a feeling right here." She patted her midsection with a pleased expression.

"I've always been taught emotions are rooted in the brain." I aimed a sly smile at my best friend. "Unless, of course, you mean your brain is in your stomach. That would actually make sense to me, since most of time your head is filled with stuff and nonsense."

Before a sputtering Nora could reply, I reached over and pulled her to her feet. "Come on, O Sybil of Portland. We need to get out there before they call your name."

"Sybil? And who might that be?"

I shook my head as I hauled her behind me. "It'd take too long to explain. Suffice it to say that you need to brush up on your Greek mythology, pal."

Someone had dimmed the lights in the main room, and a few people were scurrying around the raised dais. Thank goodness. I led the way back to our deserted table. I was more than ready to get this evening in the books and get back to Herc.

Phoebe, thankfully, was nowhere to be seen. I surreptitiously lifted the edge of the tablecloth, expecting to find her passed out once more, but the only thing I spotted was a crumpled cocktail napkin.

Sliding into an empty chair, I turned to smile encouragingly at Nora. "Ready for your close-up?"

"As ready as I'll ever be." She patted her chest and grinned. "Got my trusty phone right here, speech loaded and ready to go."

"Please tell me you're not going to fish around in your dress in front of this crowd." I could see it now, Nora's hand thrust into her neckline and a phalanx of cell phones memorializing the moment for all the world to see.

"Give me some credit, girlfriend." She slipped the cell phone out and waved it at me. "Happy now?"

"I don't know about her, but I certainly am."

Nora and I both turned around at the voice, dread already building in the pit of my stomach. Tim Lafoe stood there, his carefully arranged hair swept back from a round face, small eyes fixed on Nora's chest. Aiming a bob of his head in my direction, a movement that gave him a ridiculous, pigeon-like appearance, he focused his attention on Nora.

"I had no idea Gwen had such dazzling friends."

He leaned over and grasped one of Nora's hands, raising it toward his lips. I watched, half in fascination and half in horror, as he puckered up and aimed for the back of her hand. It was a train wreck in the making. I couldn't stand to watch, and I couldn't look away.

"And I had no idea Gwen had such uncouth acquaintances." Nora snatched her hand back just in time, giving Tim the benefit of her most regal and icy manner. Rising to her feet, she turned to look at me. "I believe it's time for us to move closer to the dais."

"Fabulous." Tim moved in behind us as we headed for another table, apparently unaware of Nora's snub. "I was going to ask you lovely ladies to join me and my parents." His voice took on a purring quality as he maneuvered his bulk between us. "This whole shindig is in their honor, after all."

"Oh, did they work at a shelter?" The words popped out before I could stop them at the gate, not bothering to hide a slight sarcasm. I wasn't sure why I'd said that.

I was well aware that his parents were some type of retired bigwigs in the medical field. Perhaps it was because Tim always seemed to rub me the wrong way when we were colleagues. Besides, Rachel's story was still fresh in my mind.

Nora gave an appreciative giggle, and Tim's cheeks bloomed with an unbecoming shade of red.

"My parents are both retired doctors, for your information. They are *volunteers* at a local shelter." He drew himself up taller, displaying the whole of his five-foot six-inch frame. "Volunteers of the year, I might add."

"How nice for them, I'm sure," Nora said abruptly. "And now, if you don't mind, I see a friend of ours. Come along, Sis."

And with a firm tug on my arm, she led me away from Tim toward a table with two empty chairs.

Louisa Lovejoy Turner, her pudgy hands clasped around a large wineglass, turned a surprised gaze on us as we sat down next to her. She was even more impressive up close than she'd been when I'd first glimpsed her. I hadn't had much experience with diamonds, but even my untrained eye could see the way the light refracted from her various rings and bracelets. Surely nothing manufactured in a laboratory could replicate that.

"I feel I should know you. I'm Louisa Turner."

This had been directed across me to Nora. I held my breath, waiting for one of Nora's verbal bombshells to be launched back in Louisa's direction. Nora held out her hand in a seemingly friendly gesture.

"I'm Nora Goldstein." Her tone was pleasant, a far cry from her earlier commentary on the logging heiress. It was too pleasant, in fact, and I should have been prepared for the next words. "And I'm just a common woman who pays her taxes." She paused a moment, her gaze fixed on Louisa's confused face. "You do know what taxes are, I assume."

To my surprise, Louisa threw back her head and gave a hearty laugh, causing many heads to turn in our direction. Nora and I looked at each other with astonishment, and my friend's cheeks reddened as the laughter went on and on. Finally, with a swipe at her streaming eyes, Louisa managed to take a gulp from her wineglass.

"Oh, that old story! I can't believe it's still going around." Louisa gave a small hiccup, covering her mouth with diamond-encrusted fingers, eyes twinkling over her hand. "Trust me, my dear. When it comes to taxes, I definitely know what they are. You should hear the way my accountant moans and groans every year when April comes around."

Satisfied nothing else exciting was going to happen, the curious heads had turned back to their own tables, and I was able to relax. Nora, the color still high in her cheeks, leaned closer and murmured an apology.

"Forget it." Louisa waved a hand as though dismissing an unimportant idea. "If I had a dollar for every person who believed that pack of lies, I'd be a far richer woman than I really am." She paused, and I thought she was going to add something else. Instead, she took another sip of her wine, her expression suddenly thoughtful.

"I'm Gwen Franklin." I startled even myself. "Are you here every year?"

Louisa transferred her gaze from her wineglass to me. Fine lines were etched around her eyes and the corners of her mouth, and underneath the glitter and glitz, I detected an air of loneliness. I'd seen enough of that in students, who could be surrounded by people but still be very much alone. Maybe money, or the legend of money, did that to a person.

"No, it's my first time at this particular event. You?"

I shook my head, glancing quickly at Nora. "We're newbies as well. Nora is going to say a few words and hand out one of the smaller awards." I smiled at my best friend and was amazed to see her blushing. "She's a natural-born speaker. She'll do great."

"And I'm sure she will." Louisa reached over and patted Nora's arm with a friendly smile. "Anyone with as much chutzpah as you have will do fine." Pulling her hand back, she added in a much more somber tone, "I guess you two have heard about what happened to the evening's main presenter."

I hesitated, unsure of how much to divulge.

Nora, however, seemed to have no such compunction. "Not only do we know what happened, we also know the person who's been accused of her murder."

Louisa's mouth gaped, and it took her a moment to compose her expression. What she had to say, though, was enough to knock me over with a feather, as Miss Marple might have said.

"I knew that woman was going to get herself killed sooner or later. She liked to dig into things that were none of her business, and I think she did it just for the fun of finding dirt on folks. Being a reporter only gave her the shovel." She shook her head in disgust and emptied her wineglass. "Personally, I could've happily shut the woman up myself."

Nora and I exchanged surprised glances. Did Louisa know something about Babs that would get Shelby off the hook?

Chapter 6

Silence fell as Nora and I digested Louisa's comment. I hadn't considered the possibility that Babs's muckraking had stretched farther than Portland's city limits. The logging community, of which Louisa's family was still a large part, was often in the news as it conducted battles about logging rights against the conservationists. Maybe Babs had discovered something underhanded among that group of folks.

Of course, there was always that phone call that had been overheard at the television station. And the possibility Babs had been delving into the local education issues and had discovered something provocative.

Beside me, Nora gave a slight jump as her cell phone began to shimmy across the table. Grabbing it, she stared at the text on the small screen and then smiled, relief flooding her face. "It's Marcus. He says he's staying overnight in the hospital, but it's only for observation, and he'll call in the morning."

"Any idea of what happened exactly? If they're letting him go so quickly, it most likely wasn't a heart attack." I smiled at Nora and put my arm around her shoulders, giving her a brief hug. "I'm guessing it was gas."

Louisa leaned in closer, her thinly plucked eyebrows lifted in surprise. "What's happening?"

"Marcus Avery, our escort for this evening, had a health scare earlier." I inclined my head in Nora's direction. "He's also a private detective and her beau."

Nora's color rose at my last comment, and she landed a well-aimed kick on my ankle with one of her stiletto heels. I stifled a yelp, and a satisfied expression crossed her face. Onlookers might have thought we were "frenemies" rather than best friends. Louisa, either ignoring or completely unaware of our juvenile behavior, turned to Nora.

"I was standing not too far away when it happened. I was shocked, my dears, absolutely shocked. I sincerely hope he fully recovers." She sent Nora a sympathetic smile and then turned back to me. "And I can't tell you the last time I heard that word 'beau.' How delightfully old-fashioned."

"Blame it on the books I read. I tend to gravitate to those written in the 'golden age of mystery,' as I've heard it called."

I gave a half smile, feeling slightly self-conscious. Beside me, Nora gave an irritated sniff that I ignored. Her reading material was typically confined to business e-mails, stock market news, and social media blurbs.

Louisa, however, nodded her head enthusiastically. "I love to read, especially books with a lot of suspense in the plot. Which brings me back to the current issue. How come I haven't read anything about the person accused of Babs's murder? Is there a 'news blackout,' or whatever it's called?"

Nora and I exchanged a brief glance, and I gave her a small nod.

"A journalist we know has been accused of killing her, so it's a possibility the paper has been keeping a lid on it. One of their own, you know. In my opinion, though, the evidence is flimsy, at best. I think it's only because the two of them had been at a press conference together earlier in the day and Babs had made a rather snarky comment about Shelby's physique."

Louisa snorted in disgust, shaking her head and causing her diamond earrings to swing like miniature chandeliers caught in a typhoon. "Typical Babs, I'd say. It wasn't a secret her tongue could be as sharp as a chef's favorite knife."

"Absolutely. You'd think that would be enough to get her fired, or at least warned. I'd stopped watching the local news report because of her." I thought about Matt and his apparently rocky relationship with Babs. Why had she been given leeway at the station? Maybe she had something on him as well. Leaning forward, I looked from Louisa to Nora, my expression and tone earnest. "And now that I think about it, I wonder if Babs had some dirt on Matt Robb as well. What else could explain his continued willingness to work with her?"

"That's certainly a possibility," Nora said. "If we're keeping track of possible perps, we need to add Matt's name to the list."

Waving down a passing waiter, she gestured toward Louisa's empty wineglass as she snagged one for herself. I'd had enough, though, and gladly accepted a tall glass of iced tea, a slice of yellow lemon clinging precariously to its rim.

"Absolutely." I fished the lemon out of my tea and dropped it onto a small cocktail napkin. "And don't forget the person she was arguing with on the phone. If we could only get the station's phone records, we'd know who it was."

Louisa's eyebrows shot up as she stared at me, but Nora only hooted derisively.

"As if, Miss Detective. And how do you suggest we do that?"

I shrugged, sipping carefully from my full glass. "It was just an idea."

"I might know someone." Louisa ran one finger around the edge of her wineglass. "She used to work for the phone company."

"Thanks, Louisa, but I don't think an ex-employee would be able to help."

Louisa smiled widely and lifted her glass in a mock toast. "Did I mention my friend was the CEO? I'm pretty sure she still has some pull there, considering her family is part owner of the company." Taking a sip of her refilled glass, she dropped one eyelid in a teasing wink.

Nora and I were speechless. Here was a ready-made opportunity to figure out who Babs's killer might be. Leaning over, I threw one arm around Louisa's plump shoulders and squeezed as Nora lifted her wineglass in a toast.

Louisa left before the program began, promising to call when she'd gotten the log of calls from her friend.

"And don't you worry," she smiled at both of us. "It'll be a piece of cake."

I always hated it when folks said that. It usually meant exactly the opposite. Still, I smiled back and assured her we'd be waiting to hear from her.

After the excitement of the Marcus and Phoebe show, the rest of the evening seemed to take a downward turn after Louisa's departure. Aside from the various speeches from presenters and thanks from the recipients, it was quickly becoming a bore. I could hardly wait for Nora to get her portion over and done with, and judging by the thin lines of her mouth, Nora felt the same.

"You're going to be fine." I gave her shoulder a gentle pat. "In the big scheme of things, who'll really care if you trip or stammer or freeze?"

"Oh, *that's* comforting." Her tone was pure Nora, though, dry as the Saharan desert. She'd be all right.

Nora's short speech and presentation to the Pet Walker of the Year was greeted with loud applause, although I was fairly certain the catcalls were aimed at her outfit and not the beaming recipient of the award. He was a short, rotund man whose equally round and dimpled face reminded me of a kewpie doll. Next to him, Nora looked like a tropical bird.

After she'd swayed her way from the dais to our table, all but kissing her hands to an admiring crowd, I leaned over.

"Let's get out of here." I motioned to my wristwatch, a slim Omega I'd inherited from my mother. "It's still early enough that we can call Shelby and tell her the great news. I'm assuming you got Marcus's keys to the van, right?"

Nora lifted one hand to her forehead, eyes closed as she shook her head. I sighed, louder than I'd intended.

"Well, don't blame me, Sis. You could've gotten them."

"I'm sorry. I wasn't blaming you. I was only thinking about Brent. Should we call him for a ride?"

Nora's eyes popped open as wide as they could go. "Not on your life, girlfriend. I'd rather walk."

* * * *

The Portland Pooch Park sat just south of Nora's luxury apartment building, its perimeters defined by a well-manicured boxwood hedge.

There were wooden benches placed around the inside of the hedge for the convenience of the local dog owners, and it was on one of these that Roger and I were currently seated, to-go cups of steaming Peet's coffee in our hands. The only thing missing, in my opinion, was a maple bacon donut from Voodoo Doughnuts, one of my all-time favorite vices.

Herc had taken one look at Roger's golden retrievers and had given a short happy bark, his tail wagging madly in an invitation to play before he shot off across the grass. With a glance at their owner as if to say, "This guy's got too much energy," they trotted off in decorous tandem after the black-and-white streak that was my dog.

"Looks like they're having a good time." Roger took a sip of coffee and turned to smile at me.

I'd never been this close to him before, and now I saw he had a web of fine wrinkles around his dark blue eyes. Smile wrinkles, I decided, or maybe laugh lines. I definitely liked the look.

"And Herc is certainly getting his exercise." I took a sip of coffee, noting that it wasn't as mellow as my favorite blend. In the world of coffee appreciation, though, I'd give it a big two thumbs-up. It really was difficult to find a bad cup of coffee here in Portland.

We both watched as my rescue dog—although it was still a tossup about who had rescued whom—continued to run in circles around the retrievers, barking with joyous abandon whenever they showed signs of play.

Herc had a good life, filled with play dates with Aggie, lots of food, and all the belly rubs he wanted. Finding him on that rainy night last year was the best thing that had come of a very scary time.

"Speaking of exercise," the lines around Roger's eyes crinkled even more, "how about a turn around the park? Since I retired from my dentistry practice, I find myself getting antsy if I don't keep busy."

"And I probably read too much, trying to make up for lost time when I had to read for work, not pleasure." I stood, shyly taking the hand he extended. "I had no idea there was such a difference between the two."

He didn't let go of my hand, so I left it there, conscious of Nora's apartment building looming behind us. Luckily, her widows were on the other side of the building, overlooking the Willamette River . . . but that wouldn't stop her from spying on us.

We'd begun strolling along the perimeter, the three dogs falling in behind us, when I heard a familiar voice.

"Hey, Miss F.! Is that your new boyfriend?"

Groaning inwardly, I turned to see Aggie, her stubby tail wagging in delight, her very unwelcome owner in tow.

I kept my gaze averted from Roger's face, not wanting to see his expression. My own face was hot and probably as red as the geraniums growing in the park's planters, and if I could have crawled under a rock, I would have in a heartbeat. Slipping my hand from Roger's, I turned to face Brent.

"Brent. What brings you here?"

Today of all days, I silently added as I waited for my grinning ex-student to finish humiliating me.

"Oh, you know." He waved around the park in an expansive gesture. "Aggie likes this place. Don't cha, girl?" He leaned over and gave Aggie's ears a quick scratch. "And I like it too." His smile widened as he looked from me to Roger and back. I could have happily taped his mouth shut. "Besides, Mrs. G. said you'd be here."

Of course she did, bless her little heart. *Not.* She and I would be having a little chat about this, the sooner the better.

Straightening my shoulders, I turned to face Roger. "I need to speak with Brent privately. Why don't you keep going, and I'll catch up."

"Is everything all right?" Roger flicked a concerned glance at Brent before looking down at me, and warmth spread up from my neck, adding to the heat in my cheeks.

I nodded, wanting him to go before Brent said anything else embarrassing. Knowing the boy as well as I did, it would be a matter of moments. As usual, I was right.

"But, Miss F., I only came here because Mrs. G. told me you'd be here with your—"

I hurriedly cut him off, grabbing his arm and all but dragging him over to an empty bench, Aggie trotting after the two of us. Pushing him onto the seat, I stood there with arms crossed and a stern expression on my face. "Well, out with it, young man. What else did Mrs. Goldstein tell you?"

Brent looked up, his expression as innocent as a newborn pup's. "You mean besides him being your boyfriend?"

I managed to bat down his hand as he began to point across the park to where Roger stood with Herc and the golden retrievers.

"Yes, Brent. Besides that little nugget." I got the last words out through clenched teeth, already scripting my talk with Nora.

He wrinkled his forehead, as if trying to call forth a long-buried memory instead of something Nora had told him less than an hour before. How the boy had managed to learn anything in school and retain it was beyond me. Of course, I'd seen him learn complex plays on the football field and then execute them flawlessly the following week, so perhaps it was a matter of selective learning.

At the moment, though, I was impatiently waiting for the other half of my message from Nora. I restrained myself from shaking the information out of him. I didn't need to further scramble what brains he had up in that great big noggin of his.

Suddenly, he sat up straighter, snapping his fingers and causing Aggie to let out an excited bark. "I've got it, Miss F. I was supposed to tell you to bring your boyfriend back to the apartment for coffee."

He looked so pleased with himself that I didn't have the heart to lose my temper with him over the "boyfriend" reference. I needed to set the record straight, however.

"Brent," I began firmly, "Dr. Smithson isn't my boyfriend. And it's hard for me to think Mrs. Goldstein sent you here to give me a message she could have texted to me quite easily."

He grinned, his mouth bracketed in deep smile lines. Bless the boy. I smiled back reluctantly. He lived in his own happy little world.

He nodded emphatically. "Actually, I was in the way, so she sent me instead of calling you. She said it was killing two birds with one stone." A small pucker appeared between his brows. "I got kinda scared she was really gonna throw a rock or something, Miss F. She was getting pretty hot under the collar." He winced slightly. "I never seen her so mad before, Miss F."

"Really." I hadn't expected that. "Do you know what the problem was?"

"Yup. It was Mr. Avery, all right. He called her cell phone, and she told him to stick *his* phone where the sun didn't shine." He reached over and scooped up Aggie, cuddling her close to his chest. "I guess she didn't like it when he didn't let her know some other old woman—oops, Miss F., I didn't mean you—was taking care of him."

"Hold on a minute." I shook my head as if dislodging Brent's very disjointed news. He'd made absolutely no sense. "What woman was taking care of Mr. Avery, and what made him call Mrs. Goldstein and tell her about it?"

Brent's large shoulders rose and fell in a nonchalant shrug. "No idea. Guess you've gotta ask her yourself when you bring your boyf—"

"Not one more word, young man."

The sound of footsteps made me look around. Roger, hands in his pants pockets and all three dogs at his heels, stood there, one eyebrow lifted and a faintly amused expression in his eyes. I had a feeling he'd heard that last exchange. Choosing to pretend he hadn't, I smiled at him.

"If you're not too coffee'd out, Nora has invited us over to her place." I motioned to the tall high-rise behind the park. "She lives across the street, and she's invited the dogs as well."

"I didn't hear nothing about that." Brent shut up when I gave his extra-large foot a subtle but well-aimed kick.

"Then I accept for the three of us." Roger leaned over and clipped a leash on each of the retrievers' collars. "Lead the way."

Chapter 7

Brent, Aggie cradled in his arms, charged ahead of us. I chanced a quick glance at Roger and saw he was smiling. Good. He hadn't been offended by Brent's commentary. Someone needed to take that boy under her wing for a lesson in social niceties, though. Maybe after this entire Babs fiasco was settled, I'd be able to find the time.

In the meantime, I'd found myself in another situation, albeit a pleasant one. Stepping out of the elevator ahead of Roger and the dogs, I saw the front door to Nora's apartment was standing ajar. Clearly we were expected, or maybe Brent had been in such a hurry to report to Nora that he'd left it open. My money, as scarce as it was, was on the latter. Turning to give Roger an encouraging smile, I led the way into the living room. Brent, as usual, made a beeline for the kitchen, an enthusiastic Aggie right on his heels.

Nora was seated on one end of her overstuffed sofa, bare feet curled up and tucked under a pillow. Her cell phone was pressed to one ear and a decidedly unhappy expression filled her eyes. Various sounds coming from the kitchen could only mean one thing. Brent was feeding his constantly hungry self and probably giving Aggie a treat as well. That boy could eat around the clock and still be famished.

Catching Nora's attention, I mouthed "Marcus?"

She nodded, rolling her eyes in response. Not an auspicious time for a visit. I turned to usher Roger back into the hallway.

"Hey, where're you guys going? I thought you wanted Mrs. G. to meet your boyfriend."

I turned back to see Brent standing in the kitchen's entrance, a donut in each hand and a tell-tale smear of red on his chin. Aggie was performing acrobatic leaps near his feet, trying to get at the treats. I was tempted to walk over and help him stuff the entire box into his blabby mouth.

"We can come back later, after Mrs. Goldstein's handled *that*." I nodded toward Nora. "And you'd probably better come with us." I noted his suddenly crestfallen expression. "You can bring the donuts, for goodness sake."

My best friend had another idea, though. With one bedazzled fingernail, Nora disconnected the call and tossed the phone on the sofa.

"There. All done." Uncurling herself from the sofa, she stood and marched over to where we stood, just inside the open door. "Well, come in, come in. I don't want to have a conversation in the hall for the rest of my nosy neighbors to hear." She glanced over her shoulder at Brent. "And take that mess back into the kitchen, boy. All I need is a houseful of dogs tackling you and getting donut innards all over my carpet."

Without another word, Brent vanished from sight. Nora gave me a shove toward the sofa, and I obliged, tripping over an excited Herc and Aggie reunion as I did. Roger, a retriever glued to each of his legs, paused to offer a hand to Nora.

"I'm Roger Smithson." His smile was relaxed, and he seemed to be at ease. "Thanks for having us over."

My face heated at the word "us." Of course, he might have been referring to his dogs, who were now cautiously advancing into to the room, both of them keeping a wary eye on the other two canines.

Still, I smiled at the possibility.

Nora, bless her little prying heart, hadn't missed a thing, and she darted a look from my warm face to Roger's smiling one, an eyebrow slightly raised. Between her and Brent, I wanted to crawl under the sofa for a few decades.

"So, moving on. Gwen, I talked with Shelby this morning. She said she'd tried to call you, but you must've been otherwise engaged."

She gave the last few words more emphasis than needed. I refused to react, instead giving her a cool nod as I settled down on the sofa.

"Did she say what she wanted?"

Nora's face took on a surprised expression. "Actually, she didn't. I was too focused on letting her know we'd made a gain last night." She shot a quick glance at Roger, head tilted in question.

I flapped one hand at her. "Go on. He's a good listener." *And a good looker*, I added silently, managing to keep my expression neutral. "I'm assuming you told her about Louisa? And sit down, for goodness sake."

Nora nodded, switching her attention back to me as she plopped down beside me. "I did. She seems to think it'll be enough to clear her name, although I reminded her not to get her hopes up."

"That wasn't very nice," I protested. "Shelby's not a killer, and we both know it. If anything, this will prove Babs had issues with quite a few people. The incident with Shelby was Babs being her typical 'better than thou' self."

Roger, seated in the armchair across from us, leaned forward, his face alight with interest.

"We're speaking of Babs Prescott, right?" He looked at me, a twinkle in his eyes. "This would be the one with the big teeth, if I'm recalling that correctly."

My heat grew hot, suddenly fascinated by my fingernails.

"Big teeth, huh?" Nora's tone was amused, and I glanced up to see her smiling widely. "I'll give her that, as well as her big—"

"Aaaand that's enough." I held up one hand in Nora's direction. "Let's just say Babs got a lot of attention, and it probably wasn't for her anchoring skills." My heart rate began to rise, and I took in a steadying breath. "And I can't imagine Shelby was important enough for Babs to acknowledge for more than a split second anyway. It was a chance meeting in that parking garage, where they found Babs, plain and simple."

Herc, sensing something was up with his mistress, trotted over and thrust his nose against my knee. I ran one hand through his fur, and my heart rate slowed down. Dogs were perfect as therapy animals, and Herc did his job effortlessly.

Thanks to whatever powers were at work that rainy night when Herc came into my life, I had a companion who would never let me down. Unfortunately, I was all too aware that humans offered no such guarantee. Poor Shelby, and even Babs, had experienced that firsthand, and I was more determined than ever to figure out who was behind the murder.

"It seems to me," Roger began slowly, "we need to take a look at Babs herself. Who she knew, as in a boyfriend, or who she hung out with the most. Those folks might be able to point us in the right direction."

I averted my eyes from Nora, not wanting to see her reaction to those two lovely words, "we" and "us." I was in no mood to be teased. Looking instead at Roger, I nodded.

"I think Matt might be able to give us a starting point." I took a chance and turned to face Nora.

Her expression was sober enough, but there was a slight twitch of her lips. At least she was controlling herself.

"Do you think you could get hold of him and set up a meeting?"

At that, Nora laughed. "If you're really asking me if I got to know him well enough to give him a call, just say it." She shook her head in mock irritation. "You English teachers talk in circles sometimes."

"I'm trying to be polite." I lifted my chin in defense. "Something, I might add, with which you seem to have a difficult time."

"Wow, Miss F. You sure do know how to use words. That's probably why you made us write so much, huh."

I hadn't heard Brent come back into the living room. Beside me, Nora let out a loud chuckle, and even Roger was smiling broadly.

I threw up my hands and let them fall. I knew when I was beaten. "Fine. I'll do my best to use colloquialisms from here on out."

"Collokey-what?" Brent's forehead crinkled in confusion. "Is that some kind of dictionary?"

"I think we're getting off the track." Nora gestured to the donut Brent held in his large hand, as gently as if it were a tiny animal. That boy certainly loved—*adored*—his food. "How about you bring the box in here and share, all right?" She looked at me and smiled. "I'm sure Miss Franklin would like to have that maple bacon donut I got for her."

"You want me to bring the whole box in here?"

I stared suspiciously at Brent's innocent face. He was doing everything but digging one toe into the floor as he looked at Nora, his eyes as wide as they'd go.

"Yes, Brent, that's exactly—"

I broke into Nora's comment, crooking a forefinger at my former student. "Brent Mayfair, front and center, please."

I pointed at the floor in front of me and watched a subdued Brent scuff toward me, Aggie bouncing at his heels. "Yes, Miss Franklin?"

I looked straight into his eyes, my own narrowing slightly. "Brent, did you eat all the donuts?"

"Wellllll," he drew out the word as if it was a lifeline. "Maybe not all of them." He held out one hand, the remains of a chocolate frosted hunk of goodness clutched in his fingers. "I still have this one." He held it toward me. "Want a bite?"

Across the room, Roger began laughing, a pleasant belly laugh that made Nora smile, and even my own lips began to twitch. Brent, however, simply gazed around the room at the three adults, his mind clearly thinking, "Old people are nuts."

"I have an idea." Roger, his face flushed from laughing, caught his breath and gestured toward Brent. "Why don't we get another box after we've gone out for lunch? My treat, of course."

Brent's face lit up as bright as the Tillamook Bay lighthouse had once upon a time.

I really liked this man. Good-looking, a sense of humor, easy to talk with, and he liked dogs. Even a committed spinster such as Miss Marple might have fallen for him.

"I'm all right with that." I glanced at Nora, waiting for her response. "Does that sound okay with you? Brent, I know you're fine with it."

The intended humor was as dry as my tone and sailed completely over Brent's head. He nodded enthusiastically as he stuffed the remains of the last donut in his mouth.

"You betcha." His expectant smile slipped a trifle as he looked at me. "Can I go? I mean, you're not mad anymore, are you, Miss F.?"

I mentally rolled my eyes but made myself smile at him. He was still such a boy in that big body, I could only hope Rachel was either blissfully unaware of it or had plans to raise him.

"No, I'm not mad, Brent." Standing, I gave him an admonitory finger waggle. "But next time, ask first before you eat it all, okay?"

"Of course, Miss F." He looked and sounded indignant. "I've got manners. My mom says all the time that I've got the manners of a wild animal."

That last comment elicited another snort of laughter from Roger and Nora and a wide smile from me.

Reaching up, I gave his cheek a pat. "And you can tell your mother she's gotten that one absolutely correct."

It was a beautiful day for a walk, but that was most days in Portland. I loved living in a city that could still feel like a small town in so many ways. The fantastic weather was a bonus, in my humble opinion. Of course, we had our share of rain—and probably the share of a few other towns as well—but overall, it was as close to paradise as one might get.

With Herc's leash held firmly in one hand, I boldly slipped the other into Roger's. I blamed it on the sunshine and the light breeze blowing in from the Willamette. Nora and Brent, walking ahead of us and animatedly discussing the merits of Voodoo Doughnuts, were too busy to notice, thank goodness. My bold move might have dissolved into acute embarrassment, otherwise. I slid a sideways glance at Roger and saw the smile that lurked in the corners of his mouth. I sincerely hoped it was enjoyment and not humor.

Nora had insisted on walking the two retrievers. She loved dogs, and I decided to work on getting her one of her own. Aggie and Herc, of course, were at her apartment so often they were practically hers anyway, but having a furry friend herself might finally make Marcus expendable.

To my embarrassment, Roger had said something I'd missed during my mental planning session. He was looking at me now with an expectant look, and I struggled to form an answer that wouldn't make me sound imbecilic.

"I'm fine with whatever."

There. That was a multi-purpose response. I must have said something amusing, however, because Roger's eyes twinkled. "So, you're okay with giving your share of donuts to the dogs?"

I stared at him and his delightful laugh lines and had to laugh at myself.

"Sorry." I gave his hand a tiny squeeze. "My mind was miles away. What was it you said?"

"I think we ought to include Nora's friend in our plans."

I stopped walking, taking my hand from his as I turned to face him. "Marcus Avery, the greatest no-show on earth? Whatever for?"

My voice had risen higher than I meant it to, and it caught the attention of Nora and Brent. Backtracking, reluctant dogs in tow, they came back to where Roger and I were standing. The shade from an overarching elm tree made shadows on their faces, and I noticed Nora's eyes looked a tad sunken, as if she'd not been sleeping well. I'd have to ask her later, though. Right now, Marcus was hot topic number one.

"Did I catch something about Marcus?" Nora's eyebrows lifted in question as the retrievers moved over to press themselves against Roger's legs.

Leaning over and gently caressing their fine silky ears, he restated his suggestion.

"I know he can be a complete pain, Nora, but he's good at what he does. As it pertains to detecting," I said hastily as I saw her eyes narrow. Yes, I was doing an about-face, and I expected Nora to point that out. When she said nothing, I continued, pointing out that four heads would be much better than three—here I gave Roger a brief smile—and that we'd cover more ground more quickly. "Shelby's situation can't wait much longer. And I'm positive that, between us, we'll be able to find out who might have had the opportunity to kill Babs."

Nora's expression was difficult to read in the shade, and beside her, Brent, still cradling Aggie, had looked bored. If it wasn't about food or Rachel or animals, he was ready to check out. When I mentioned murder, though, he perked right up.

"Maybe you should get Rachel in on this too." He looked from one face to the next and beamed proudly. "I mean, she's practically a detective herself, Miss F."

"Just because she lives with one doesn't make Rachel a detective," I said firmly. "It's not an airborne allergen, Brent."

"Allergy? Who said anything about allergies?" Now Brent sounded indignant, and Aggie gave a little whimper as she licked his cheek. To my amazement, he kissed her back and then added, clearly still miffed, "Rachel is the wellest person I know. She never even sneezes, not even when Aggie shakes her fur."

"It sounds like you've got a keeper." Roger smiled at Brent as he reached out and gave Aggie's soft head a little pat. "And, of course, she'd be welcome to join us. The more the merrier, right?"

That last comment was directed at me, and I reluctantly smiled in agreement. Rachel, to her credit, had been helpful in the past, and she would probably be the same this time around.

"You're probably correct." I smiled sheepishly around at my companions. "With six of us, surely we'll be able to get to the bottom of this. The police, of course, will most likely beat us to the answer, but at least I'll feel useful. Nora? What do you think?"

I was almost certain she'd actually welcome the excuse to be around Marcus. When I saw the flush appear on her cheeks, I knew I was right. Oh, well. It could be worse. If he could get his penchant for flirting and his bad taste in clothes under control, Marcus wasn't such a bad guy.

"Shall we?" Roger extended one hand in the direction we'd been walking before the impromptu confab.

Crooking one arm at me, he smiled, and I slipped my arm through his. I might as well get it out in the open.

"Close your mouth, boy, or you'll catch flies." Nora gave a gawking Brent a poke in the back and prodded him forward.

Looking over her shoulder, she batted her eyes at me. I rolled mine at her.

The small café we chose was a family-run affair, dog-friendly, and fairly inexpensive. I gladly took the chair Roger pulled out and tethered Herc's leash to the table leg. Nora sank into the chair next to mine, and Brent settled in across from me, a curious Aggie on his lap.

The smiling waitress who approached our table paused to give the golden retrievers a quick scratch between their ears. There was something familiar about her face and her red hair, and when she turned to stare at me, I instantly placed her: second-hour American lit, several years past. Her name, however, was lost somewhere among the thousands of others I'd once known and then forgotten when the next batch of students came along.

"Miss Franklin! How good to see you again." With a wide smile on her freckled face, she came around the table to give me an exuberant hug.

I said what I always did whenever I came across a student whose name I couldn't recall, which was all of the time. "Hey, you! How're you doing?" I glanced around the café and noticed a few others with the same red hair and made a quick deduction. "Does this place belong to your folks?"

She nodded, pointing to a large woman standing just inside the swinging kitchen door.

"That's my Grandma Ginnie, and Uncle Lewis is back there cooking." She nodded toward the man at the cash register and the woman behind a glass-fronted counter filled with various pies. "And those are my dad and mom. Grandma Ginnie is my dad's mom, and Uncle Lewis is my mom's brother." She grinned around at us. "It's a real family business."

Brent had been staring intently at the waitress the entire time she'd been speaking. Now he cocked his head to one side. "You're Addie's little sister. Emily, right?"

To my astonishment, Emily teared up and dropped her gaze to her clasped hands.

Nora gave Brent a disapproving glare and reached out for Emily, patting her gently on the arm. "There, there. It's all right."

When Brent began to protest, she raised a finger in his direction, instantly shutting him down. I had to admire her technique. For someone whose experience with children revolved around brief spates as a stepmother, Nora sure knew how to handle them.

"Emily," I said softly, "why don't you pull up another chair and join us." I glanced over at the counter, where her mother stood watching us, and gave a waggle of my fingers. "I'll go clear it with your parents, okay?"

Without waiting for an answer, I headed straight for the counter, my friendly parent-teacher conference face firmly in place.

Chapter 8

"I'm Gwen Franklin, one of Emily's high school teachers." I thrust out my hand in greeting, first to her mother and then to her father.

Both shook my hand, mild curiosity in their expressions.

I hurried on. "Emily seems to be upset about her sister. Would it be all right for her to join us for a few minutes? I'd like to speak with her, if that's fine with you." I included both parents in that last statement, looking from one to the other.

After a short hesitation, Emily's father shrugged and gestured at his wife. "She's the boss when it comes to the waitstaff. It's fine by me, but . . ."

His voice trailed off, but I knew what he meant. In all my years of attending staff meetings, I had developed the skill of reading between the lines, so to speak, and I was reading this line loud and clear. Emily's mom wasn't just the boss of the restaurant's waitstaff; she was also the boss of the house.

"I'd appreciate it." I turned to look at Emily's mom. "And I know Emily would appreciate it as well." I smiled at her, hoping I still had that indescribable "teacher's aura," the one that made most folks stand straighter and answer politely.

"I'm not sure I want you talking to my girl." Emily's mom, apparently, wasn't in that category.

Out of the corner of my eye, I saw her husband shifting sideways and out of sight. Smart man, but definitely not a good sign for me.

"She's supposed to be earning her paycheck, not sitting around gossiping about Addie." She glanced over my shoulder toward Emily, her mouth pressed together in disapproval.

Emily's dad was nowhere to be seen.

"It'll only take a moment," I urged. "And I won't keep her from her job, I promise." I turned and waved at the almost-empty room. I was tempted to point that out but managed to keep that observation from crossing my lips. Discretion, I knew from experience, was the better part of valor, and it certainly was the better part in this particular situation.

"Five minutes. And you tell that girl I'm taking it out of her pay." Without another word, Emily's mother returned to her task behind the counter.

I hustled back to the table, not wanting to waste a second of the allotted time. I was beginning to understand Addie's absence. If I was in her shoes, I'd probably be out of here as well. Slipping back into my chair, I turned to Emily. "Your mom said we can have five minutes, so talk fast, okay?"

She sniffed, whether from crying or directed at her mother, I couldn't say. Taking in a deep breath, Emily settled back into the chair and began to speak.

"Addie moved away last year, right after her second year at the college." She looked at me. "She went to the local junior college, the one downtown."

"Hey, that's where Rachel goes." A proud expression crossed Brent's face. "She says she hates it."

Emily gave a short laugh that sounded more like a sob. "Yeah? Well, so did Addie. Hated it, I mean. Especially that one teacher." She slid a quick glance in my direction. "Sorry, Miss Franklin."

I waved a hand as if brushing away her words. "Not a problem,. I'd be the first to admit not every teacher should be in the classroom."

I glanced at my watch: three minutes and forty seconds left.

"Well, this guy shouldn't even be allowed on this planet." Emily's voice was rough with tears, and she appeared to be getting upset again.

Time to channel my inner Dr. Phil. "Emily, I need to hear exactly what this teacher did. Or didn't do." I wanted to appear fair. "Was he a poor teacher? Or did he leave the teaching to his assistant and sleep in his office?" It had happened before and probably would again.

She shook her head vehemently, sending her ponytail whipping from side to side, like a windsock in a hurricane.

"No, that wasn't the issue, Miss Franklin." Leaning forward, she glanced quickly over her shoulder at the front counter. "She didn't say anything bad about his teaching. It was just that, well . . ." She hesitated, her face reddening, and my stomach began to roll.

I knew what she was going to say.

"Addie told me he wanted to trade her grade for . . . for . . ." The words trailed off, and she stared at the table as if it was the most fascinating thing she'd ever seen.

The silence was acutely uncomfortable, practically thick enough to scoop up with my hands, and my heart picked up speed. Roger, who had been listening quietly with the retrievers leaning against his legs, reached out to touch Emily's hand, an expression of sympathy on his face. She started, drawing back from him as if bitten by a rattlesnake. It didn't take a genius to read between these lines.

"It's okay, Emily," I said soothingly. "Dr. Smithson is a friend of mine."

I waited a moment while she shot a quick glance at him before lowering her gaze again. Whatever Addie had told her, it hadn't painted men in a positive light.

An exaggerated cough from the front of the restaurant sent Emily leaping to her feet. I still needed to know who it was that had frightened her sister Addie, although a suspicion was growing as rapidly as a sinkhole in Florida. Grabbing Emily's arm, I asked, "Can you remember the name of the teacher?"

She started to shake her head and then hesitated. "Something that sounded like 'laffy.' Maybe 'la-something.' I can't remember exactly, sorry."

"Was it 'Lafoe'?" I held my breath, waiting for her answer.

She shrugged. "Maybe. It sounds kinda like it." She looked over at her mother again and then back at me. "Listen, I gotta get busy or my mom'll skin me alive."

I flinched at her words, trusting it was only a figure of speech.

"I'll be back with your orders in a few minutes, okay?"

And with that, she was gone, almost running to the kitchen.

Nora, who had sat unnaturally quiet during the entire exchange, shifted in her chair, a thoughtful expression growing. I turned to look at her, hoping she'd thought of something significant about this latest development and not just something about the menu.

"Yes?" I snapped my fingers in her direction. "Any thoughts, oh guru of the geriatrics?"

Brent looked puzzled at my comment, and Roger leaned over to give his dogs another hug—and to hide a smile, I was pretty sure.

Nora, for once, ignored my gentle dig. Tapping the tabletop with her rhinestoned nails, she glanced over her shoulder for eavesdroppers and then leaned forward. "I think I see a common thread here, Sis." She looked around at the three of us. "I'm pretty sure Babs had the goods on Tim Lafoe." When none of us responded, her face took on a mulish look, chin jutting and mouth puckered as if she'd tasted something rotten. "Fine, then. You guys are so smart, you figure it out."

Nora, in one of her pouts, could either be downright hilarious or supremely irritating. I was trending toward the latter at this moment, and Herc must have sensed my exasperation. Lifting one shaggy paw and placing it on my lap, he nuzzled my leg and whined softly. Without thinking, I wound my fingers through his thick fur, gently patting my personal canine comforter.

Taking in a steadying breath, I turned to Roger. "Do you see any connection between a poorly behaving teacher and a murder?"

When Nora began to splutter before he could answer, I held up one hand to stop her.

"I'm being serious, Nora. We do need to look at every possibility, no matter how ridiculous it might sound. After all, WWMMD?"

"WWM what?" Brent sounded as nonplussed as he appeared, an everyday occurrence for the boy. "Is that some sort of secret code, Miss F.?"

Across the table, Nora snorted derisively. "Only if you don't know your Agatha Christie, kiddo."

Now Brent was doing his best tennis-match impression, his neck swiveling from Nora to me and back again in rapid succession. I winced as I watched him, hoping he didn't develop whiplash or further scramble those brains of his.

"I don't know no Agatha What's-her-name, Mrs. G.," he said after a moment. "I only took the easy classes so I could play football."

"Didn't you have him in one of your classes?" murmured Nora at me, giving me a sly smile.

I gave her a not-so-sly kick in the ankle.

Roger didn't bother hiding his amusement this time. I only hoped he was laughing at Brent and not at the ongoing Gwen and Nora show.

"Brent," I said in my practiced lecturing voice, "Agatha Christie was a British mystery writer during the early part of the twentieth century."

"Oh, so like in the time when we fought against them in the revolution?"

Roger almost choked on a laugh. Nora chuckled outright. Giving her one of my laser stares, I shook my head. No need to discourage the boy. So his knowledge scaffolding was a little shaky; at least he was trying to make a connection.

"No, not that early. Closer to when most people began to drive cars." I hated to mention anything about driving to someone who was a terror behind the wheel, but he seemed to get my meaning. "One of her main characters was named Miss Jane Marple." I shot Nora another look and caught her in mid eye roll. "I said 'WWMMD' because Miss Marple was a crime solver."

He still appeared baffled.

"It means 'What would Miss Marple do?'"

"Oh, I see, Miss F." A broad smile broke out, and Aggie reached up to lick his chin. "So, are we gonna call her? I'm pretty sure we could use her help."

Nora leaned over and placed one hand on Brent's arm. "My boy, if you can get hold of either Agatha Christie or Jane Marple, you let me know pronto. I've got a few questions I'd like to ask those two."

It was my turn for the eye roll. "Oh, really, Nora. Don't tease him. Brent, Agatha is dead, and Jane is fictional. That means that she's not a real person."

To my amusement, Brent gently placed one large hand over Aggie's furry ears. "I don't think you should talk about things like that in front of Aggie. She might think you're talking about her being d-a-i-d."

Most of the time I was able to understand "Brent speak," but this gem had me stumped.

Nora gave another laugh and reached over to pull Brent's hand off a squirming Aggie's head. "Number one, that dog may be smart, but she won't be able to make a connection between 'Agatha' and 'Aggie,' not to mention being 'd-a-i-d.' Trust me on that, kiddo. And number two, she only answers to her name because it's a sound that has food attached to it."

Brent's expression grew solemn, and he looked dangerously close to tears at Nora's words. He hugged Aggie even tighter to his chest, and the dog gave a surprised yelp.

I looked for a distraction, something to coax Brent back to his normally happy demeanor. The swinging kitchen door opened, and Emily backed into the restaurant, both arms laden with plates.

Smiling in relief, I nodded at Brent. "Our food's on the way. Maybe you should put Aggie down with the other dogs, all right?"

"Sure thing, Miss F." He leaned over and gently lowered the small animal to the floor. "Besides, I don't want her eating off my plate."

"And quite right. It's not good for dogs to eat people food."

"It's not?" Brent's forehead furrowed in concern. "I was gonna give her some of my fries on the floor."

I was spared any more of this inane conversation by Emily's arrival.

Deftly unloading the plates from her arms and handing them around, she smiled at us. "Can I get you anything else? Maybe some ketchup?"

"I'll take mustard, if you've got it." Brent seemed to have already forgotten about sharing his food and sat with one arm curled around his plate as if guarding it from invaders. "I don't like ketchup no more, not

since my friend Jeremy made it come outta his nose at football camp."
He wrinkled his own nose in disgust. "It made him look like he had a—"

"Aaaand that's enough, thank you very much." I was pretty sure I knew
where that tidbit was headed. "Let's just let Emily get the mustard and get
on with our lunch, all right?"

The remainder of the meal was pleasant.

Roger amused us with stories of patients whose extreme fear of the
dentist caused them to do odd things, such as the time one patient showed
up with his college-aged son in tow. "He told me his son was studying law
and he wanted him to be there in case of malpractice. When I asked him
what he meant by that, he said, 'In case I start crying.'"

Nora and I laughed while Roger shook his head.

"As you might imagine, I suggested he find another dentist pronto. His
son was mortified by his dad's behavior, I can tell you that."

"I'm not afraid of the dentist," offered Brent around a mouthful of
hamburger. "I like it when I get to use that stuff that makes me feel all
floaty." He looked at Roger, his head tipped to one side in question. "You
got any of that stuff at your house?"

"Good question, kiddo." Nora grinned at Roger, her eyes twinkling
mischievously. "Maybe we could use some on that Lafoe creature, see if
we can make him talk."

"Oh, come on, you two." My cheeks were getting hot, concerned Roger
would begin to think I was as kooky as they sounded. "I don't think he
kept any laughing gas as a retirement memento."

"No. Sorry, Brent." Roger shook his head. "I didn't bring home any
laughing gas. However, I do know a way to get some information about
Babs, if that's what you're aiming for."

This last comment was directed to me and I nodded.

"Absolutely. If we could get someone, anyone, to tell us about Babs's
research into education, I think we might be able to start honing in on who
killed her. Or at least who might have wanted her silenced."

Nora leaned forward on one elbow, resting her chin on her hand and
nearly upending my glass of iced tea into my plate. I grabbed it as it
wobbled and frowned at her. For whom was she posing? I didn't care for
this particular situation one bit.

She ignored me, gazing instead at Roger with a sultry half smile. "Don't
tell me. You've got a secret dungeon in that house of yours."

I knew my best friend well enough to know what sordid path that
little brain of hers was taking, and I was tempted to give her another kick
under the table.

"Oh, cool!" Brent's eyes lit up, and for once, I was glad for his interruption.

Nora, however, looked a little put out, and I couldn't hold back a smile of satisfaction. I'd make sure Brent got his share of Voodoo Doughnuts and more.

"Can I see it? Me'n Aggie sure could use it to hide out from my mom. She's always trying to make me do stuff, like make my bed and take care of my little brother."

"I'm afraid I've only got a small garden shed, and that's full of things like rakes and grass seed."

Brent's mouth drooped in disappointment. "Guess I'll have to find somewhere else to hide out."

"If it's all right with everyone, I'd like to get back to how we can get someone to talk. Roger, you were saying?"

I gave Brent and Nora both a stern look before turning to face Roger. Instead of responding, he gestured to something behind me. Twisting around in my chair, I saw what he was pointing at, or rather, *whom*.

Matt Robb, erstwhile partner of the late Babs, sat at small table outside the café, legs crossed and with a pleased expression as he busily scribbled in a notebook. Across from him sat none other than Louisa Lovejoy Turner, Portland's logging heiress, and, more importantly, our connection to Babs's phone records.

Without thinking, I jumped up from my chair and headed for the door. If Louisa had any important information, I planned on being there to hear it.

Chapter 9

"Well, if it isn't my good friend from the shelter event. How are you doing this glorious day?"

She smiled at me, sweeping one hand around in an expansive gesture. I had to agree with her assessment. Portland's skies were a clear blue, and the light breeze blowing in from the Willamette River was refreshing. This was a good as it got anywhere in the world.

I smiled back, wondering if she had forgotten my name. I recognized her use of a euphemism such as "my friend," after all. I had my own tried-and-true "Hey, you" I used with former students.

Turning, I greeted Babs's news partner. "I'm sure you don't remember me, Mr. Robb. I'm Gwen Franklin. My friend Nora Goldstein and I had a chance to speak with you at the same event."

The light dawned in his eyes, along with a slight panic. I wanted to chuckle, but he didn't need to worry. I wasn't going to mention Phoebe, at least not if I could avoid it. Some things were better left unsaid.

"Gwen, why don't you join us?" Louisa nodded at an empty chair. "I'm sure Matt won't mind, and it'll save me a phone call."

So I was right. Louisa was here to spill the beans, although why she hadn't called me or Nora first, I couldn't imagine. Sliding the chair out from under the table, I sat down, both hands folded primly on my lap, my feet planted side by side. I was getting ready to ask Louisa what she meant when the door to the café opened, discharging Nora and a dancing Herc.

"And here's my other pal." Louisa moved out the last empty chair with the toe of one shoe. "Have a seat, Nora. My, this really is fortuitous." She winked at me and hauled a large leather bag to her lap. "I was actually on my way to see you after this. I've got those phone records you asked for right here."

"What phone records?" Matt's eyes narrowed in question as he stared at Louisa, and it hit me he had no idea what Louisa was talking about. I had no idea why the two of them had met, but it certainly wasn't Babs.

"Oh, it's just something Nora and I needed to look at. Nothing that would interest you." I attempted a casual attitude, looking hard at Louisa's confused face and trying to send her a mental message to follow my lead.

Nora glanced up from tying Herc's leash to the arm of her chair, both eyebrows lifted in surprise. I slid my foot sideways and hit hers, shaking my head slightly at the same time.

"I see." Matt's tone, however, showed he clearly did *not* see, and I could tell his newshound's nose had picked up the scent of a possible story.

Louisa, one hand still hovering above her bag, hesitated before withdrawing it and smiling around at the rest of us. "It's girl stuff, Matt. You wouldn't get it—right, girls?"

Nora and I nodded obediently, and I let out a sigh of relief. If Matt had no idea what we were doing, it was better to keep it that way . . . unless we needed him.

Nora and I sat quietly while Louisa and Matt wrapped up their conversation concerning modern logging activities and the effects it had on the local economy. When at last he capped his pen and slipped it back into a small loop at the top of his notebook, I silently applauded Louisa's adept handling of what could have become an awkward situation. I had a feeling this was a woman who could run a company with one hand tied behind her back and an adult beverage in the other.

When Matt finally left, heading toward a sleek convertible parked across the street, I turned to Louisa and held out my hand. "Thanks a lot for not giving us away."

She reached out and took my hand in hers, pressing it gently as she smiled. Withdrawing it, she reached down and gave Herc's ears a soft pat. "Call it woman's intuition, my dear. Besides, I don't think that man could see anything except his own ego. Did you see that horrible job someone did on his hair plugs?"

Nora burst out laughing. I shook my head uncertainly at Louisa's observation, unsure of what a hair plug might look like to begin with.

"It looked almost as bad as my third—no, my fourth—husband's hair." Nora wiped tears of amusement from her eyes, leaving behind twin streaks of mascara down her cheeks. "Why any man thinks that mess will look any better than being bald, I have no idea. I mean, really!" Here she began laughing again. "It looked like a patchy sod job gone wrong."

Louisa chortled loudly, causing a passing family to steer clear of us. I automatically ducked my head, hiding my face in case it was someone I knew. Blame it on two decades of sneaking about in public, trying to escape running into a student or, even worse, my principal.

"All right, ladies." I impatiently drummed my fingers on the table. "Let's get down to business. Nora, remember we've got two people waiting for us inside, okay?"

"Want me to get them?" She half-rose from the chair, but I waved her off.

"No, not for this. We'll see what it is and then tell them if it helps with anything."

"Well, let's take a look, shall we?" Louisa began rummaging in her large bag once more. "Ah. Here it is."

She drew out a thick stack of paper bound together at the top with a large binder clip. I took it from her outstretched hand, running my gaze down the information, flipping through each page, looking for a pattern.

When I saw it, I looked up from the paper and gave the stack to Nora. "Check out the third and fourth pages, as well as the next-to-the-last number on the final page. Tell me what you think. And, Louisa, if this is what I think it is, we might have spotted our killer."

Louisa's cheeks turned pink with pleasure, and she smiled widely. "Do you think so? And trust me, it's not that I liked that gal one iota. But to help solve a murder, well, that practically sends chills down my spine." She gave a little wiggle, demonstrating her excitement. "So very Agatha Christie."

Nora looked up sharply from her perusal of the phone records. "Oh, not you as well." She had an almost comical expression of dismay. "I get enough of that from little Miss Detective over here."

The café's front door opened once again, and Roger and Brent, followed by the trio of dogs, emerged onto the sidewalk. Herc, sensing possible play time, began barking and pulling away from where he was leashed. Aggie, not to be outdone, added her high-pitched yapping to the cacophony, her stubby tail wagging fast enough to cause a breeze.

"Brent, get that dog of yours under control, please." Reaching over to grab Herc's collar, I pulled him into my lap, a squirming bundle of black-and-white fur. "And you can be quiet too, mister."

"Goodness," laughed Louisa. "My Pickles is almost as noisy. I got her at my local shelter, which is how I got involved in the whole Clear the Shelter caboodle to begin with."

The two golden retrievers, standing quietly near Roger's legs, sighed deeply and lay down on the sidewalk. I completely understood. Sometimes the young ones could wear a person, or a dog, out just by watching them run and jump around.

"Now that's a great dog name," commented Nora. "These two are saddled with Hercule and Aggie, if you can believe that."

Louisa clapped her plump hands together in delight. "How absolutely wonderful! Maybe I should change Pickles's name to Miss Lemon."

Nora snorted as I beamed at Louisa. I never imagined in my wildest dreams I'd have anything in common with an heiress. Before I could say anything further, however, Roger took the chair vacated by Matt.

"I think we might have interrupted you ladies." He included Brent in his gesture. The latter was squatted beside the retrievers, patting their soft fur with one hand while holding Aggie steady with the other. "Is that perhaps something about the murder?"

Louisa's thinly penciled eyebrows rose in question as she glanced at me.

I nodded briefly, gesturing at the packet of phone records. "Yes. This is a record of phone calls made and received by Babs at the television studio." I opened it to the third page and handed it over for his perusal. "Take a look at this page and the next, and tell me what you see."

It didn't take him long to see what Nora and I had spotted. "There were quite a few calls from one number almost exclusively." He flipped back and forth between the two pages. "By my count, there are around ten." Lifting his head, he looked around the table at the three of us sitting there, his gaze level. "It doesn't take Sherlock Holmes to see the possibilities here. It could be anyone, right? Maybe a secret boyfriend or the local pizza delivery. Or—and this is a big 'maybe'—she was calling the person who killed her."

"At last, someone who doesn't evoke Miss Marple every dang time," muttered Nora under her breath.

I chose to ignore her. Sherlock Holmes was every bit as canny as Hercule Poirot, but I wasn't going to tell Nora that.

"I think," I began hesitantly, not wanting to insult him, "it's more a situation of the killer, if that's who it was, contacting Babs. Those calls are all incoming. All except one, that is."

"I noticed that," said Nora. "If you look at the next-to-the-last call documented, you can see it involves the same phone number, only it's outgoing."

Louisa smiled all around. "You guys are amazing. Now, do you want to know whose number that is?"

I stared at her, my eyes widening and just catching my mouth from following suit. "You mean you know? How?"

"I think you mean 'who?'" Louisa dropped one eyelid in a conspiratorial wink. "According to my friend, it belongs to the main switchboard at Portland Junior College."

"That's where Rachel goes. And Emily's sister." Brent looked up, a pleased expression on his face. "Or at least she did. Emily's sister, I mean. Rachel still goes there, although I—"

"Thank you, Brent," I said firmly. "I think we know that already."

Before he could lapse into a sulk at my comment, Roger leaned over and patted him on the shoulder. "You must be really proud of Rachel." He smiled. "I can hardly wait to meet her."

"Yeah," Brent agreed. "I already told her about how Miss F. has a boyfriend."

Brent shot a broad grin in my direction, and I wanted to crawl under the table. Embarrassed, I turned to explain Brent's error only to find Roger was looking directly at me with a smile that suddenly made my breath catch. If I had to speak at that moment, I wasn't sure I would be able to get any words past my lips. Louisa, thank goodness, had no such issue.

"I think that's wonderful, Brent. But right now, we need to focus on why the college might have been calling Babs." Louisa shuffled the stack of phone records with a busy air as though calling a business meeting to order. "Any ideas?"

Louisa's words cut through the awkward moment, and I gave an inward sigh of relief. To my disappointment, Roger was already looking at Louisa, anticipation clear on his face.

"I would think it had to do with something she'd discovered or maybe it was a whistleblower situation." Roger looked around the table, including all of us in his suggestion. "You hear about things like this all the time, employees finding out that illegal activity is happening at their companies."

Louisa nodded enthusiastically. "Absolutely. Possibly someone found out money was being misused, maybe for personal reasons. I can see that happening with the bunch we've got on this current board of regents. You can mark my words on that."

By this time, I'd recovered my composure. I shifted in my chair, lifting my feet to rest on the table's lower crossbars. "Do you know any of the board members?"

Louisa snorted loudly, and Aggie gave a startled bark. I hid a quick smile by ducking my head and pretending to adjust my Birkenstock sandals.

Roger, I saw, had leaned over and was doing something with the retrievers' collars. Brent was simply staring at her, his mouth hanging open.

Louisa, thank goodness, didn't appear to notice the rest of us. "I'll say I do. The biggest nincompoop on the board is my brother-in-law." She shook her head with a look of disgust. "How he got voted on, I have no idea. That man couldn't run a bingo game, much less an educational entity."

"Do you think there might be, I don't know, dishonesty with the board and its leadership? Would that sound like a story Babs might have gotten hold of?" Parallel lines appeared between Roger's straight brows. "Or maybe it doesn't have anything to do with the board. From what I know of the business world, most shenanigans tend to come from the financial departments."

"As in the financial aid office?" I wrinkled my forehead in thought.

Three heads nodded back at me. Brent, however, was busy scratching Aggie under her chin. Bless his heart. The boy was doing a good imitation of a placeholder. At least he wasn't out causing trouble, though, or driving. That last thought made me shudder, and Roger looked at me with a concerned expression.

"Chilly? I can get you a coffee, if you'd like. And the rest of you as well," he offered.

As we waited for him to order, Louisa gave me a knowing smile. "He's quite the gentleman, isn't he?"

My face heated. "Yes. And he likes dogs."

It sounded inane, but Louisa seemed to know what I meant. Nodding her head at me, she leaned over and patted my hand. "A perfectly matched set, I'd say."

I wanted to ask if she meant Roger and me or the retrievers, but Roger was back, with a pleased expression.

"You look like that cat that got the cream." Nora lifted one eyebrow in question. "Care to share?"

"Coffee and fresh apple pie are on their way." He rubbed his hands together. "I ordered mine with cheddar cheese melted on it, but she's going to bring dishes of vanilla bean ice cream for the rest of you."

"You eat cheese on pie?" Brent's brows wrinkled. "I put it on baloney sandwiches."

"I like that as well," Roger smiled at him. "But nothing beats melted sharp cheddar on warm apple pie."

Nora screwed up her face in disgust. "That's like slapping an onion on a pan of brownies."

"You sure do eat some weird things, Mrs. G." Brent's eyes were solemn as he looked at Nora. "Can we still go to Voodoo Doughnuts after this?"

Nora stared at Brent, her mouth dropping open in amazement. "And you sure do eat a lot, Brent Mayfair. Yes . . ."

He began to protest.

". . . we'll get more donuts. Sheesh! You keep eating like this, and I'm going to start taking a food allowance out of your pay."

"Speaking of pay," I broke in, "what's up with our pet valet business?"

"Nothing's up with it. I took the liberty of declaring a vacation for two weeks." A crafty expression briefly crossed her face, and I knew what she actually meant was she'd only just thought of that. Well, that was fine with me. I'd prefer to concentrate on Shelby anyway. And more dates at the dog park sounded pretty good too.

"You're the boss. What about, you know," I inclined my head at our dog walker as he sat stroking Aggie's soft ears. "He'll ask sooner or later."

Nora made an impatient gesture. "We give him a paid vacation, of course. Besides, we might need his help in this investigation we've got going."

"And mine?" Louisa leaned forward as far as her bulk allowed, a hopeful expression on her face. "I've got quite a few connections, you know."

"And so do I," Roger said. "You might be surprised at whose mouths I've seen over the years."

"Like lots of mouths?" Brent's eyes widened. "That's pretty gross, Dr. S."

"Lots of them." Roger agreed with an amused tone. "And yes, some were fairly unpleasant. But that's why they came to me, so I could fix them."

"All right, all right, enough of this dentist talk." Nora sounded brisk, but I knew the real reason behind her comment. She was deathly afraid of going to the dentist and only visited whenever I prodded her into it. "Let's get back to the college."

The café's door swung open, and Emily appeared, a large tray balanced on one arm. That girl either lifted weights or she was incredibly coordinated. "Fresh coffee and apple pie. Ladies, you get ice cream with yours as well. And for you too," she said to an anxious-looking Brent.

She looked and sounded much more cheerful than she had earlier. Staying busy was probably a great way to forget about her sister. Balancing the tray, she swept around the table, setting a steaming ceramic mug in front of each of us.

"We've got cubes if you want it, but Mom thinks it's easier to serve packets." She placed a small container of fresh cream and a container of multi-colored sweetener packets in the center of the table. She cast a disdainful glance at the rectangular container. "Me, I prefer sugar cubes. When my grandma makes us tea, that's what we use."

"I do as well." Louisa smiled at the girl as she picked up her coffee. "I drink my coffee with cream only, though, just enough to cut the bitterness."

"I like sugar," Brent announced as he dumped his bowl of ice cream on the slice of pie sitting in front of him. "I'm good with any kind, really."

"What a surprise," Nora muttered under her breath, and I stifled a laugh.

Emily disappeared back inside the café after making sure we were set. It suddenly occurred to me Roger must have settled the check for lunch as well as this lovely treat. Reaching into the small purse I sometimes carried, I drew out my wallet. Before I could say anything, though, Roger had already spotted what I was doing and had waved my gesture away.

"My treat, Gwen, and no argument." He smiled around the table, including Louisa in his generosity. "You can't imagine how nice it's been, having someone else to talk to except the boys here." He gave them a fond look as he stirred his coffee. "Max and Doc are good company, but they never answer back."

Before anyone could think of something to say, Emily flew out of the café, one hand waving a cell phone in a sparkly pink case.

Chapter 10

"Miss Franklin, you're not going to believe this. You're just not."

I could see she was close to tears and automatically reached out one hand to steady her. "What's happened, Emily?"

"Yeah, what's up, Em?" Brent's fork hovered in midair as he stared at her with concern. "You get fired or something?"

I wanted to reach over and put my hand over his mouth. Instead, I pushed his plate closer to him and waited for Emily to answer.

"It's Addie." She held her phone out so I could see the small screen. "She just sent me a text!"

"Cool beans." Brent, his mouth full of apple pie, grinned at Emily. "Tell her I said hi." He lifted one of Aggie's front paws and moved it in a waving motion. "And tell her Aggie says hi too."

"I will." She spoke automatically, her gaze still fixed on me. "Miss Franklin, what'll I tell her?"

"About what?" I was momentarily stumped. Maybe she thought I could read minds. "Are you speaking of the college incident?"

Roger sat silently drinking his coffee, with a thoughtful gaze on Emily. Brent was carefully scraping up the remainder of his ice cream as he eyeballed the pie that sat untouched in front of me. I slid it toward him, smiling inwardly as he dug his fork into the flaky crust without lifting his head.

Beside me, Nora and Louisa snorted in tandem, twin expressions of disdain on their faces.

"Incident, my eye! Just call a spade a spade, Sis." Nora's nose wrinkled as she spoke, her repugnance clear. "The man took advantage of a young girl and needs to be called out on it."

"And I agree," chimed in Louisa. "If you'd like, I know someone who might be able to help."

Emily looked around, hesitation clearly marked on her face. "I guess you could," she began tentatively. "I mean, I don't want to get Addie mad at me, you know?"

"Emily," I said firmly, "your sister was mistreated by a very unscrupulous person. If anything, she'll be happy for the help."

"You really think so?" Emily's eyes filled with tears, and she lifted the edge of her apron to wipe them away.

She wore no makeup, and the tears made her eyes seem brighter. Even Nora's, with all of her tricks with mascara and eyeshadow, didn't have the same brilliance. Of course, there was the age difference. Maybe Emily would give in one day and turn to artifice. Maybe I should. I chanced a quick peek at Roger and saw his expression was still thoughtful, one hand slowly stroking Max (or was it Doc?) between his ears.

Herc, his emotional radar on high alert, padded over and nudged Emily's leg with his nose. A tiny smile flickered at the corners of her mouth as she leaned over to run gentle fingers through his fur.

"Aw, he's cute." She looked at me with a ghost of a smile. "Is he yours?"

"That's a great big 'yes.'" I leaned forward and gave Herc a fond pat on his head. "He's a rescue dog, of sorts. And it's a long story," I added before she could ask for the particulars. "Right now, though, we need to think about your sister." I paused, taking another sip of my cooling coffee. "What was it your sister said in that text?"

"She, well, she wanted to know if it was safe to come back." Emily gave a helpless shrug. "I honestly don't know what she means, Miss Franklin. That's why I don't know what to say."

"Safe?" Roger leaned forward and indicated an empty chair. "Please, sit down. Don't worry about your mother," he added when Emily protested. "I'll take care of it."

"As will I," I added. "Sit down and tell us what you think she might mean. Maybe she's said something to you in the past about feeling afraid."

With an uneasy glance toward the café's large picture window, Emily slipped into the empty chair indicated by Roger, her hands twisted together in her lap. Herc managed to follow her, despite being tethered to my chair. He rested his head on her lap, looking at her with his large brown eyes. That dog was more perceptive than most humans.

Except Brent, it would seem. To my astonishment, the boy hit the problem on its head, and even his comments, although grammatically painful to my ears, made sense.

"Addie must've told someone about that college teacher, and now he's threatening her." He took the last bite of my donated slice of pie and exhaled with satisfaction. "If I was you, Em, I'd tell 'er to stay outta sight."

He grinned at his somewhat speechless audience, and I noticed a smear of dried ice cream on the front of his shirt. His poor mother. No wonder he wanted to hide out. She'd probably had it up to her eyeballs with him.

"I hate to admit it, but that actually sounds quite sensible." Nora's smile negated the sarcasm in her words, and she reached over to thump Brent on his shoulder. "If that's the case, Sis, I'm thinking Rachel might be in the same boat, now she's told us about her run-in with the dimwit."

I stared at her for a moment, thinking it through. If Rachel hadn't told anyone else except those of us here, I couldn't see the problem.

"I'd think she'd need to tell someone who'd run straight to Tim." I shrugged slightly, reaching for my coffee mug, finding it empty. Emily jumped up, ready to run for more, but I motioned her back in her seat. "It's fine. I've probably had more than my quota as it is."

"Is there really such a thing here in Portland?" Louisa lifted her own empty mug, her head tilted to one side. "Somedays I feel as though I drink my weight in the stuff."

Brent's eyebrows went up, and I hurriedly spoke up before he could make one of his typical "ready, aim, fire" comments. I turned to Emily. "You know, maybe another round of coffee is just what I need. Roger? Nora? How about you?"

They all agreed that more coffee would be perfect.

I was tempted to go inside with Emily to make sure she was able to get our refills and return without trouble. I didn't need to worry, though.

When she'd passed out the refilled cups and taken her seat once more, she looked more relaxed than before. "Mom told me to take the rest of the day off. I guess that's cool. Unless it's her way of getting rid of me." A momentary frown formed between her eyebrows and then quickly smoothed out.

"Right on, Em."

Brent and Emily sounded more like leftovers from the sixties than what they really were, products of the new millennium. Well, my grandad used to say, "Everything old is new again," so perhaps I'd soon be hearing teens spout things like "Hang ten, man" or "Gag me with a spoon," a personal favorite from the neon eighties.

"If you two hippie wannabes don't mind," I said briskly, "it's time to get some real work done here." I turned to look at Louisa. "You mentioned you knew somebody who might be able to help us with Addie and Rachel's situation. Do they work at the college?"

Louisa gave a modest shrug. "In a way you could say that. He's mostly in his office uptown, although he will make a trip to the various campuses as needed."

Nora made an impatient movement with her hands. "Well, spit it out already. Who's the lucky guy?"

Louisa shot Nora a hurt glance. "I'm getting to it, Miss Sassypants."

I wanted to laugh at the surprised expression on Nora's face. Only I had ever stood up to her—in a semi-joking, best-friend sort of way, of course. Louisa, Portland's answer to Gloria Vanderbilt, had quite the personality underneath all those jewels.

"All right, now." I spoke quickly before Nora could turn this into a test of wills or Brent could make one of his inane observations.

Emily, I noticed, was watching the show with an amused expression in her eyes. Hopefully, she wasn't thinking all women of a certain age acted like overgrown children in public.

"Louisa, let's hear it."

"Why, it's Mayor Dinwitty, of course. Or, as I like to call him, Mayor Hot Pants."

"Indeed." Nora tilted her head to one side, with a dreamy smile. "That man can have my—"

"Aaaaaand that's enough of that. Nora, keep those thoughts where they belong, please. Remember, we've got other ears present."

I shifted my gaze toward Brent and Emily and back to Nora and Louise. All four of them were staring back at me with matching expressions as if a third hand had just popped out of my head. Out of the corner of my eye, I saw Roger's amused expression.

"I don't know what you're getting so worked up about, Sis." Nora crossed her arms. "I was just going to say he could have my vote any day of the week." Unfortunately, she emphasized her statement with a suggestive wink, sending Louisa into a fit of giggles.

"Is that what you call it? Well, he can have mine too," said Louisa, and, before I could stop them, the two hormone-addled gals were leaning on one another, clutching each other's arms and howling with laughter.

Fabulous. Now Nora had a partner in her craziness.

I frowned around the table, purposely bypassing Roger. I did *not* want to see his face at that moment. It was a case of "if I don't see it, it didn't happen," and I was perfectly fine with keeping it like that.

"So, you say the mayor might be able to help. Details, please?" I directed this comment to a still-chortling Louisa, my arms crossed and my body language clearly set on disapproval mode. When I said nothing else but continued to stare, the two merry maniacs attempted to compose themselves.

"Gosh, I had no idea voting was so much fun. Maybe I should try it too." Brent's comment sent them into near hysteria once more, and I heard Roger emit a noise that was close to a gargle. At the rate this conversation was going, they'd be ready for the loony bin soon, and I'd be right behind them.

"You need to loosen up, Sis," gasped a red-faced Nora between fits of giggles. "Voting's your civic duty."

This comment induced another round of howls and uneasy looks from the few people that dared to edge their way past our table.

"Fine." I lifted my hands in the air and let them drop back on my lap. "I give up. Never mind the fact that Shelby is being blamed for something she didn't do. Never mind that Tim is still walking around, free to bother some other young student. You two nutcases keep laughing it up, all right?"

That did the trick. At the mention of Shelby's name, the gasps and guffaws died away, and the mood became somber. Emily, still holding her phone, looked at it as it gave a tinny cricket's chirp.

"Addie's texting me again, Miss Franklin." She thrust the cell phone toward me, her eyes large in a tense face. "You talk to her, okay?"

And say what, exactly? I wanted to ask, but I obediently took the pink cell phone from Emily and held the screen closer to my eyes than I might have a decade ago. Oh, the vagaries of getting older! If someone could only create a pill where the wisdom of age and the brashness of youth could be melded together, I'd be the first to ask for a lifetime's prescription.

I could feel the gazes of five pairs of eyes on me as I read the message once, then once again to make sure I hadn't misunderstood. In the ensuing silence, Emily's eyes began to tear up again, but she didn't make a sound. I reached over and placed my hand over hers, giving it a gentle squeeze. This poor child was really going through it.

"It's all right, I promise you." My voice carried more assuredness than I was feeling, but there was no need to stir things up further. Besides, the text really *was* innocuous. "Addie wants to let you know she's heard about, ah, the current hoopla and she might have some information about it."

Across the table, Louisa gave a very inelegant snort, all traces of hilarity gone. "'Hoopla'? That's putting it mildly. And if your sister has information, I hope she intends to share it with the proper authorities."

This last comment was aimed at Emily, and I watched as the girl nodded automatically. I suspected she was programed to be agreeable, especially after observing her parents. Until she, and I, knew exactly what

Addie had to say, I wasn't ready to force anyone into confidences of any sort, and I said so.

"Let's see what Addie knows first, Louisa. She might have something important to add, and then again, she might not. And I really don't see a need to add to Shelby's troubles with unverified 'information.'" I gave the last word a set of air quotes, a bad habit I'd picked up from Nora and Brent. "Emily, why don't you text her back and ask her what she knows."

I offered the phone to her, and she took it into a hand that shook slightly. Giving her a reassuring pat, I waited for her to type in her message, admiring her dexterity. I was strictly a one-finger texter and couldn't imagine using my thumbs as quickly as she was doing.

"Okay, done." Emily looked up, the pink cell phone hanging loosely from her hand.

"Hopefully, she'll give us something to work with." Roger leaned forward and smiled at Emily, and I saw that his expression was gentle. "If your sister—Addie, correct?—has information that will help clear up Babs's murder, it'd be deeply appreciated. I'm sure I speak for everyone here." He aimed his smile at me.

My cheeks grew warm, and I was glad to hear Emily's phone begin to chirp again.

"Well, what's the scoop?" Nora set down her coffee cup and looked across at Emily, her eyebrows lifted in question. "Anything worthwhile?"

"Maybe. I'm not sure. Miss Franklin, will you read it, please?"

Once again, the sparkly phone was thrust out in my direction.

"Read it out loud, Sis," Nora commanded and, beside her, Louisa nodded vigorously. "We all want to hear this."

I shot her an irritated glance as I moved the phone closer to my face and then away, trying to find my focus again. Paying no attention to my best friend's muttered comment about "some women being too vain to wear glasses" (never mind the fact that she needed them as much as I did), I began to read the text aloud.

"'I remember the anchorwoman came out to the school with a lot of questions about money and how it was spent. I had no idea, but I know some students were eager to speak with her. She was with the mayor most of the time.'"

I handed the phone back to Emily, smiling slightly. "She must have done well in her English classes."

Nora quickly turned a laugh into a cough as Brent gave me a puzzled look. His texts were enough to send me running to find the nearest grammar book to assure myself the language and its structure hadn't changed when I wasn't looking.

"So, this whole thing is possibly about money?" Louisa made a sound of disgust, and her double chin shook along with her head. "That figures."

"Sounds like someone had their hands in the school cookie jar." Nora's lips tightened, and I knew she was thinking about the bevy of stepchildren constantly asking her for handouts. "Money can make some people crazy."

"Crazy enough to kill that reporter?"

We all turned to stare at Brent. Trust him to hit the nail on the head. Was it possible Babs had uncovered an illegal scheme concerning finances? Perhaps she'd been silenced before the information could be exposed.

"I need to talk to Addie. Please ask if she'd be willing to speak with me, all right?" I gave her an encouraging smile. "I'd be grateful, and I know Shelby would be as well."

"Do you think Addie might know who the killer is?" Emily's eyes grew large, and her voice trembled. "I'm not sure I want her talking to anybody, Miss Franklin. It might not be safe."

Emily's words sank like stones in a murky pond, and the merriment from earlier was gone, replaced with a heaviness that encompassed us all. Even the dogs seemed to feel it, and Aggie gave a small whimper and cuddled closer to Brent's chest.

A bank of clouds moved across the sky and blocked the sun, and I shivered as I hugged my arms tightly against my body. Someone had been deranged enough to kill once, and if they thought someone else might have knowledge about them, they probably wouldn't hesitate to kill again.

Were Addie and Shelby next on the killer's list? Not if I could help it.

Chapter 11

We promised Emily we wouldn't do anything to endanger her sister, and she assured me she'd do her best to convince Addie to speak with me.

"If she agrees, Miss Franklin, it'd probably be better to meet here. Can I have your cell number? That way I can get hold of you when she shows up."

"Of course." I held up my phone so she could copy the number into her contacts list. "And you've got my permission to share it with your sister as well."

With final goodbyes exchanged, we began the walk back toward Nora's place. Louisa decided to join our little party, declaring she'd leave her car right where it was. I didn't blame her. Street parking in Portland could be sketchy at best, and the closer one got to the river, the more difficult it was to find a parking space.

She and Nora kept up a steady stream of gossip as we made our way back to the apartment building. Roger and Brent stayed busy with Herc and company, trading the occasional comment about the four dogs. I was quiet, however, my mind whirling with ideas. If Addie had pertinent information that could exonerate Shelby once and for all, I'd be more than happy to carry said info to the Portland Police Department and personally deliver it.

"Hey, Sis," called Nora. "Cat got your tongue?"

"I'd say it has Addie's." I stepped to the side, letting the canine parade pass me by. I exchanged a smile with Roger and ignored Brent's grin as he watched us. "Something's keeping her from talking about what she knows, and I want to find out what it is."

Although the clouds had moved in, it was still a pleasant day, according to Portland standards. If nothing was coming from the sky, most people found their way outdoors. Louisa, Nora, and I walked slowly, maneuvering carefully around tree roots that had pushed up the sidewalk in places, creating abstract formations in the concrete.

Louisa gave me a sidelong glance as she stepped over a concrete hump. "I'm fairly certain I can find out what's been going on without bringing in the mayor."

Nora smiled at Louisa's words but thankfully made no comment. I wasn't sure if I could take another giggle-fest about voting.

"Do you think your brother-in-law might have information?" I moved to the side as I spoke, allowing a young mother pushing a double stroller to pass.

I wiggled my fingers at two solemn-faced toddlers, alike enough to be twins, and smiled at their mom before moving back beside Nora.

"Are you two even talking?" Nora blurted out the words, and I saw Louisa wince at the blunt inquiry. Nora tended to use the "ready, aim, fire" conversational method, usually taking others aback before they realized this was simply her style.

Louisa shrugged, her lips pursed. "Possibly. Actually, probably, but only if I give in to his latest request." She wrinkled her nose in distaste. "Seems like dear brother-in-law wants me to underwrite his campaign for reelection to the school board. That's because no one else will give him money." Her tone was scathing. "The man's a complete idiot and refuses to see it."

"Or admit it," chimed in Nora. "I've got a few of those in my bunch, believe you me. I'd swear some of them were born with their hands out."

A picture of Phoebe curled under the table at the shelter event flashed into my mind. Whenever someone made a comment about Nora's wealth and how she'd gotten it, I was quick to point out she'd more than earned it, having had to care for a succession of imbecilic husbands as well as their offspring.

"If you think it'd be worth the effort," I said, "please do try. Shelby's freedom could be riding on this."

We'd reached the corner adjacent to Nora's apartment building. Roger and Brent, along with their four canine companions, had already crossed the street. I tried not to be obvious, but I couldn't help staring at Roger as he stood with the retrievers' leashes looped over one arm, his silver hair catching the last rays of sunshine. Whoever said sixty was the new forty hadn't met Dr. Roger Smithson. He was a walking, talking argument for sixty being the new thirty.

Brent was saying something, with an earnest expression, as he gesticulated with the hand not holding Aggie's and Herc's leashes. Roger seemed to be listening intently as Brent spoke, and I sent up a silent prayer that my former student wasn't telling tales about me. I would really hate to waste my last fancy duct tape, the one embellished with classic books, on a gag for the boy. The light changed.

"Hey, Miss F.!" Brent's voice was raised loud enough to be heard at Multnomah Falls, not just across the street. "Dr. S. says you can make fake teeth for dogs! Isn't that cool?"

"Yes, that's very cool." I shot a smile at Roger. "Do you have a particular dog in mind?"

Before Brent could respond, we stepped out into the street and were almost hit by a pair of giggling teens balanced on an electric scooter. Those things were a menace to pedestrian traffic, not to mention an eyesore. Most riders simply discarded them whenever they arrived at their destination, leaving the lime green scooters scattered about like fallen leaves.

Nora raised her three middle fingers and yelled something about "reading between the lines" at the pair while Louisa and I hotfooted it to the opposite sidewalk. I'd rather save my breath and my life than remain in the middle of a Portland street.

"Are you all right?" Roger held out a hand, and I took it as I stepped up to the sidewalk.

Standing there for a moment to catch my breath, I watched Louisa frantically fan her face as if she'd just run a marathon.

Brent, waving his hands animatedly, kept talking as we headed for the building's entrance. "Dr. S. says it's a real thing, making teeth for animals."

He gave Roger the same look I'd seen on Nora's face at the beginning of a new relationship. I tipped my head back to look at the building's broad expanse of windows, camouflaging an amused smile as a sun-dazzled grimace. I could tell Brent was developing a serious case of hero worship.

"And I know just the one who needs some, too." His tone became as serious as his expression. "That little poodle from the house next to the dog park, the one named Fifi? He needs teeth real bad."

Badly, my mind corrected automatically. He needs teeth *badly*. Aloud, I said, "Don't you mean 'she'? I'm not sure I've ever heard of a boy dog with that name."

This wasn't the first time a dog's name had confused the masses. I liked to point out that a certain famous television canine was called "Lassie" for a reason and not "Laddie," but all I usually got in response was a disinterested, "Oh, is that right?" For some reason, most thought only the male of any species could rescue Timmy from the well or the damsel from the dragon.

Brent's forehead wrinkled in consternation, and his eyes narrowed. "No, Miss F., it's a boy for sure. The first time I walked it I saw the—"

"And I believe you, I really do." I spoke quickly, interrupting Brent before he could give us a lesson in canine anatomy. "I just happen to think it's odd, giving a girl's name to a boy dog. Call me a purist, all right?"

Leaving Brent to puzzle out the meaning of that comment, I followed Nora and Louisa as they swept past the concierge station and into the well-appointed lobby. Roger came next, Max and Doc edging closer to his legs as they took stock of their new surroundings.

We managed to squeeze into the elevator, Herc sitting on my feet and Aggie riding on Brent's shoulders, the two retrievers standing stiffly as the elevator gave a jerk and then began to rise.

All that was missing was Marcus and his ubiquitous plaid jacket.

As usual, I spoke too soon.

Leaning against the wall across from Nora's apartment stood Portland's man about town, a legend in his own mind, the one and only—thank goodness—Marcus Avery.

Behind me, Nora began to simper. She brushed past the rest of us, her lower half wiggling in a manner than even Babs couldn't have duplicated.

"What's wrong with Mrs. G?" Brent's question, voiced in a loud stage whisper, slipped out before I could prevent it.

If Rachel wasn't there to stymie such comments, I usually tried to think one step ahead of the boy and his vocalized thoughts.

"She's walking kinda funny, like she's got something—"

Without thinking, I clapped one hand over his mouth, reaching up as high as I could to accomplish this. Roger smiled broadly, and Louisa laughed outright. Nora and Marcus only had eyes, and ears, for each other.

Louisa's cell phone began to warble a tinny rendition of "Don't Worry, Be Happy," one of those songs that could become an earworm without much effort. I closed my eyes and hummed Handel's "Hallelujah Chorus" under my breath, my go-to method for combatting such invasions.

When I heard Louisa give an excited gasp and then drop her phone, my eyes popped open, and I left off my musical counterattack.

Nora, one hand planted firmly on a plaid-covered arm as if its owner was a flight risk, looked around with a frown of annoyance. Clearly, she didn't appreciate having her romantic reunion interrupted. "Are you going to answer that sometime today?"

Ignoring the comment, Louisa bent down to retrieve the singing cell phone, panting slightly as her considerable chest pressed against a substantial middle. I eyed her with concern, not wanting to witness yet another person in health crisis mode. Marcus's experience among the wine bottles at Coopers Hall was enough for me.

"It's my friend from the phone company," she managed to wheeze out before poking the screen with one pudgy finger and placing the phone to a diamond-encrusted ear. "Hey, gal! What's shakin' in your neck of the woods?"

For once, Brent refrained from sharing his inane viewpoint. Of course, it might have been because my hand was still firmly held over his mouth. With a warning glance, I slowly let it drop, bringing a rush of blood back to my extended arm. Brent gave me a hurt look and began mumbling into Aggie's ear. I disregarded him, turning instead to see what the newest commotion was all about.

We stood with our gazes fixed on Louisa's animated face as she carried on a friendly chat. I wanted to shout at her and encourage her to get to the point. Before I could give in to the impulse, though, Louisa's expression changed, and her voice took on a serious note.

"Are you sure about that? You double-checked? Yes, of course, of course." A pause. "Well, if that's what it says, that's what it is." Another pause as she listened, shaking her head. "Live and learn, as my old man would say. *C'est la vie* and all that jazz. You just never can tell about people."

She spoke for a few more minutes, promising to swing by for a visit soon and sending her love to someone named Mel, then disconnected the call. When she turned to face her apprehensive audience, I could clearly see she was more than disturbed by what she'd heard.

"Is everything all right?" I stepped closer to Louisa and put an arm around her shoulders in a gentle hug. "Was that bad news?"

She gave me a sardonic smile as she waved away my concern. "Yes. Maybe." She cleared her throat unnecessarily, plainly in a dilemma over what she was about to say. "It seems that His Honor the Mayor was a frequent flyer on Babs's phone records."

I let out a gasp and saw Nora's eyes widen.

Before anyone could say a word, Louisa continued, her tone suspect in its lack of expression. "And it seems he was the last call she took on her cell phone the day she died."

The silence that followed her remark was louder than the proverbial elephant I imagined I could hear stomping its way down the corridors of the building. Mayor Dinwitty, he of the Hollywood looks, a killer? I'd heard stranger things before, of course, but the man I'd seen seemed harmless enough. With the requisite toothy smile and carefully coifed hair, he was the quintessential politician.

Of course, I thought as I shivered, that description could have fitted Ted Bundy as well. I instinctively hugged myself with goose-pimpled arms. Nora, I noticed, was now huddled inside the circle of Marcus's arms, her expression a mixture of anxiety and building hysteria. That was the classic Nora response to anything that affected her deeply.

And personally. How personally, I couldn't guess, but I sincerely hoped it hadn't gone past the occasional wave in passing whenever they'd met.

Somewhere down the hall, I heard the sound of a door opening and closing, then footsteps headed in our direction. The noise seemed to galvanize Nora from her thoughts and propel her into action. She produced a key from somewhere in her skintight outfit, I really didn't want to know where, and threw open the door to her apartment with a dramatic flourish.

"Let's take this party indoors, folks. Can't stand out here and entertain the neighbors." She stepped in ahead of the rest of us, Herc and Aggie at her heels. "Brent, grab a few mixing bowls and fill them with water for the dogs. Marcus, be a dear and start a pot of coffee, will you? And get that strawberry coffee cake from the fridge."

She moved into the kitchen. Brent wanted to know where the promised donuts were, and Marcus told him to get happy with whatever he was offered. Aggie trotted after them, hoping for a handout, followed closely by Herc, who was determined to get his share. As usual, Max and Doc stayed close beside Roger.

I sat on one of Nora's overstuffed sofas, curling my legs up under me as I leaned into the soft cushions. Roger sat beside me, close enough that if I chose to stretch out my legs, they'd be in his lap.

Believe me when I said I was tempted.

"That boy sure likes his food." Louisa, shoehorned into the armchair across from me, said with admiration. "I wish I could eat like he does. He must have the metabolism of two people."

"And zero brain cells," I muttered.

"I think he's on to something," said Roger.

I turned to stare at him. Brent? On to something? How was that even possible? In my experience, if something didn't focus on food, animals, or Rachel, Brent wasn't interested.

"Care to share, as they say on those sappy reality shows?" Louisa kicked off her shoes and attempted to tuck one foot under her bulk before giving up.

I pretended I hadn't noticed.

"Yes, I'd love to hear it." I leaned over and gave Roger's arm a gentle poke with one finger. "Being 'on to something' and 'Brent' usually don't run concurrently."

Roger captured my hand before I could withdraw it, and my cheeks heated. Louisa, bless her heart, returned the favor of not noticing what was happening, although I thought I spied a small twitch in one corner of her generous mouth.

"He's got me thinking, I have to admit," Roger smiled at me. "If one dog needs help with its dental health, how many more are there in Portland?"

Before we could explore the idea further, the genius himself returned to the living room, Aggie and Herc close on his heels. He plopped down on the floor, and Herc made a dive for his lap. Aggie, used to being queen of the castle, wasn't sure she cared for this and issued a few irritated barks in his direction.

Max and Doc ambled over, lured by the large slice of pastry Brent was holding above his head. Aggie, sensing possible competition for the treat, made one heroic leap and managed to nose the plate from his hands.

The ensuing commotion brought Nora and Marcus running from the kitchen. Marcus's tie was askew, and Nora's cheeks were pink, and I sighed. That woman collected men the way I collected mystery novels. Inwardly shaking my head, I unfolded myself from the sofa and headed over to grab an unwilling Herc by his collar, pulling him away from the mess on the floor.

By the time we'd corralled the animals and cleaned up the remains of the pastry, Louisa looked ready to collapse, and I was right there with her. Dogs could be as energy sapping as a houseful of toddlers.

"I don't suppose you can make that call right now, can you?"

I looked across at Louisa, her face flushed, one hand placed on her rather impressive bosom as though playing a part in a Victorian melodrama.

Without opening her eyes, Louisa made a noise I interpreted as consent, and I watched in fascination as she began fishing around in the large handbag she'd dropped on the floor. She reminded me of my brothers when the four of them were small: "If I can't see it, it isn't happening." Louisa, however, seemed completely able to function with her eyes closed, a talent I'd have given anything to have during my teaching years.

I'd also give my firstborn, if I had one, for a steaming cup of coffee. I smiled to see Roger headed over to where I sat, carrying two mugs of the ambrosial stuff. I smiled my thanks through half-closed lids as I cradled the cup to my nose, inhaling the energy-restoring brew with the fervor of a . . . of a what?

While my caffeine-deprived mind attempted to settle on the appropriate comparison—a disciple? an addict?—Louisa began to speak in a tone I often referred to as a "telephone voice." My school department had been rife with teachers who could be in the middle of a volatile gripe session—the parents, the work load, the administration—and instantly channel professionalism if the classroom phone rang. Louisa could have written the handbook.

"May I speak with Jim Chase? Let him know it's Louisa Lovejoy Turner calling." I thought I heard a squeak from the other end of the line, and a wide smile spread across Louisa's face. "Of course, I'll wait. Tell him I need to speak with him concerning business. Pronto."

More squeaking and then the distinct sound of canned music. Louisa certainly kept her earpiece volume on high. As I watched her, she opened one eye and directed a shark-like smile at me. I smiled back in admiration. The woman was the master of the ambiguous: business indeed. The rattled secretary at the other end of the line must have assumed she'd meant the massive family logging business. Lovejoy Turner was a name that still carried a lot of weight in our part of the state.

Poor Jim was in for a surprise of the not-so-nice kind, however. If he had information that might uncover the reason behind Babs's murder, he'd better be ready to divulge it or he'd have to deal with a monstrous regiment of women, Portland style.

Chapter 12

Thanks to the loud volume on Louisa's phone, I could almost hear her brother-in-law's responses. When he finally came on the line, the first thing out of his mouth was a question that ended in a noise not unlike a guinea hen's querulous squawk. Louisa's return volley wasn't much different. By the time they'd exchanged thinly disguised insults and a few other barbs I pretended not to hear, I was concerned she'd never get to the reason for the phone call.

"Some families," murmured Roger behind his coffee mug. "Makes me glad I was an only child."

"Lucky you," I said before I could call the words back. "I've got four brothers, all younger, and all married with enough children between them to start their own small country."

Roger laughed and patted my knee. A tingle jumped from my leg to my brain, leaving me speechless. Was that what they meant by electricity between two people? Before I had the chance to think this through, Louisa finally got to the meat of the call.

"Look, Jim," she impatiently twirled one finger in the air as his voice rambled on, "I didn't call to argue with you, believe it or not. I need some info on, let's say, a mutual friend."

There was a moment of silence as if he needed to process her comment. Maybe having a regular conversation with Louisa was something that didn't happen that often. When he didn't respond, Louisa rolled her eyes to the ceiling and mimed smacking her forehead with one hand. This was better than afternoon television.

Beside me, Roger chuckled as we listened to our end of the phone call. I turned to smile at him, staring into his gorgeous eyes with those wonderfully placed laugh lines. Had any man ever aged better than this? Before I could answer myself, an interruption wearing skintight yoga pants and a top that looked like it'd been painted on that morning strolled in, Marcus in tow like a well-trained pet.

"So, what's cookin'?" Her sharp eyes took in my warm cheeks and the lack of space between me and Roger. "Anything I should know about?"

Before I could stammer out an answer, Roger said smoothly, "Only that Louisa's brother-in-law seems to be on the lower end of the family appreciation spectrum. I'm almost feeling sorry for him."

Nora dismissed the idea with one sweep of her manicured fingers. "That man? Trust me, he's a total dimwit. I'm pretty sure he weaseled his way through the board elections on the Lovejoy Turner reputation." She plopped down on the second sofa with Marcus obediently following suit. "If I was Louisa, I'd wring his scrawny neck."

"And believe you me," Louisa dropped her cell phone onto her lap, "I'm tempted to do just that at least twice a week." She shook her head emphatically. "What my sister ever saw in him is beyond me."

"Love is blind," said Nora blandly.

Beside her, Marcus blushed as he tentatively put out a hand to touch her shoulder. I sighed inwardly as I watched. The man had succumbed to Nora's many charms, not the least of which was her eye-catching wardrobe. Nora, however, was focused on Louisa with the concentration of a cat watching a mouse hole. Marcus's face fell as she all but swatted his hand away.

"Well, give it to us already. What'd the poor excuse for a family member have to say?" Nora wiggled her fingers at Louisa in a "come on, let's have it" gesture, the blood-red tips of her fingers moving like the legs of an exotic spider. Come to think of it, Nora *did* remind me of a spider at times. She was sometimes benevolent and kind, like Charlotte in the famous children's book, and other times she was downright deadly. Marcus had better stay on his toes.

"He gave me next to nothing, quite honestly." Louisa readjusted herself in the chair. "If truth be told, the only thing he said that might be of interest is this. Babs never toured the campus alone."

She grinned around the room, shark-like similarities flitting across her face. Fabulous. I'd become friends with a spider and a shark. All I needed now was a defenseless fly and a curious goldfish to complete the metaphor.

At times, my thoughts seemed to conjure themselves out of thin air. I turned to see Brent ambling into the front room, a look of complete food ecstasy on his face.

"Gosh, Mrs. G. I hope it's okay I ate most of that cake."

Nora's head swiveled to stare at Brent, her mouth compressed into a tight line. *And here comes the fly, walking right into the web.*

"I sincerely hope that the operative word there is 'most,' young man, and not the entire thing."

"Of course it is," he said indignantly. "Whatta you take me for?" He lowered himself to the floor, all gangly legs and arms. "I saved you a piece."

One piece? Had he really consumed almost a whole coffee cake on top of the luncheon and desserts he'd had less than an hour before? Something wasn't right there. Maybe I should talk to his mother and get her take on the issue. Maybe he had an unknown disease that caused him to eat around the clock without gaining weight. Did we have tapeworms in Portland?

Louisa cleared her throat loudly, and all eyes turned back in her direction. "If you're interested, folks, I can tell you who Babs's escort was."

Brent's hand shot into the air as if he was still in the classroom. "What's an escort, Miss L.?"

I'd been wondering how long it would take Brent to assign Louisa her own alphabetic label. To my amusement, the newly christened Miss L.'s cheeks turned pink as she looked frantically around the room for help.

Nora, of course, couldn't resist a wisecrack. "I think that's something your mom should talk to you about, kiddo. It's one of those grownup things, you know?"

She elbowed Marcus, and they both guffawed. I frowned in disapproval at their antics and took in a breath. It looked like my teaching days weren't over yet.

"An escort," I began in a pedantic tone, "is someone who accompanies a person when they go places. Sometimes it's as a favor, and sometimes you need to, uh, offer remuneration." At Brent's confused expression, I said, "That means you have to pay for it, Brent."

Here, Nora and Marcus gave a whoop of laughter, leaning on each other as if I'd just told the funniest joke they'd ever heard. Louisa's entire body was shaking with suppressed merriment, making her look as though she was sitting on a vibrating chair. Even Roger was chuckling, a pleasant sound that reminded me of the Columbia River during its summer flow.

Only Brent appeared to be deep in thought, tapping his chin with one finger as he stared at the ceiling. A sudden flash of understanding crossed his face, and he looked pleased as his brain seemed to produce its own illustration.

"It's like when me and Rachel go places. She's my escort 'cause I sometimes pay for her food and all that." He paused a moment, considering. "Well, sometimes she pays, so I guess I'm her escort too."

I covered my face with one hand, unwilling to let him see my smile. Just when I thought he'd moved on to the territory marked "adulthood," Brent could surprise me. His genuine innocence at times made me thankful for Rachel, and I wondered if she realized she'd need to keep an eye on him for as long as they both should live. Or at least as long as they were a couple.

I didn't need to worry about Brent dwelling on the topic, though. Aggie and Herc were now wrestling for a spot in his lap, and it appeared his attention had already pulled up stakes and moved on. Oh, for the attention span of the young. It might have saved me from quite a few tedious department meetings.

"As I was saying," Louisa continued, "Babs's companion was none other than the mayor." She hiccupped and clapped one ringed hand over her mouth. "I swear I've never laughed so much as I've laughed today. You folks are good medicine."

"I couldn't agree more."

Roger aimed a sideways glance in my direction. Of course, my face heated. I didn't give Nora a chance to tease me, though.

"It's getting a little silly, don't you think?" I threw my question out to everyone, not looking at Roger, for fear I wouldn't be able to string together a sentence. "Mayor Dinwitty seems to be at the center of everything that concerned Babs. Don't you think it's time for the Portland PD to invite him over for a little chat?"

"Nope." We all looked at Marcus as he shook his head adamantly. "No way. In my book, it's never that obvious. I mean, come on, people. Do you think a killer would leave a trail like this?"

Marcus flashed a disdainful glance around the room. He was, after all, a private detective, and he never lost an opportunity to remind the rest of us. We sat silently for a moment.

"If not the mayor, then who?" Nora's usually smooth forehead was corrugated.

"It's 'whom,' my dear." I disregarded her scowl. "And I agree. If it's not the mayor, I can't think of anyone else who might have the motive to kill her."

"Oh, puhleeze," drawled Louisa, both hands lifted. "That woman was a one-person wrecking crew when it came to relationships."

"And what do you know about her relationships?" Nora demanded, brushing off Marcus's hand as she leaned forward. "I didn't realize you knew her that well."

It was Louisa's turn to scowl. "I think it's obvious the woman loved only herself, Nora. That would make any relationship with her a little crowded, don't you think?"

The two women glared across the room at one another, their expressions reminding me of teen girls vying for the title of "most popular." In this case, though, it was "most know-it-all," and it was getting old very quickly.

"Let's focus, shall we?" I turned a stern look on the two women and one on Marcus and Brent for good measure.

All four shut their mouths in unison. Roger chuckled under cover of taking a sip of coffee.

"Now," I began, "let's start again. Is the mayor in the clear?"

Nora lifted one shoulder in a shrug. "If you say so, Sis. Just because he's good-looking doesn't make him innocent. I mean, think about Ted Bundy. He was hot."

I stared at her in amazement. Trust my best pal to focus on physical appearance. Of course, physical evidence was usually the best way to nab a criminal. I'd never heard of letting someone go because they were pretty.

"There has to be something else," I objected. "Either he had the opportunity or he didn't."

"And I say he didn't." Nora glanced around at the others.

Again, a unified reaction as all heads bobbed in unison.

"Fine. Let's drop him from the list for now. But if we found out something to put him back, I say we do it."

"Sounds good." Roger gave me smile that sent a delightful thrill through me. Time enough for that later, though. Right now we had a killer to unmask. I cleared my throat and continued.

"Good. The next question, I believe, is who else had a motive to kill Babs?"

I paused, thinking back to something Miss Marple said about secrets having roots that go down a long way. Had Babs Prescott died because of someone's secret? In her job as a reporter, had she discovered a root and tried to expose it? I gave an involuntary shiver. We all had secrets, didn't we? The thought had made murder almost sound sensible.

"Do you think jealously might have played a part?" Roger's calm voice interrupted my bleak thoughts, and I watched as he stretched out his long legs, gently nudging aside the retrievers. "From what you ladies, and gents, of course, are saying, it sounds as though she thought of everyone else as a competition."

"Maybe someone wanted her spot on the news desk." Marcus attempted to mirror Roger's easy posture and succeeded in looking like an overstuffed Elf on the Shelf, ready to fall forward at the slightest touch. "I mean, I heard she was making a pretty penny. That might give someone a reason to scoot her out of the picture."

"That wouldn't mean they'd make the same amount even if they, whoever 'they' are, got her job." I took another sip of coffee, enjoying the smooth taste of the Ethiopian blend Nora and I both favored. "But I get what you're saying. Babs certainly flaunted her position as a lead news anchor, didn't she?"

"Made me stop watching that channel altogether." Louisa gave a small grunt as she attempted to rearrange her position. "One thing I can't stand is a skinny woman pushing it in your face, present company excepted, of course." She shot a mischievous smile at Nora. "You've got the kind of panache I like, pal."

"Right back atcha." Nora's cheeks got a little bit pinker under the usual smudge of blusher. Marcus slipped a proprietary arm around her shoulders, looking proud.

"Do you think it was someone in her line of work? I think that would be the police department's first line of questioning and not our poor Shelby."

The mention of work caused my memory synapses to fire up, and I all but slapped my forehead as I suddenly remembered a message I'd meant to share with Nora hours ago. "Speaking of work, one of our clients sent me an e-mail earlier requesting a sitter tomorrow for her Siamese. She's willing to pay extra since she knows we're closed for vacation."

"What's so special about a cat?" The comment earned Marcus the sharp end of Nora's elbow in his side. "Hey, watch where you're pointing that thing, woman. I happen to think a cat doesn't need anyone to 'watch' them." He gave the word air quotes and received a second round of elbow from Nora.

"This one does." I spoke quickly before he and Nora could get into a spat. "Isis is a purebred with her own social media following. More to the point, she's expecting several bundles of joy any day now."

"A cat has a social media following?" Marcus looked astounded, his eyes opened as wide as they could go. "Now I've heard it all."

"From what I've been told, she does quite well on Instagram." Nora slipped her cell phone from its usual spot inside her top and began swiftly tapping on the screen. "Look. What'd I tell you?" She thrust the phone out for Marcus to see, and I watched in amusement as he sat shaking his head, dumbfounded.

"Maybe I should open an account for the boys." Roger leaned over and ruffled the ears of his dogs. "Herc could be a guest star." He looked at me and smiled, and my heart did a nosedive straight into my stomach before launching itself back into my chest. "And maybe you could join him."

I laughed, willing my heart to settle down before Roger noticed its acrobatics. "No thanks. I'm only on there because it gives me a way to stay in touch with my students. I like hearing about how they're doing and how many children they have now. Even if it does make me feel a tad ancient."

"Hey, you guys. Look who else is on Instagram."

We all looked at Brent as he held up his phone. Smoldering out from the screen was the unmistakable face of Babs Prescott. My shock was mirrored on the faces of the rest, and I could have kicked myself for being so remiss. Why hadn't we thought of that already? After all, Instagram was where I'd spotted Shelby and Babs's picture at the very start of this entire mess.

Before anyone could comment, Nora's front door opened a crack, and Rachel stuck her head in, smiling hugely. "Hey, everyone. Hiya, Brent." Rachel squatted down to hug Aggie and Herc, both of them vying for attention from one of their favorite humans. "Thanks for texting me, Mrs. Goldstein. I was sitting at home bored to death."

Brent, with a ridiculously wide grin, got to his feet and swept Rachel into a bear hug as he did, lifting her off the ground.

"I was gonna call you." He put her back down, one arm still around her waist. "It's almost like a party over here. We're talking about murder and things like that."

Rachel looked at me and rolled her eyes, but her grin negated the action. "And who better to call than the detective's daughter?" She twirled out of Brent's encircling arm and took the mug of coffee Nora held out for her. "Thanks, Mrs. Goldstein." She took an experimental sip, her eyes widening slightly with delight. "This is really good! Where'd you get it?"

"It's just something I picked up from The Friendly Bean." Nora's tone was casual, but she looked pleased.

Coffee appreciation in Portland was an art unto itself. Discovering delicious new blends was as good as finding a twenty-dollar bill tucked in a pair of old jeans.

Rachel took a seat on the floor next to Brent, holding her coffee mug out of the reach of inquisitive Aggie and Herc. Taking another sip, she offered it to Brent.

He shook his head. "I'm startin' to feel kinda full." He grinned sheepishly. "Maybe give me a few minutes, okay?"

Nora and I looked at each other and laughed.

"What?" Brent looked at the pair of us, his forehead wrinkled in question. "What'd I say?"

"Never mind." I slid my gaze to Rachel. "Have you heard anything else about Shelby's case?"

She shook her head. "But I did hear my dad say they're close to figuring out why it happened." She paused, a tiny furrow appearing between her eyebrows. "I'm pretty sure they think it was something personal, like maybe a relationship gone bad. Something like that. So they seem to be straying from Shelby . . ."

I puckered my brows in thought and stared at Nora. She was looking back at me, and I could see we were on the same wavelength.

"I'm not sure Babs had a relationship outside of her work peers and maybe the few family members she had scattered around the state."

Rachel shrugged, expertly drinking coffee and holding both dogs at the same time. "That was just something I overheard my dad saying. He didn't mention any names."

Louisa had been watching this exchange with an expression of bewilderment.

I decided to put her out of her misery. "Rachel's father is a homicide detective with the Portland Police Department."

"Is he now?" Louisa surveyed the young woman with half-closed eyes, one dimpled finger tapping her chin. "Would he happen to know a Leroy Turner?"

"Uncle Leroy? I love him!" exclaimed Rachel. "He's my dad's training officer from a long time ago, and he was always over at our house when I was little."

Louisa smiled delightedly. "He's my cousin once removed, or something to that effect. And I agree with you, young lady. He is a wonderful person."

"Oh, this is Rachel." I'd forgotten Louisa hadn't met her. "She's another of our dog walkers when she's between classes."

"And she's my girlfriend." Brent's smile couldn't get any wider. "We went on vacation together and everything."

Rachel looked at him, a mischievous expression on her face. "And how he got past the gauntlet of my dad and my brother I'll never know."

"I second that." I bent over to scratch the ears of the nearest retriever.

Beside me, Roger chuckled quietly.

"I have an idea," said Nora abruptly. "Let's have the two young folks comb through Babs's social media accounts. Maybe they'll spot something that will help us figure out this mess."

"And a very good idea that is," agreed Louisa. "I'm as lost as a goose in all that Instagram this and Facebook that."

Rachel and Brent looked at each other and laughed. Aggie and Herc joined in, emitting excited barks and running in furry circles.

"So, I'll take that as a 'yes,'" Nora said dryly.

"If there's anything in there to find, we'll find it." Rachel's confidence gave me a small twinge of hopefulness.

I had a feeling a publicity-loving person such as Babs would take for granted that anyone who followed her was a fan. From what I understood about the social media world, though, it wasn't just fans who posted in their idols' accounts. There was always a nutcase doing their best to earn the "rude badge" or someone posting a personal opinion just because they could. Some of these were annoying. Others, however, were downright threatening. Did the police have specialists who checked on things such as this? I sincerely hoped so, especially since it seemed so many people conducted their entire lives on social media.

Maybe our killer had left a trail of vitriol that would lead straight to a motive . . . and to them.

Chapter 13

"Do you want us to make a list of any names if we spot something suspicious?" Rachel was already busy scrolling through her phone, thumbs moving at a pace I couldn't imagine achieving. "I was thinking that if I do one list and Brent does one, we can compare and maybe hone in on a suspect account."

Louisa clapped her hands, sending an armful of gold and silver bracelets jangling like the long-ago sleigh bells on my granddad's horses.

"Perfect." She beamed at Rachel and Brent. "Nora, do you have any paper and pens these two can use?"

I watched in amusement as the two young folks exchanged glances.

"We don't need any, thanks anyways." Rachel's expression was polite, but her eyes were twinkling.

I could tell that she wanted to laugh. I did it for her. "I'm pretty sure they'll just copy and paste the names and move them into a Google doc."

I felt smug at how up-to-date I sounded and decided not to disclose I'd only learned how to use Google docs during my last year of teaching. While it was admittedly convenient and took away the age-old excuse of "my dog ate my homework," it had opened up a whole new can of worms. Students now said things like, "My computer got a virus and lost all my work" or "I left my flash drive at home."

Oh, for the days of tangible data. I sighed inwardly, but I knew it was inevitable. After all, we'd stopped using slates and primers long before my time, and I was certain Google docs would most likely go the way of its paper and pen ancestors before too many years passed.

"Miss F.? You okay?"

I snapped out of my reverie over the good old days that never were and smiled at Brent. "Yes, thanks." I held up my coffee mug and gave it a little waggle. "I think I need some more get up and go."

"Well, get up and go get it," Nora drawled.

Funny it was not, but we all laughed anyway. With my coffee refilled and the two sleuths busily trolling social media, I decided to send a quick reply to the client who needed a cat sitter. Opening the icon for e-mail, I tapped on COMPOSE and then paused, looking at my business partner. "What do you think I should tell Mrs. Petty about Isis?"

Nora disentangled her hands from Marcus's grasp and reached over for her iPad. "Let me check my calendar. I might be able to do it."

"Why don't we do it together?" I smiled, recalling a few of our earlier jobs. "Remember that awful parrot? It was a good thing we were both there, right?"

Nora gave a small grunt as she scrolled on her iPad. "If I never see that rotten bird again, it'll be too soon for me. Okay, here we are." She tapped the screen and then looked at me, smiling widely. "Looks like it's a go, Sis. Tell her we'll be there in the morning with bells on."

"You've got it."

I hurriedly tapped in a confirmation and hit SEND. To tell the truth, I could use a day of brain rest. I felt as though I'd done nothing but immerse myself in this Babs issue for years when it really had been less than a week. And what harm could a pregnant feline cause, really? Anticipating a relaxing few hours hanging out with my best friend, I closed my phone and tucked it back into my pocket.

"Anyone interested in a game of gin rummy?" From somewhere in her capacious handbag, Louisa produced a deck of cards.

"Sure," I smiled. "I haven't played that since college." I looked at Roger, one eyebrow raised as I trotted out one of my few Latin phrases. "*Et vobis?*"

Nora groaned before he could respond. "Oh, don't drag that dead language out, Sis. I can't understand a word you say."

Roger laughed and looked at me, a mischievous glint in his eyes. "There's always *veni, vidi, vici*, right?"

My face was flaming hot.

Nora cleared her throat loudly. "If you two are through showing off, I suggest we take the game into the kitchen."

I had more fun playing cards at Nora's kitchen table than I'd had in a while, and it felt good to do something besides worry over Shelby. Of course, her plight was never far from my mind, but even Miss Marple took some time off occasionally, right?

We'd played several rounds of gin rummy when Rachel strolled into the kitchen, her eyes bleary from staring at a small screen. Brent was right behind her, Aggie tucked under one arm.

"I've gotta get home, Mrs. Goldstein." She laid down her phone and stretched her arms above her head. "I can do this later, right?"

"Yeah, I gotta get home too." Brent went through his own stretching routine, Aggie acting as a counterweight. "My mom'll kill me if I don't come home for dinner."

"We wouldn't want that," I smiled brightly.

"What—his mom bumping him off or the boy missing his chow?" Nora got to her feet and placed both hands on her lower back, giving it an experimental twist. She grimaced. "I've got to get to the masseuse and soon."

"I don't charge very much." Marcus waggled his eyebrows suggestively as he flexed his fingers.

Nora rolled her eyes, but I could tell she was tickled. Well, I intended to be long gone before any of their hanky-panky started, and I said so.

I stood, tipping my mug back for the last bit of delicious Ethiopian coffee. Herc, not wanting to be left out, bounced over and nudged my leg with his wet nose.

I reached down and gave his ears a fond ruffle. "Let's get out of here, boy. Ready for a nice walk home?"

"If you can wait until I leash these boys up, I'll walk with you," Roger offered.

"And if you two can wait for me to visit the ladies' room, I'd like the company to my car." Louisa stood and groaned as she put weight on her feet. "If I can walk that far."

"I can run you to your car," Rachel offered. "I was going to take Brent and Aggie home, but I can do that after I drop you off."

"Great idea." The words popped out before I could stop them, and my cheeks grew warm again. I didn't want to sound as though I didn't want Louisa along for the walk with us.

Okay, I didn't. But I didn't want Louisa feeling left out, either. She was not only becoming a good friend, she had also proved to be a great help when it came to gathering information.

With Rachel and her passengers gone, I took a moment to chat with Nora, planning our cat-sitting job for the next day.

"I can be here by nine," I offered. "Mrs. Petty's house is only one street behind the Portland Pooch Park."

"Come a little earlier, and we can have coffee and croissants at The Friendly Bean." Nora leaned over and gave Herc's ears a gentle tug. "And you'd better stay at home, sir. There's no telling how that cat will react to a dog in her territory."

"Absolutely," I agreed. "The last thing I want is for Isis to have those kittens while we're there."

Nora gave a shudder. "Ugh. I'd be out of there in a heartbeat. Trust me. Nowhere in our contract does it agree we'll deliver babies."

"And we're not starting now," I said firmly. "It'll be a nice, easy day. Maybe we'll be able to come up with more ideas for tracking down Babs's killer."

I looked over at Roger, standing at the door with Max and Doc already leashed. He and Marcus were laughing at something, and my heart gave an acrobatic leap. Could it be I'd finally become that elusive creature called "one half of a couple"?

"He is nice-looking, Sis." Nora gave me an impulsive hug and whispered into my ear. "Keep it going."

"Oh, that's the plan," I murmured under cover of hugging her in return. "That's the plan."

The walk home that night was way too short, but my dreams were very, very nice.

* * * *

The sun was playing hide-and-seek behind a bank of dark clouds when I left my house the following morning. Herc had been fed and watered and seemed perfectly content to be left lying on my bed, already drifting off into the first of many naps. With the doggie door giving him access to the backyard, I was certain he'd be fine while I was off seeing to Mrs. Petty's cat.

I was nearly at Nora's building when my cell phone began a musical riff in my pocket. Pulling it out quickly, I stopped walking and squinted at the number marching across the screen. It was no one I knew, so I hit DECLINE and slipped the phone back in place.

Instantly, it began its musical call again, and this time I answered. If it was a wrong number, I was going to let them know so they'd quit calling. If it was a telemarketer, well, they'd better hang on to their ears. I was going to give them the full "Miss Franklin is not happy" treatment.

"Hello." I spoke more brusquely than I normally would, expecting to hear the sound of a hang-up click or the robotic voice of the spam caller.

"Is this . . . is this Gwen Franklin? Miss Franklin?"

It was definitely the season for forehead slapping. I'd completely forgotten I'd not only given my number to Emily, I'd also told her to share it with her sister.

"Addie? Is that you?"

"Yes, ma'am."

There was silence on the other end of the line, but I could hear her breathing, so I knew we hadn't been cut off. I waited a moment longer to see if she would say anything. When she didn't, I said gently, "Addie, Emily said you might want to speak with me. Would you like to meet somewhere today?"

"Yes, please." Her voice was quiet, almost a whisper. "I'm going to be in town this afternoon." She paused and then added in an even softer voice, "Could we meet at my family's café? Maybe around seven?"

Seven. My mind ran swiftly over my calendar for the day. It took less than a second. Aside from taking care of Isis and getting home to feed and walk Herc, I had no other plans.

Aloud I said, "Seven sounds fine, Addie. And may I bring my friend Nora Goldstein with me? Emily's met her, and she knows all about the—the issue you had at the junior college."

This time, the silence dragged on for so long I thought I'd lost the connection. I was just getting ready to hang up and redial the number when Addie answered.

"Sure, that's fine. No one else though, okay?"

This time there was no question. Addie had disconnected the call. Slipping my phone back into my pocket, I hurried as fast as my Birkenstocks could go without falling off my feet. Nora was going to flip when she heard this bit of news.

I was right.

"*Who* called you?" The question came out in a screech, in spite of the piece of scone in her mouth.

I'd kept the phone call to myself until we were seated in The Friendly Bean enjoying a warm cranberry scone and a café au lait, hoping the treats would act as a deterrent to a scene such as the one currently unfolding.

I leaned in closer, overlooking the several faces that had turned in our direction. "Addie called. Emily's sister. From the café yesterday, remember?"

Nora's thinly plucked eyebrows met over her nose in a scowl. "Of course I remember, nitwit. I'm not senile, at least not yet."

"And I'm not deaf, so I'd appreciate it if you'd keep your voice down a few decibels." I broke off a corner of the scone and popped it into my mouth. Slightly sweet, crumbly, and full of luscious fruit, it was the perfect counterpart to my coffee.

My human counterpart sat across from me, still frowning over her coffee mug. I sat silently, placidly enjoying my morning treat. If she had a comment, I had no fear she'd share it soon enough.

She did. "I get she needs to talk to someone about what happened to her. I'm just wondering if this isn't something for a counselor to handle." She paused and stared at me, her expression solemn. "Besides, don't we have enough going on with this Babs thing?"

"This 'Babs thing' may send one of our friends to prison," I said heatedly.

A few more curious faces turned our direction.

Lowering my voice, I leaned closer. "And quite honestly, this might be connected. In fact, I'm sure it is."

"How do you know it is?" Nora sounded incredulous, as if I'd produced a magic wand and made a unicorn appear. "Don't tell me you're going to get all psychic on me after all these years."

I rolled my eyes and popped another piece of scone into my mouth. If it had something else to do, it couldn't let fly the comment currently tumbling around in my brain.

"Well?" Now she sounded indignant.

I almost expected her to put her hands on her hips and stomp her stiletto-encased foot.

"Cat got your tongue?"

"No," I replied calmly. "And I can't explain why I feel the way I do. Call it intuition, but I have the feeling Addie and Rachel's bad experiences at the college might coincide with Babs's investigation into the school's funding."

Nora took another bite from her scone, followed by a sip of café au lait. I could almost see the thoughts spinning in her brain, trying to make the same connection I was feeling. Of the two of us, Nora had always been the logical one. I was more of an abstract thinker, working with feelings as opposed to facts.

Finally, she sighed, sat her coffee cup down, and looked me straight in the eyes.

"I absolutely do not see how you came up with the conclusion you did, Sis, but for argument's sake, I'll go with it."

I stared at her for a moment, trying to find any hint of sarcasm in her words. I decided she meant what she said.

"So, does this mean you'll go with me to meet up with Addie?"

"I just said that, didn't I?"

No, she hadn't, but I decided to pretend she had.

"Great." I craned my neck to check the time on the iconic Felix the Cat clock hanging on the back wall. "We'd better get going if we want to get to Mrs. Petty's on time." I smiled as I ate the last bite of scone. "Can't keep a pregnant gal waiting, right?"

Nora's sarcastic response was muffled behind the rim of her coffee cup. I smiled sweetly in response.

Mrs. Petty was a small woman in every sense of the word. Not only was she short, well below the five feet mark; she also had small eyes set deep in their sockets, a small, pursed mouth, and a tiny, pointed nose. She reminded me of the china doll my great-grandmother had played with as a girl, its face smoothly painted and its real hair carefully arranged.

This morning, however, Mrs. Petty's hair looked like it had been styled with a jolt of static electricity. She'd clearly made an effort to smooth it back into a clip, but a crop of short hairs had come loose and surrounded her face like a spiky lion's mane.

"Oh, thank goodness." She opened the door with one hand on her heart, her eyes opened as wide as they'd go. "Poor Isis isn't doing well this morning." She motioned us inside and closed the door. "Can you hear her? My poor, poor baby."

I could definitely hear a sound coming from somewhere in the back of the house. It reminded me of the time one of my brothers had accidentally slammed the screen door on our cat's tail. It sounded like a cat in pain.

Or in labor.

"Mrs. Petty," I began, careful not to sound panicked. "Are you sure you should leave her with us? It sounds to me like Isis needs her mommy, not a babysitter."

"You've got that right, Sis." Nora's arms were crossed over her chest, one foot tapping her irritation. "I am *not* going to stay with an animal in the middle of having a baby. Or babies."

"Oh, please, can't you stay?" Mrs. Petty's hands were clasped as if in prayer.

To tell the truth, I felt like praying myself. I was in no frame of mind to deliver kittens. Neither, it seemed, was Nora.

"Not on your life," Nora said firmly. "Gwen, we're out of here." She turned back to the door, ready to make a quick exit.

I watched as two large tears slid down Mrs. Petty's face, and my treacherous heart began to capitulate.

"Nora, don't you think we could just stay for a little bit? Just to make sure everything goes all right?" Now it was my turn to beg.

"Oh, great." Nora threw up both hands and let them drop to her hips. "Now my own partner is blackmailing me."

Mrs. Petty, sensing victory, looked pleadingly at Nora. I added my own pitiful look and watched as Nora's willpower began to crumble.

"Fine. Fine, we'll stay." Nora's tone wasn't pleased. "But one of those kittens gets named after me, understood?"

Mrs. Petty nodded vigorously, and I smiled.

Later, we all agreed Goldie was the perfect name for one of the mewling kittens, its soft baby fur a dark tawny color. Nora, in spite of her reluctance to remain with Isis and Mrs. Petty, was clearly besotted.

"You know Herc will be insanely jealous." I leaned over the box holding the proud new mama and her three babies. I was never a cat person, but these tiny Siamese were adorable. "And Marcus might be allergic to cats."

"As if I care," Nora sniffed.

I sighed deeply. So much for Magic Fingers Marcus.

We left Mrs. Petty cooing over the new kittens, the proud mama cat watching through half-shut eyes. I didn't blame her one bit for being tired. It had looked like a lot of work to me, and now Isis had the task of taking care of those babies. It made me wonder just how exhausted Brent's mom was after nearly two decades with the boy.

I parted from Nora with the promise I'd be back a few minutes before seven.

"We can call an Uber if you don't want to walk there."

I paused a moment in front of her building's entrance, glancing at Nora's newest pair of stiletto heels. They were bright fuchsia pink with red leather roses on the closed toes. They certainly provided a pop of color to her tight black jeans, a change from the usual spandex yoga pants and sleeveless black top that might have been painted on that very morning. Aside from the few cat hairs she'd collected at Mrs. Perry's, she looked catwalk-ready.

I decided not to look at my own ensemble—faded denim capris and a flowing cotton top over a pair of my favorite Birkenstocks. Not the most stylish look, of course, but certainly comfortable and more suitable to walking than Nora's outfit.

"Thank goodness Brent seems to be settling down a bit." Nora smiled.

"Amen to that." I'd seen him in action for several years, beginning in high school, and I had to agree with Nora's assessment.

"Rachel is a good influence on that young man." Nora tilted her head to the side, with a thoughtful expression. "Of course, her dad probably had something to do with that."

"Probably so. I'd have some conditions as well if my daughter was dating Brent."

Giving her a quick hug, I headed toward home. I lived in a small bungalow set on the end of a quiet, tree-lined street, bought when I'd first begun my teaching career. Herc would be waiting, and I was in the middle of reading a book by another Golden Age writer, Josephine Tey. I picked up the pace, my Birkenstocks slapping on the pavement as I walked.

I had a date with Alan Grant, Josephine Tey's intrepid Scotland Yard inspector.

Chapter 14

As promised, I was back at Nora's building a little before seven. The evening had turned chilly. A stiff breeze was blowing in from the Willamette River, and I'd worn my favorite poplin jacket. I'd found it on one of my many shopping trips to our local Goodwill, and with my twenty percent teacher's discount, I'd bought it for a fraction of what it had cost when brand-new. Never sneer at a bargain, I always said.

"Well, don't you look cozy, Sis." Nora strolled out of the lobby, her black moto jacket fitting as snug as a glove above her extra skinny jeans. She'd changed her shoes to a more manageable three-inch heel and added a sweep of lavender shadow on her eyelids. With the earrings swinging against her cheeks, she looked ready for a fancy dinner out, not a meeting at a mom-and-pop restaurant.

"And don't you look snazzy." I glanced from my ever-present Birkenstocks to her shoes and smiled smugly. "Looks like one of us will be ready to run when Addie's mom chases us out of the café."

"Honey, I can walk in these heels faster than you can run in those medieval flip-flops you insist on wearing." She reached out and hooked one arm through mine. "Come on. Let's quit arguing and get going. No one will be able to run us out if we never get there."

The walk was pleasant, in spite of the heavy breeze. Stars were beginning to appear in the twilight sky, something we didn't see that often because of river fog. We chatted about Herc and Aggie, laughing at their antics from the night before. Talk soon turned to Goldie, with Nora admitting the temptation was real when it came to the kitten.

"I could put a litter box in the laundry room. Surely one cat couldn't make that much difference."

I hooted. "Keep on thinking that, oh deluded one. Did I ever tell you about the cat my brothers brought home?" I wrinkled my nose as I recalled the kitty "presents" it had left in various spots to await unwary toes. "Just wait until it gets mad at you. You'll see just how much difference one cat can make."

Nora stopped walking. I stopped as well since she still had my arm entwined with hers.

"Seriously? One little cat? I've never heard of a cat getting mad at an owner."

I shrugged, untangling my arm from hers, and began walking again. "I'm just saying you should probably talk to other cat owners first. We know quite a few of them." I paused and waited for her to catch up, smiling inwardly as she teetered slightly on her heels. So much for being able to run.

"All right, smarty-pants, I will." She slid her arm through mine again, and we walked in silence for a few minutes.

"What do you think Addie will have to say?" I glanced sideways at Nora, curious to see her response.

"I don't know. Maybe nothing useful. Of course, she might have the info to blow this thing wide open."

"Wouldn't that be nice." To be able to clear Shelby's name and put the real killer behind bars would be amazing.

After spending the afternoon with Inspector Alan Grant and reading about his exploits, I was ready to gather clues and solve crimes. Miss Marple would be so proud of me.

The café's windows were lit from within, the tables clearly visible from the street. As we opened the door and walked inside, inhaling the mingled scents of freshly baked bread and brewing coffee, I spotted Addie.

She was sitting near the back of the café at a small table, bent over her phone, forehead wrinkled as she stared at something on the tiny screen. A tall glass sat in front of her, a slice of lemon hanging precariously from the rim. I almost shivered when I spotted ice cubes floating inside the glass: I needed something to warm me up after that walk.

I approached her as cautiously as I would a skittish animal, not wanting to startle her. She must have seen us from the corner of her eyes, though, and she glanced up quickly from her phone.

I hadn't seen her in years. The Addie I recalled from the school corridors was outgoing and full of life, always surrounded by a group of giggling, chattering friends. This Addie was the direct opposite. Although she couldn't have been more than nineteen, she had the expression of a much older woman in her eyes, and the skin beneath them was dark and paper thin.

"Addie? How are you?" The words sounded inane to my ears as soon as I'd uttered them. Addie, however, didn't seem to notice and smiled up at me wanly.

"Hey, Miss Franklin. It's nice to see you again." She glanced at Nora, one delicate eyebrow lifted. "Is this . . ." The words trailed off into awkward silence, and I hurried to make the introductions.

"Addie, this is my friend, Mrs. Nora Goldstein." I gave Nora a little nudge forward.

They shook hands, Addie automatically responding when Nora reached out first.

"Emily must have told you why she's here with me." I said that as a statement, not a question, and Addie nodded. Thank goodness. Having to explain Nora's presence was one less thing to deal with. From all appearances, getting information from Addie was going to be difficult enough.

Nora and I sat down, one on each side of Addie. She was focused on her phone again, intently typing something with both thumbs. I exchanged a look with Nora and gave a small shrug. I'd give the girl a few more moments to acclimate herself to our presence before plunging into the reason we'd come here.

"Want some coffee, Miss Franklin?" Emily appeared at my shoulder, the welcome aroma of coffee wafting from the carafe.

I nodded vigorously, turning to smile up at her. "That would hit the spot. It wasn't too bad outside, but I did get a little chilled."

"Oh, sorry about that." Emily's eyebrows drew together in a frown as she glanced from me to her sister.

Addie's head was still down, and Emily didn't look pleased.

"Well, give me a sec to grab a couple of mugs, okay?" With another critical stare at Addie, she took off for the kitchen, the door swinging behind her.

"Addie," I began gently, "Mrs. Goldstein and I are here because you wanted to tell us something."

I waited a moment to see if she'd respond. When she didn't, I sighed. It wouldn't bother me one bit to play the old lady card with this girl. Okay, so being in my early fifties wasn't old. I got that. But to anyone younger than thirty, I was antique.

Clearing my throat, I added in a slightly quavering voice, "And it was a very long, cold walk for two elderly women." I wanted to laugh as Nora's thin eyebrows shot sky-high, a retort clearly on her lips. Giving her a little shake of the head, I continued, this time a bit more firmly. "If you're not going to tell us what you know about the college, then we'll leave and give you some space."

I made as if to push my chair back and nearly collided with Emily, a tray of coffee and brioche balanced on one arm.

"Oops, Miss Franklin. My fault." Emily maneuvered deftly around me and placed the loaded tray on the table. Before I could reassure her it was fine, she put both hands on her hips. "Addie, you're being just plain rude to these two ladies. If you aren't going to talk to them, I am."

"You've got that right." Nora reached for a full mug of coffee and a generous slice of warm vanilla brioche. "At least I'll get some food out of it."

"Be nice." My tone was mild, but I agreed with her. I'd finally get to taste some of the pastry the café was famous for in our neck of the woods.

"Fine. I'll talk." Addie's voice was rough, cracking as if she hadn't spoken in a while.

I didn't say anything but took a long sip of the deliciously warm brew. As far as I was concerned, I'd already helped her as far as I was going to.

"Addie?" Emily's voice was gentler now, coaxing her older sister into revealing whatever it was she'd learned. "Why don't you tell them where you were when, you know, you heard about the–the—"

"The professor who liked to trade grades for 'favors'?" Her fingers came up to make air quotes. The nails were bitten to the quick, cuticles red and peeling. This girl clearly had something bothering her.

I stepped into the conversation, carefully placing my nearly full mug down first. "Addie, before we get started here, let's get something straight, all right?" I had her attention.

Emily's eyes widened slightly at my words, but she remained silent.

"If you want us to help you, we can't have any of this." I mimed the air quotes, smiling to show her I wasn't mad. "Just say what you have to say and don't worry about what we'll think. Deal?"

Addie nodded slowly, her cheeks reddening as she glanced around the table at three interested faces. "Okay. Just don't blame me if I embarrass you."

"This is probably where I leave you three to chat." Emily smiled uncertainly around the table, but I made a shooing motion with my hand, laughing in amusement at Addie's words.

"Trust me when I say I've probably heard it all already. High school students aren't the best at using a social filter when they talk." I reached over and patted her hand gently. "Just tell us what it is you know."

"Yes," Nora chimed in. "Tell us in your own words."

That phrase, "in your own words," had always been one of my pet peeves. Every time I heard someone say it, I was tempted to ask, "And whose words will they be using if not their own?" It took some willpower, but I managed to disregard Nora and focus on Addie. At this point, she was the only one with firsthand information concerning the college and Babs's delving into its financial secrets.

"Addie?" I prompted her. "Why don't you begin with what you know about the mayor and Ms. Prescott?"

"Why would I know anything about the mayor?" Addie sounded puzzled, her eyebrows puckering together as she looked at me. "The only thing I know is Mr. Lafoe was getting ready to have his name all over the news for what he was doing."

Ah. Now we were getting somewhere.

"Why was his name going to be on the news?" Nora's tone was casual, but I could see the sides of her neck tightening as she spoke. "Was he cooking the grade books or something?"

Addie stared at Nora as if she'd sprouted horns. "If that was all he was doing, well, he'd be like dozens of others on that campus. Talk about a corrupt system!" She snorted in disgust. "That college is a microcosm of everything that's wrong in this world, I'm telling you."

"Then what was it?" I was beginning to feel impatient again, and I looked around for Emily. Maybe a refill of coffee would help.

"Just what I said. Tim Lafoe." Addie's smile was thin, without a shred of warmth in it. "He played these stupid games with grades. He even had a barter system that was absolutely disgusting. He'd give a girl an A, even if she didn't show up to class, if she'd—"

I stuck a finger in each ear and closed my eyes. I really didn't want to know. My stomach was rolling at the thoughts that had formed in my mind, however, and Nora's reaction seemed to be much the same.

"Did you tell anyone, Addie? A counselor, an administrator, anyone?"

She gave a small laugh, one completely empty of mirth. "Really, Miss Franklin? And have to tell them over and over what some of my friends had done in his class?" She shook her head adamantly. "No way. That's why I left. I figured if I wasn't there, no one could ask me questions, especially not that nosy newswoman."

Nora and I exchanged a look. This sounded promising, in spite of the gut-churning information.

"Do you mean Babs Prescott?" I knew that was who she meant, but I needed to hear it for myself.

"Yep. Ms. Plastic herself." Addie laughed again, this time sounding close to hysteria. "You should've seen her walking around, her pretend boobs leading the parade. She sure seemed to eat up the attention she got from all the guys on campus. Especially Mr. Lafoe."

Nora, rather proud of her non-fake assets, gave a satisfied smile. I wanted to cover my nearly-not-there chest.

Instead, I leaned closer to Addie, my voice and expression serious. "Addie, did Babs know about Tim Lafoe's so-called barter system?"

She shrugged, reaching out for her iced tea. "Maybe. Actually, I'm pretty sure she knew something. I think that's why he was constantly swarming around her."

"What makes you think that?" Nora leaned in as well. "Did you hear her saying something to that effect?"

Addie nodded slowly. "One day when I was in the library, I heard arguing coming from the stacks in the very back of the room." She gave a small shrug, with a half smile. "I was bored with what I was studying, so I snuck back there to listen."

"And you overheard Babs and Tim?" I tried to keep the eagerness out of my voice. "Did you hear what they were saying?"

Addie nodded. "And how! She was practically hissing, telling him she'd already gotten the goods on him from some of his students." She reddened slightly. "I heard the names she gave, but there's no way I'm telling that part."

"And you don't need to," I assured her.

If the police wanted to grill her for the information, they were welcome to it.

"What was Tim's response to that?"

"He told her she'd publish it over his dead body."

Nora hooted in laughter. "Well, he got that one wrong, didn't he?"

I frowned at her. "That's not funny. Someone *did* die."

"But nothing got published, did it?" Addie's words made Nora and me turn to stare at her. She was absolutely correct.

"Nora." I spoke carefully, not wanting to appear too eager. "I think we need to find out where Tim Lafoe was on the day Babs died."

"And I agree." Nora took the last sip of her coffee and grimaced. "Ugh, I can't stand cold coffee."

"Let me top that off for you, all right?" Emily was at my elbow with a carafe. Her expression was carefully neutral, but her concern was obvious. I smiled at her as brightly as I dared, without appearing manic.

"That would be lovely." I held out my mug for her to refill. "Nora?"

The atmosphere became lighter, and we enjoyed a few minutes of easy gossip with Emily and Addie, the sisters telling funny stories about their time in high school. I laughed the loudest, recalling exactly what they were describing. It made me realize how much I still missed the students.

I didn't miss the ever-present politics, though. And I definitely didn't miss the few unscrupulous educators I'd met over the years. It was time to find out exactly what Tim Lafoe was up to and get that news story out there. Shelby Tucker would be just the person to do that.

That thought made me smile with glee. Justice would be served up in black and white, the perfect end to a bad situation.

Chapter 15

"So now what? Do we call the police? Good grief, I'm cold!" Nora pulled her jacket closer about her body, shivering as we quick-stepped our way back to her apartment building.

You need more body fat, I wanted to tell her, but I answered her question, letting my own jacket fly open in the breeze. "I think we should, don't you? Addie's practically handed us the killer on a silver platter."

"Or on a plate of brioche. That was really good stuff. Kinda woke up my sweet tooth. Should we swing by The Friendly Bean? Maybe grab a few chocolate croissants to take back to my place?"

Yes, my traitorous stomach screamed. "No, that's okay. The brioche was enough."

"Really?" I could feel Nora giving me an appraising look. "Would this happen to have anything to do with a certain dog owner?"

"What makes you say that?" I was glad it was dark because my face was on fire. "I just don't want anything, that's all."

"Uh huh." Her tone was as dry as the dust in my house.

I'd neglected routine housecleaning lately in favor of anything except housecleaning. I figured the dust would wait but other things might not, such as a good book, a coffee date with a certain man, and clearing Shelby's name.

The building's entrance was brightly lit, a bank of spotlights trained on several pieces of art that sat in niches around the lobby. If I didn't know it was an apartment building, I might have thought it was a luxury hotel.

"Have a nice evening, ladies," chirped the building's new concierge, her bright pink nail polish shiny under the lights. "And don't forget that next month's talent show still needs a few more acts."

"I'll sure take that under consideration." Nora waggled her own brightly painted nails as we headed for the elevator.

Once we reached it, Nora turned to me, "There's no way on God's green earth I'll be doing that any time soon." She pushed the button to summon the elevator.

I gave her arm a poke. "What about having Marcus perform a tango with you? It seems you two are pretty good at that sort of thing."

We stepped into the elevator, and Nora pushed the button for her floor. The door closed with a soft hiss.

"Indeed," was all she said, but a smile lurked in the corner of her mouth. She might have been thinking of the dance, or it might have been a different sort of tango on her mind.

If I was a betting woman, I'd put all of my chips on the latter.

After a quick cup of hot tea—chamomile with lavender, a perfect way to end the day—I said my farewells and began the walk home. We needed to make a personal visit to the Portland Police Station and had agreed on taking an Uber together to save a very long walk.

"I'll text when we're on the way," she'd assured me. "And don't tell Brent what we're doing or he'll insist on driving."

"Not to worry," I laughed. "He's the last person I'd tell."

I slept well that night, in spite of the brioche. Sugar didn't sit well with me at times, especially when eaten later in the evening. If I had to guess, I'd say the tea had done its job.

I didn't bother to set an alarm, knowing Herc would be more than happy to wake me well before Nora made an appearance. I'd always been an "early to bed, early to rise" person, even when younger, and Herc's nudges didn't inconvenience me.

I hadn't counted on Nora, though. When my cell phone began to announce a text long before I was ready to get out of bed, I was disoriented, reaching for the nonexistent alarm clock I'd tossed out on my first day of retirement.

Rise and shine, it read, followed by a series of tiny pictures.

With one eye opened, I recognized a cup of something that looked like coffee and a croissant. The line of red hearts that followed these was as loud as Nora herself, and I could have sworn the phone had added the ability to actually project the aroma coming from the tiny food pictures. It was too early, however, and I groaned, letting the phone fall from my hand.

"Hey, boy," I said as Herc's snuffling nose bumped the side of my bed.

He still looked sleepy, as if the idea of food hadn't entered his doggy brain yet. He slept on the braided throw rug beside my bed, ignoring the deluxe cushion I'd found for him at the local Goodwill. It had been sanitized and cleaned, I'd been assured, but apparently it wasn't up to Herc's standards. I was all right with the current arrangements, to be honest. It was comforting to hear his soft snores when I awoke in the night. I wasn't certain he'd be much of a deterrent if a burglar ever showed up, though.

The cell began chiming again, this time indicating an incoming call. I picked up the phone and looked at the time: five minutes after six. What in the world was the woman thinking?

This had better be good. "I was asleep. And that begs the question: why aren't you?"

Nora's laugh echoed strangely in my ear. If I didn't know better, I'd have guessed she was standing in my living room.

She was.

"What in the Sam Hill are you doing here? And how did you get in?" I clutched the covers to my neck, glaring as Nora waltzed into my room.

She carried a tray. It hadn't been the emojis I'd smelled. A carafe, two cups, and a plate of something tantalizing was deposited on the small nightstand next to my bed. Herc's tail, always a good indicator of his mood, was thumping a rapid staccato on the floor as he sat eyeing the tray. At least one of us was happy.

"We've got a date with the boys and girls in blue, remember?" She poured a cup of coffee and handed it to me. "Drink this and wake up, buttercup. You are one grumpy bunny in the morning."

I wanted to ignore her, turn my back, and pull the covers over my head. She and her pal Herc could enjoy the morning together without me. Instead, I took the cup from her hand and grunted my thanks.

"You still haven't answered my second question." I eyed Nora over the rim of my coffee cup, feeling more awake but still, as she'd so eloquently put it, like a "grumpy bunny." "I don't recall giving you a key to my house."

"I didn't need a key, goofy. Remember this?" She withdrew a small metal object from the velvet fanny pack she'd fastened around her waist. "I guess I forgot to return this after our little adventure last year."

I closed my eyes and shivered. To call it an "adventure" was a gross understatement, to say the least. It was typical of Nora, though, to save a memento. She'd had the largest accumulation of ticket stubs I'd ever seen when we were teens while I'd been into growing my collection of mystery books. I guess I should have been thankful it was only a lock pick and not something else, considering what we'd experienced.

"Is it okay for me to come in now?"

I started and almost dropped my coffee on my favorite duvet cover, the one sprinkled with violets and tiny green leaves.

Rachel's smiling face peeked around the corner of my bedroom door, her cell phone held up in one hand. "Have you told her yet, Mrs. Goldstein?"

"Mrs. Goldstein," I said sharply, "hasn't told me much except to admit she picked the lock on my front door." I glared at Herc. "And thanks to this amazing guard dog here, I feel as safe as a fish in a roomful of cats."

"Aw, don't blame him." Rachel edged her way in and squatted by my dog. He looked at her with an adoring expression as she began scratching between his ears. "He's a lover, not a fighter."

"That figures." I swung my feet over the side of my bed. "I can't even choose a dog properly." I looked at my rather ratty nightgown and motioned to the robe hanging on the back of my door. "Nora, hand me that robe, please. And you two," I looked at Rachel and her furry shadow, "can wait in the kitchen. We might as well eat at the table."

When we'd seated ourselves at the table and had passed the fresh, chocolate-filled croissants around, I looked pointedly at Rachel, one eyebrow lifted. "Okay, I'm listening. Let's have the big news."

"I promise you're gonna like this, Miss Franklin. It might even save us a trip downtown to my dad's office."

"To your dad's—oh, you mean to the police department." I gave Nora a not-so-happy look. "And for this you woke me before the crack of dawn? It couldn't wait?"

Nora shrugged as she bit into a croissant, but she didn't look one bit sorry. In fact, now that I looked at her properly, she appeared downright elated about something.

"All right, you." I pointed one finger at my best friend, feeling as though I'd fallen down the rabbit hole and back to my classroom. "Talk. And I mean now."

She lifted both hands in the air. "It's not my news, Sis. It's Rachel's."

"Like I was saying, Miss Franklin, I found out something really interesting." Rachel's fingers moved deftly over the face of her smartphone. "And ta-da! Take a look at this."

I squinted as I looked at the picture she was holding up. Babs's smug smiling face stared out at me, and my blood pressure began to rise. Perhaps I needed more coffee.

"Explain, please." I reached for the carafe and poured the last of the aromatic brew into my cup. "I'm listening."

Rachel set the phone down and leaned forward, eager. "I found someone who isn't much of a fan. And whoever it is, they've commented on almost every post she has—had," she corrected herself. "Listen to this."

Rachel began to read some of the comments, and chill began to work its way down my spine. This could be the very person who'd hated her enough to get rid of her permanently.

"And Mrs. Goldstein's already called Miss Louisa." Rachel beamed at Nora. "Isn't that awesome?"

Nora's modest smile made me want to laugh out loud. If there was any credit to be had, Nora would make sure she got it.

I refrained from rolling my eyes. I turned to look at my oldest friend. "And just what does Louisa have to do with this?"

Nora gave another suspiciously nonchalant shrug. "She knows someone who can track down the ABC."

Rachel giggled and leaned over to snag the last croissant. "You mean the IP address, Mrs. Goldstein."

"Whatever. She's headed over here, by the way." Nora glanced at the clock on the face of my microwave, another acquisition from Goodwill. "In fact, she should be here in the next few minutes."

I threw up my hands and let them fall with a thump to the table, making the cups rattle as I glared at Nora. "Don't let me get in the way. It's just my house."

"Eat your breakfast, Sis. Sounds like you're running a bit low on sugar this morning." Nora gave me a cheeky grin as I stared at her, trying to stay angry.

I never could stay mad at her for too long, though. I could, however, put her to good use as long as she was here.

I pushed back from the table. "Well, before the rest of the gang arrives, I'm going to get a shower. Could someone please feed Herc? Oh, and feel free to put the dirty dishes in the sink and run some soapy water." I gave Nora my own sassy grin. "The word 'dishwasher' in this house means the two-handed human variety, by the way."

I left them to it, smiling all the way to my room. This was almost as good as having a live-in maid.

* * * *

By the time I'd showered, dressed, and dried my hair, I had a houseful of guests. Louisa and Nora sat side by side on the sofa, laughing like two crazed loons over something on Louisa's phone. I really didn't want to know what it was. Rachel was nowhere to be seen. I posed the question of her whereabouts to the queen of comedy as I settled into the only other piece of upholstered furniture in the house, a rather battered armchair inherited from an aunt.

"Oh, Rachel took Herc for a walk." Nora looked away from Louisa's phone, her eyes still glinting with humor. "She said to tell you you're almost out of dog food, by the way."

"And good morning," said Louisa. "Thanks for having all of us over this early. Not many folks would be so kind." She smiled. "Nora told me that you're an early riser anyway, though."

"That's me all right, the quintessential early bird. Gotta love getting up with the sun." I glowered at Nora, waiting for her to say something.

She, however, was staring intently at her nails, suddenly finding them mesmerizing.

Louisa, oblivious to my sarcasm and Nora's discomfort, smiled widely as she produced a sheaf of papers from her large handbag. She glanced through them briefly before handing them across to me.

"Here's a copy of Babs's phone records. I thought you might want them for your files or wherever you keep evidence."

I smiled at her choice of words and watched as she scrabbled around in her bag again, a tiny frown puckering her forehead. Rachel's dad would split a gizzard, as my granny would say, to hear it called "evidence." He'd probably split that same gizzard again if he knew we were meddling in police business, to be honest.

An uneasy feeling settled on me momentarily, and my smile faded. Was it evidence? And the big question was did I have the legal right to keep it? Probably not. I mentally shrugged, shaking off the uneasiness. I'd most likely do worse things before I eventually bought the farm, another one of granny's rural euphemisms.

"Now what did I do—aha! Here it is." She waved a single sheet of paper in the air with a pleased expression. "My friend, the computer savvy one I spoke about earlier, e-mailed me the instructions on how to find an IP address." She beamed at Nora and me. "Isn't that amazing?"

"Amazing." Nora was still examining her fingers. She was going to have to look up eventually.

"Wait a minute. Are you telling me anyone can find out that type of information?"

"Well, maybe not anyone, but *we* can, thanks to my pal at TeleTech." Louisa laid the paper on the coffee table, a relic from my childhood home. "And as soon as Rachel gets back, we'll get started."

"In the meantime," I said, "what'll we do with the information about Tim Lafoe?"

"Tim Lafoe? What information?" Louisa sounded baffled, and I was beginning to explain when my front door opened and in walked Herc, head down and tongue hanging out, followed by a smiling Rachel.

Herc looked exhausted, but Rachel looked energized, her cheeks pink from the morning coolness.

"Let me get him some fresh water, and then we can talk." Rachel led a plodding dog into the kitchen.

"You betcha," Louisa answered, with her gaze still on me. "What did you find out?"

Water began running at the kitchen sink, and Rachel talked to Herc in a singsong. Why did folks feel the need to use baby talk with animals?

"Find out about what?" Rachel, wiping her wet hands against her jeans, walked over and dropped to the floor between the sofa and the armchair, Herc right on her heels.

Nora looked at me with wide eyes, her nails forgotten. I wanted to smack myself: I'd mentioned "that name" without first warning Rachel.

"Rachel," I began gently, "we had a chance to speak with Addie, a student who used to attend the junior college."

"Okaaay." Rachel's confusion was clearly written on her face, and Nora wasn't going to jump in and help. Taking a deep breath, I told her about the conversations we'd had with Emily and then Addie.

"It seems Tim has a nasty habit of making his students feel uncomfortable, to put it mildly." I paused and watched Rachel for a moment, trying to gauge her reaction.

She said nothing.

"Addie happened to overhear him and Babs arguing in the college's library. It seems Babs was letting him know some of his students had talked, whatever that means."

The room was silent, except for Herc's soft panting. Hopefully, I hadn't upset Rachel too badly. It was too early in the day for bad news.

When Rachel finally spoke, her gaze was level and her voice calm. To anyone who didn't know the situation, she'd appear to be the picture of tranquility. The only giveaway to how she must really be feeling were the hands twisted tightly into a very patient Herc's fur.

"Do you think Professor Lafoe killed her? Is that what you were talking about when I came in?"

"Yes," said Nora in a decisive tone. "We, Miss Franklin and I, that is, think we ought to tell someone at the police department about this."

Rachel smiled grimly. "And I'd be more than happy to pass this on to my dad. In fact," she got to her feet, "if I go now, I can catch him before his shift meeting."

"Wait, Rachel." I looked at her, my neck held at an awkward angle. "I thought you were going to show us the address, the one you spotted on Instagram."

She slapped her forehead and sank back down to the floor beside Herc. "Gosh, I'm getting as forgetful as Brent. Must be the close proximity, or whatever the saying is."

"I think it's 'birds of a feather flock together,' and you two couldn't be more unalike if you tried."

Rachel quickly opened an icon on her phone. "I've sent the screenshot to Mrs. Goldstein."

Nora held up her phone. A text notification was on the screen.

I shrugged, smiling sheepishly. "You need to make allowances for the technologically inept, my dear."

"Just drop the 'technologically,'" muttered my very best friend in the whole wide world.

She managed to duck as I sent my "Welcome to Oregon" pillow sailing across the room.

Chapter 16

After Rachel left, promising to let her dad know what Addie had said, the three of us got to work.

"What does the screenshot tell us?" I looked hopefully at Nora, waiting to hear something that might reveal the person behind the posts. "What's the user name that caught Rachel's eye?"

"It says . . . hang on a sec." Nora played air trombone with her phone until she got the focus just right. "It says fedupwithfakenewsanchors." She looked up, frowning slightly as she refocused her gaze on me. "Think they liked Babs much?"

"It sounds to me like they didn't want to hear all the crazy stuff going around these days. You know, the 'fake news' or whatever they call it." Louisa sniffed as she fished in her handbag once more. "Good thing I thought to bring my iPad."

"I don't think it's the news they meant," I said slowly, thinking aloud. "They said 'fakenewsanchor,' as in the person reading the newscast."

Nora emitted an inelegant grunt. "Well, who was faker than Babs? I mean, that woman replaced or added to nearly every part of her body that we could see and most likely to some we couldn't, if you get my drift."

A sassy wink followed this comment, and I had to shake my head. Louisa, of course, laughed loudly enough to startle Herc from beside my chair. With a look of clear doggy disapproval, he headed for the back door's flap and into the backyard.

"All right, you. We get your drift. You need to float back this way, okay?" I picked up the e-mail that held the instructions on retrieving an IP address and studied it for a moment. It didn't appear to be that complicated, and the thought we might be mere minutes away from finally discovering Babs's potential killer made my heart pick up the pace.

"Give me just a moment to get this open." Louisa typed carefully with one finger, her bottom lip held between her teeth. "Okay, I'm in. Gwen, can you give me the web address?"

I scanned the e-mail quickly. There it was: How to Trace an IP Address, followed by a rather long series of numbers and letters. I cleared my throat and then began to read them out, careful to enunciate.

"Aha—and here it is, bold as brass." Louisa looked up from her tablet and grinned broadly. "Just give me the steps one at a time."

In the time it took Nora to brew a fresh pot of Ethiopian blend coffee, Louisa had opened up the page needed to identify "fedupwithfakenewsanchors."

"And here we go." She turned the iPad around so all three of us could watch the screen as it did its job of revealing Babs's detractor. When the information finally popped up, I gasped, not believing what I was seeing in black and white. The address now on the screen was one we'd come across before. And the person attached to it was as familiar as the local news station.

"It's Matt Robb?" Nora sounded shocked, her mouth hanging open in the most unbecoming way.

I knew what she was probably thinking, and I didn't have to wait that long to hear her say it.

"How can someone that good-looking do something that stupid?" She shook her head vigorously. "Uh-uh. No way, no how."

"I can call him," Louise offered. "Maybe act like I'm from Instagram and need to verify his phone number or something."

Nora snorted, still not happy with the outcome. "As if that'd work. He's gotta be too savvy to fall for that."

"He was silly enough to choose a user name that pointed straight back at him," I said mildly. "Think about it, Nora. Who else would get that articulate except another news anchor? Most folks use handles like 'moonpiemama' or 'nascarfan.'"

"Maybe." She sounded doubtful, but I could see the wheels turning in her head, shifting her opinion from "good looker" to "possible killer."

I wanted to remind her about Ted Bundy, one of the most dapper-looking serial killers of the modern age. He had to fake an arm injury, get out in public, and make direct contact to get his victims alone. Now a killer could hide behind a social media post and attack without warning. That thought chilled me more than a day at Seal Rock or Pacific City.

We sat in in silence for a moment, sipping the fresh coffee and trying to sort out our thoughts. When I set my cup down on the table, Nora and Louise both looked at me with identical expectant expressions.

"What?" I stared back at the two of them, my forehead wrinkled in question. "I don't have the slightest idea what to do, so don't look at me."

"So, what do we do with this new information? Rachel's dad isn't going to thank us for getting in his business, especially when he discovers how we got the info." Nora placed her cup next to mine and leaned back against the pillow depicting Multnomah Falls. "What do you think, Sis?"

"I think," I began slowly, "we should check out Matt's movements on the day Babs died. That's got to be fairly simple, considering he's a public figure. Right?" I looked hopefully at my guests, waiting for their assurances.

To my relief, both Nora and Louisa seemed to agree with me. I figured if the three of us worked together to uncover the information, we'd soon uncover any shenanigans. If there were any, that was. In this country, I reminded myself, it was still "innocent until proven guilty." Just because a person appeared guilty didn't make it true.

It sure made it easier to blame him, though.

Did I believe he could do the deed, so to speak? I let that thought roam around unfettered for a moment while I examined it from all angles. The answer was a big, fat "yes." Anyone at any time could do anything. If there was any lesson to be learned from Miss Marple, that was it.

"Hello, Sis? Anyone at home in there?"

I started as Nora leaned toward me, snapping her fingers to get my attention. "Yes. Sorry. I was thinking about Shelby."

"Poor kiddo." Nora shook her head sadly. "I hope to goodness we get this solved before they throw her in the slammer for good."

"Why would they do that?" Louisa's gazed darted between Nora and me. "I thought she didn't do it."

"She didn't." I spoke with more firmness than I was feeling. "I'm just thinking they're going to want to pin this on someone quickly, and she's as good as anyone to blame. Especially since she was right there. Actually, according to Miss Marple, anyone can do anything if the circumstances are right. Even," I said solemnly, "the three of us."

Nora groaned. "Can't you get through one day without quoting that woman? Who, in case you didn't know, isn't even real."

"Hey, I happen to like Miss Marple!" Louisa reached over and gave my shoulder a comradely squeeze. "And any idea is as good as another right now." She looked at Nora and me, her eyes troubled. "So, thoughts?"

Nora and I exchanged glances. I gave a small shrug. She returned it. Louisa sighed loudly.

"Well, this isn't going to get us anywhere." Louisa looked at the bundle of phone records. "For what it's worth, we could go back through the phone records again."

"We've done that already," protested Nora. "What else will we find out? We already know Matt was the last phone call Babs got that day."

I slowly held up one finger, and the other two looked at me expectantly. There was something in the back of my mind, something troubling me about that call. What was it?

And then it hit me. "How do we know it was Matt on the other end of the line?"

Nora stared, but Louisa clapped her hands together and all but crowed. "That's it! Just because it was his cell phone doesn't necessarily mean it was him who used it. I mean, I've let others use my phone before. Haven't you?"

Nora and I both nodded in agreement.

"As a matter of fact, I let the boy use it last week." Nora wrinkled her nose. "He said he was calling his mom because his phone was dead. He could've been calling China for all I paid attention."

"See? It could happen." I felt jubilant now, almost as if the answer was right under our collective noses. "It might have been anyone using his phone. That's what we need to find out."

"No time like the present," said Nora. "Louisa, can we ride with you? Rachel was my ride here, and I'm sure Gwen's car hasn't been driven in months."

"Walking's good for the body," I retorted. "Besides, all those rides with Brent have completely put me off vehicles."

"Well, it'll be a mighty long walk to the television station." Nora's tone was as sassy as her grin.

Louisa put both hands on the table's edge for support as she rose to her feet. According to the man at the Goodwill store, it'd come from a house full of antiques.

"Like the owner," he'd chuckled as he'd given the table a final swipe with a dust rag. "None of her family wanted anything less than twenty years old, so we got this little gem."

"Do you think he's at the station this early?" Nora asked doubtfully.

It was still early in the day, relatively speaking, and Matt's news slot wasn't until five in the evening. Of course, I knew nothing about how a television station ran or when its employees showed up to work.

Louisa batted the question away with one plump hand. "Oh, sure. He's gotta get his stories together first, right?"

"I thought he had an assistant for that sort of thing. You know, the research part, the dirty work."

Herc's head appeared inside the doggy door, and I patted the side of my leg, calling him in. With a wary glance at Louisa, he walked over to me and plopped his head on my lap with a sigh.

"Maybe we should talk to his assistant first," suggested Nora, "and see if she—"

"It could be a 'he,'" I objected, and she wrinkled her nose at me.

"Okay, Miss Proper, we could see if *he* has a list of Matt's appointments, maybe a Day-Timer or something."

"Does anyone still use a Day-Timer?" I stared at my cell phone. I'd gotten used to plotting my plans in the calendar, grateful for the reminders that sounded whenever I had something I needed to do. "I figured those went the way of beepers and car phones."

"Oh, don't be so difficult, Sis." Nora's tone was exasperated. I leaned over and pushed her cup of coffee closer to her. She grabbed it with a scowl, taking the last bit in one gulp and setting the cup down with a thump.

"Better?" I asked sweetly.

Her reply, suffice it to say, showed she was going to be a handful until this mess was resolved, and I couldn't blame her. Thinking about Shelby's situation made me antsy as well, although I did try to keep my word choice socially acceptable.

"Are you two really friends?" Louisa looked at the pair of us, eyebrows lifted in mock disbelief. "Anyone who listens to you might think it's the opposite."

Nora and I looked at each other and laughed.

"I think we had our first argument in kindergarten." I leaned over to give my best friend a quick hug. "Something about which one got to use the play kitchen first."

"I think it was over which one of us got to sit next to Danny Ferguson during snack time," Nora said. "You remember. The boy with the red hair and all those freckles."

I put my hands up, smiling at Louisa. "And as you can see, we can't even agree what the first disagreement was about."

Louisa shook her head, sending her earrings swinging like mini pendulums. "And if I didn't know better, I'd have thought you two really *were* sisters." She hefted her large handbag to one shoulder, her car keys in hand. "Ready?"

After a brief stop at the local Dutch Bros' drive-thru for something called a Flap Jack Breve for Louisa, a White Zombie Mocha for Nora, and a bottle of water for me, we headed toward SW Columbia Street and the television station. Parking, of course, was nearly nonexistent, but Louisa spotted a car leaving and managed to maneuver her car into the spot with only minor swearing.

It made me glad I'd decided to let my car sit in the small unattached garage. Driving in Portland could be a hazard at the best of times. Besides, I reminded myself smugly, walking not only did the body good, it was good for the environment.

We paused for a moment before entering the building, staring at the ever-growing skyline around us. From where I stood, I counted no less than three high-rises in progress, each topped with a bright yellow crane. I shivered as I watched the long arms swinging precariously. How anyone could work that high up was beyond me.

"So much for worrying about my carbon footprint," I muttered to myself. With all of the machinery it took to grow a city, my little contribution seemed almost silly. Still, I had to admit, I'd never really liked driving, not even as a teen, and claiming I was parking my car for a greater cause made me feel normal, whatever "normal" meant.

"Quit daydreaming and move it." Nora gave me a poke in the arm, walking past me and through the automatic door. I followed her, rubbing the spot where her nails had nearly pierced my skin. Those things were almost as lethal as her stiletto heels.

The lobby was rather plain Jane, with pieces of furniture that looked like leftovers from the seventies. A burnt orange sofa sat dumpily between two brown-and-tan-striped barrel chairs, and the oblong coffee table placed in the middle of the arrangement was piled high with magazines that could have been collector's items. So much for a glamorous business. This place made my living room look as good as Buckingham Palace.

One wall, though, was thoroughly covered in framed photographs that ranged from black-and-white studio shots to full-color candid poses, each face representing a news anchor, past or present. It amused me to see the timeline of workplace equality. It had taken five rows of photos for me to finally spot a woman's face among the cadre of men.

Babs Prescott, however, was easy to see. Her face, in all its technicolored glory, had been removed from the lineup and rehung in a place of honor near the wood-paneled reception counter. A vase of roses sitting beneath it added to its shrine-like appearance.

I pointed at it with my chin, catching Nora's arm in one hand. "It looks like they've got the queen bee front and center. She'd have loved that."

"Shhh," Nora hissed, jabbing my side with one bony elbow. "I heard someone moving behind that wall."

The short wall that formed the reception counter, high enough to make me stand on my toes, was a relic from the days before the public smoking ban. The idea, I supposed, was that cigarette smoke would think twice before crossing the great paneled divide between the news room and the waiting area.

"May I help you?" The thin voice of an even thinner woman standing just inside the blocked-off reception zone made me jump, and I nearly knocked my chin on the Formica-topped counter. If her compressed lips were anything to go by, she wasn't a happy camper when she took in my appearance.

"Yes, ma'am. I'd like to see Matt's assistant for a few minutes, if that's all right."

She opened her mouth to speak, but I cut her off at the verbal pass.

"I don't have an appointment."

"Hmmph." She shuffled her way over to the surprisingly modern laptop on a scarred wooden desk, prodding at the keys with one arthritic finger. Good grief. The woman must have arrived here with the first station owners.

Finally, she glanced at me. She had applied a thick application of makeup in an apparent attempt to disguise the age spots scattered over her face. I almost gulped in dismay. I'd discovered the beginnings of one below my right cheekbone just that morning.

Well, I was going to do something about it. Nothing fake on my face, thank you very much. I'd resort to my newfound love of all things homemade and natural. Age spots? Not a problem. Just point me in the direction of vitamin E oil mixed with a few drops of tea tree oil. According to *Sara's Herbal Remedies*, a show on the local public television station, there was a concoction available for every ailment known to womankind.

"She's in a meeting with Mr. Robb," announced the ancient receptionist. "I'll go and see if she can give you a few minutes of her time." She glared at me over the counter. "And if you're someone from the *print media*," the words were spat out as if she'd bitten into something sour, "you'll be out the door before you can say time waster."

With that, she headed back through the doorway and disappeared into a low-lit corridor.

"She sounds like a real sweetie." Louisa's mouth twisted in a grimace. "Must've got up on the wrong side of the cot this morning."

"Reminded me of the nurse we had a few years ago at school." I sat in one of the chairs and felt myself sinking lower as the cushion gave up the ghost. "She was so mean, the poor students would rather sit in class puking their guts up than go to see her."

"Thanks for the visual." Nora's tone was light, but I thought I saw a tinge of green in her cheeks. It might have been the poor illumination, though.

I wondered if the cost of keeping the star anchors happy had drained the budget set aside to drag the office into the twenty-first century.

Swift footsteps sounded down the hall and into the front of the office. It wasn't the receptionist. The feet were moving too rapidly to be her, unless she'd discovered the fountain of youth in the back rooms of the station.

I moved to the counter and peered over. A youngish woman, dressed from head to toe in clashing animal prints, stood there, one hand holding a thin cell phone to her ear. Holding up one finger, she turned her head and murmured into the phone and then disconnected the call.

"I'm Kenzie, Matt's general gofer." Her broad smile displayed a mouthful of whitened teeth. I wondered if she was practicing for her turn before the camera. "Moira said you needed a few minutes?"

The last sentence came out as a question, and I nodded.

"If you don't mind." I motioned for Nora and Louisa to join me at the counter. "We've got a few questions you might be able to answer."

"Good morning, Kenzie." Nora thrust out her hand toward the assistant. "I'm Nora Goldstein, an old friend of–of . . ."

"Of Bud and Susie Greenworth," chimed in Louisa.

Both of Kenzie's eyebrows made a valiant attempt to lift, a clear indication Louisa had just produced a pair of very important names.

"The station owners?" Kenzie managed to squeak out the words, her eyes widening ever so slightly.

"Yes." I nodded, holding up my smartphone in one hand. "In fact, we've managed to uncover a very interesting social media account that might just require an explanation."

I'd read descriptions claiming someone's face became instantly pale, and, in the space of one point five seconds, I'd just witnessed the phenomenon. Kenzie's complexion was now the color of a frog's underbelly, a sickly hue that made my stomach turn cartwheels. Was she going to pass out? Have a heart attack?

Before I had a chance to scoot around the wall and offer her a sip from my water bottle, though, Matt appeared, the wizened Moira right on his polished heels. He took one look at Kenzie's face and grabbed her around the waist as she began to sag.

"Move that chair," he barked at Moira.

The woman scurried to do as he asked, her expression clearly blaming our intrusion for the current hoopla. I stared over the counter as Matt lowered his assistant to the floor, careful to cushion her head with one hand.

Without looking at us, he asked, "Why did you really come here? And who sent you?"

I exchanged a baffled look with Nora, who gave a tiny shrug. Louisa, however, went into "Lady of Portland" mode, her voice as haughty as her expression.

"My name is Louisa Lovejoy Turner. My friends and I wish to speak with someone who can give us the information we need." She stared at Matt. "And since it has to do with your whereabouts on the day Babs died, I'd highly suggest it be you who does the talking."

I have to say it wasn't a pleasant sight watching Matt, news anchor extraordinaire, with his mouth agape. Did he realize the silver filling in the back of his mouth showed up when the light hit it?

And more importantly, had Louisa hit the proverbial nail on its head? Hopefully, we were about to find out.

Chapter 17

To our collective relief, Kenzie's color soon returned to normal, and she was able to sit up in Moira's desk chair. I noticed, though, she leaned against Matt's arm as if she still felt dizzy. He obligingly allowed her to do so, and the look of bliss in Kenzie's eyes gave away her feelings for her boss.

Don't do it, I wanted to shout at her. Employer–employee relationships rarely succeeded, at least not the ones I'd witnessed.

Take, for instance, a certain math teacher and a principal. It was only at the insistence of the principal's wife, who happened to be one of the school's counselors, that the teacher was transferred out of the district.

I shook my head inwardly, thinking about the scuttlebutt that went around and around the school for several semesters. It was enough to put me off men forever.

Except for Roger, of course. The thought of his kind smile made my cheeks grow warm. Looking up, I saw Nora watching me from the corner of her eye, the edge of her mouth twitching in a repressed smile. That woman could read me, all right. She'd known me for far too long and far too well. I wanted to give her a hug.

"Let me make sure Kenzie is okay," Matt said. "Then we can talk in my office." He gave a perfunctory glance at his assistant. "You'll be fine. Just sit there a while."

His voice was as rigid as his back, and Kenzie stiffened as he all but pushed her away from his side.

Better get used to it, girlie. Unless something out of the ordinary happened, that would probably be the full extent of the relationship.

Leaving Kenzie to the not-so-tender attentions of Moira, Matt led Louisa, Nora, and me past the reception area and down the corridor. The narrow hallway was carpeted in an olive-and-tan pattern, the loose threads and faded color showing its age. If I had to make a guess based on the color, I'd have said it was brand-new during the Nixon administration.

"In here, please." Matt paused beside an open door, the word "please" clearly a habit and not meant as true politeness. This man was angry, and it showed. From the top of his shellacked hair to the toes of his tasseled shoes, Matt signaled fury. I gulped as I edged past him, careful not to trip over his professionally shined loafers or touch a thread of his immaculately laundered shirt.

Closing the door with a sharp click, he marched to the business side of a large teak desk and sat. Only two chairs were placed at angles facing him, so one of us was going to have to stand.

Once Nora and Louisa were seated, I propped myself against the wall nearest the desk. Thank goodness, I'd worn my sensible Birkenstocks. Of course, I wore them every day, but right now I was grateful. I couldn't have stood one minute in Nora's ankle killers.

I looked from face to face, waiting for someone to say something. It was a classic standoff, with neither side giving in to the other. Sighing loudly, I tapped one foot and put my hands on my hips, ignoring the new roll that had recently developed there. "Look, you three. I may be retired, but I don't have all day to stand here and play childish games. Mr. Robb, we have a few questions for you."

He opened his mouth, but I held up one hand to stop him.

I wasn't finished giving directions. "Louisa, you start. Be sure to let him know exactly how we focused on him."

When she began to speak, I gave her the same stop sign.

"Nora, you and I will jump in and fill in any gaps."

This time all three of them stared at me.

I nodded my head in my most regal manner. "Louisa, you may begin."

She looked at me blankly.

Giving another exasperated sigh, I prompted her. "Rachel was looking through Instagram . . ." I patted her on the shoulder, ready to give another cue if needed.

"Yes, through Instagram," she repeated.

"And?" It was Matt who interrupted this less-than-stellar recitation. "Who is Rachel, and what has Instagram got to do with me?"

Nora and Louisa looked at me in one perfectly synchronized movement.

I wanted to say, "I'll give that a ten out of ten," but instead, I nodded at them and stepped closer to the desk. "Rachel is one of our employees. We asked her to take a look at the social media accounts of Babs Prescott and report back to us if she discovered anything, for the lack of a better term, unsettling. She did."

Matt's reaction was Oscar worthy. "Whoa whoa whoa, ladies." He stood up so quickly his ergonomically designed chair tipped backward, hitting the wall behind it. "First of all, and I mean this with all respect, but what the heck does Babs's social media accounts have to do with you?" He planted both hands on the desktop and leaned forward, eyes narrowing in a not-so-friendly manner. "And secondly, if you don't have a really good lawyer, I'd suggest you get one pronto. This little stunt is gonna cost you big-time."

"Louisa?" In spite of my jumping heart, I managed to sound cool as I turned to face her. "Maybe you could reintroduce yourself?"

It was a low blow in the Portland society world, but it was the only one I had. And she didn't let me down. I wanted to applaud.

"I, young man, am Louisa Lovejoy Turner." She paused a moment, haughtily waiting for the full effect of her name to hit a fuming Matt where it hurt. When his mouth gaped open yet again, she smiled in satisfaction. "I have as many lawyers as I need, ready to drop whatever they're doing to make sure that I. Do. Not. Lose." She leaned slightly forward, her eyes narrowed. "I trust I'm making myself clear."

Matt ran a finger around the inside of his collar as if his tie was suddenly too tight. "Yes, ma'am. Clear as Waterford crystal."

Nora and I smiled at one another behind Louisa's back. This was getting to be fun.

Louisa's nod was stately, a queen in her court dealing with a recalcitrant subject. "So, let's back up a bit, shall we? I believe my friend here was telling you about a little something that was found online."

That was my cue. "As I was saying, Rachel discovered something very interesting." I paused for effect, adding, "Does the user name fedupwithfakenewsanchors ring a bell?"

Matt stared at me, his eyes as wide as they could go and his lips working without a single sound escaping them. Dear Lord, was the man having a fit? Maybe his collar *was* too tight.

Before I could voice my concern, a knock at the door startled all of us. "Should I get that?" I motioned to the door.

Matt waved away my question and walked around the side of the desk. I watched him carefully, calculating his current state of health. If he was moving in a normal manner, surely he was all right. Maybe I'd only stumped him with that user name nonsense.

To my surprise, Moira and Kenzie stood there. Moira's angular face stiff, her thin lips clamped tightly shut as if trying to keep in a flood of words. Kenzie, however, looked as if she'd been crying with the floodgates wide open, her mascara leaving twin smudged tracks under her eyes.

"What?" barked out Matt, which sent his assistant into another round of weeping.

Moira, her cheeks mottled red, yanked on the girl's arm and shoved her into the office.

"Mr. Ro-obb," hiccupped Kenzie, furiously scrubbing at her face with the back of one hand. "I ne-eed to tell you so-omething."

"Indeed you do, girl, and you'd better make it snappy. You're going to need some time to clear out that desk of yours." Moira's tone was both triumphant and angry, and Matt's color rose as he glared at the two standing before him.

"I'll be the one to decide who'll be clearing out a desk here, Moira." Matt's voice had moved from flaming to icy, and Moira flinched.

Could the receptionist actually see herself as a rival with Kenzie? This was getting "interestinger and interestinger," as Brent would say.

"Well? Out with it already. I'm dealing with one crisis, and I don't need another."

I'd been closely watching Kenzie's face, and her gaze darted from me to Louisa and then to Nora. Call it intuition or suspicion, but I had a gut feeling this gal had a good idea of what we three had come to talk to Matt about.

"I–I think I know what this is about, Mr. Robb." Kenzie looked briefly at me and my two friends who, for once, stood silent. "I did it." She gave another gulp and managed to stop another bout of crying. "I posted those things about her, okay? I thought she was mean, and she never had a nice word to say about anyone, especially you."

"What in the world are you babbling about?" Now Matt stood with his hands on his hips, his expression baffled. "I swear. If I ever learn to understand females, I'm writing a book."

"And good luck with that little project," Nora said under her breath.

Louisa, of course, laughed.

In spite of the drama, I was getting antsy and wanted to go home. Herc would be expecting a walk soon, and I was dying to crack open the new-to-me Josephine Tey book *The Man in the Queue*. Inspector Alan Grant was starting to give Hercule Poirot a run for his money. Miss Marple, however, still reigned supreme.

I decided to take the situation in hand and move things along. "What I think Kenzie is saying, and please correct me if I'm wrong," I glanced at Kenzie, "is she's the one who posted under the name fedupwithfakenewsanchors. Is that about right?" As far as I was concerned, this was the most viable answer.

I looked into her eyes and watched them fill with tears once more. Case solved.

With an "I knew it" shrug, I said to the room in general, "And that's it in a nutshell. Kenzie made some rather unwise comments on Babs's Instagram account. I'm having a hard time thinking she's the killer, though."

This last comment was directed to Nora and Louisa. They both nodded their agreement, and I could see that they were feeling as sorry for Kenzie as I was.

"Wait a minute." Matt held up both hands, palms facing outward. "Wait just one minute." He stared from me to Kenzie and back. "Are you telling me *she's* the one who killed Babs? Over some stupid posts?"

He could have sung second soprano, judging by the range of notes his voice hit. Or shattered glass. It certainly did a number on my sensitive ears.

All bedlam broke lose as Nora and I defended Kenzie. Kenzie began sobbing again in earnest, and Louisa added to the noise with her offer of a lawyer "for the poor dear." It was some time before order was restored and Kenzie was sufficiently calm.

"Why did you feel the need to follow Babs's account to begin with?" Nora's voice was kind, and I could tell she felt sorry for the girl. "Did she know you were using that name?"

Kenzie looked shocked, placing one hand on her animal-printed shirt. "No way! She woulda killed me!" As soon as the word was out in the open, she clapped one hand over her mouth, eyes wide. "I didn't mean that. She wasn't a nice person, but she never would've killed me or anyone else."

"It would've spoiled her manicure." Nora waved her own decorated nails in the air.

"At this point, Kenzie, that's moot, especially since she's the one who was killed." Matt's tone was just this side of sarcastic, and I cringed inwardly as Kenzie flushed, her expression miserable.

Poor girl. I wished, with all my heart, that the man would tumble from that ivory pedestal where she'd placed him. The more I saw of him, the more I wasn't impressed.

"Back to the posts for a few more minutes, Kenzie. Then we'll leave you in peace." I waited a moment for her to recompose herself. "Did you think she'd eventually find out who was behind the comments?"

To my surprise, Kenzie gave a short laugh. "Her? She was lucky if she could use a smartphone properly. Talk about a dumb blonde. Babs was the poster child. And she wasn't even really a blonde, if you can believe that."

"You don't say." Nora stood and rested one hand on an out-thrust hip. "I'm shocked, I tell you. Completely shocked."

Louisa, of course, fell into a fit of not-so-regal giggles.

I wanted to laugh as well when Matt lifted one hand and smoothed back his dark blond hair, its tresses artfully streaked with a touch of ash. I wondered if he used the same hairdresser as Babs.

Before he had a chance to say anything, though, I spoke up hurriedly. "One more thing, Kenzie. Where were you on the morning Babs died?"

To my surprise, she laughed again, and this time it was lighter, almost coy. "That's easy." She shot a flirtatious glance at Matt, and he flushed a bright pink as he twisted the gold band on his left hand. "I was right here in this office. Mr. Robb and I were, ah, a little busy all that morning, you might say."

I turned to face Matt, both of my eyebrows raised. "And can you corroborate her story?"

His face became even redder, and that finger made a pass around the inside of his collar once more. It occurred to me this was probably his "tell," the movement that would really ruin a poker game or police interrogation for him.

"I think this conversation is over." Matt Robb sounded as though he was strangling on the words, and he appeared to be doing his best to not look in Kenzie's direction.

Kenzie appeared much more relaxed and poised. If I was a betting woman, I'd lay my money on Kenzie having the upper hand after we left, especially since the cad was apparently married. I hoped a hefty raise was in her near future.

Moira's sour smile was the last thing I saw as I walked out of the station's front door. I was thankful I didn't have to deal with her equally sour personality on a daily basis. I'd take crazy conversations with Brent any day over two words with her.

And as usual, I'd either managed to conjure up the boy or had a finely tuned warning system leftover from my classroom days.

"Hey, Miss F. and Mrs. G." Brent grinned widely at the three of us as he leaned against his car, Aggie cuddled in one arm. "And Miss L. too. How cool is this?" He threw out his unoccupied arm in a welcoming gesture. "You ladies wanna ride? I've got my chariot here, ready to roll."

I managed to put on my saddest expression as I gave Aggie's soft head a scratch. "I'm sorry, Brent, but I've already made plans to go with Mrs. Goldstein and Miss Louisa. But thanks for offering. It's very sweet." I began to turn away, heading for Louisa's car, when a thought hit me right upside the head. "Brent, how did you know we were here?"

He shrugged carelessly and leaned down to nuzzle Aggie. "Oh, that was easy, Miss F. I was with Rachel at her house, and I heard her dad talkin' about what you were up to, 'cause Rachel had to talk to him and he was getting pretty loud, and she told him what you were doing, and he said you three are the most—"

I waved a hand in his face, hoping to ward off the ever-growing run-on sentence. He froze mid-flow, giving me a chance to catch my breath. Listening to him talk sometimes made me feel as though I was on a treadmill with an increasing speed and no OFF button.

"Thanks for the update. Really. And thanks again for thinking of us."

Before he could launch into another sentence without punctuation, Nora spoke up. She paused beside Brent's car and peered inside with a look of disbelief. "When was the last time you cleaned this thing out, kid? It looks like you live in it."

A hurt expression crossed Brent's face. "It's just my stuff from the garage sale, Mrs. G."

"*From* the garage sale?" Now Louisa was caught in the Brent tractor beam. "Is it still for sale?"

"Nah." A secret smile appeared on his lips. "It's stuff I told my mom I was gonna dump, but I'll just keep it in my car and she'll never see it."

The silence that followed this pronouncement was a typical reaction to anything to do with Brent. Louisa was going to have to get used to this soon or risk having her brain turned inside out on a regular basis.

"And how does Rachel feel about riding in a vehicle that looks like this?" I couldn't help asking as I began to recover.

Louisa still looked stunned, but Nora had a grip on her arm and was leading her away from Hurricane Brent. She'd be all right in a moment.

Brent gave another shrug. "It's okay, Miss F. We just use her car."

A Brent Mayfair–inspired headache was beginning to form behind one of my eyes. With a self-preserving wave of farewell, I almost pushed the other two toward Louisa's sedan. If I was going to help catch Babs's killer, I'd need all my little gray brain cells to be in working order.

Hercule Poirot would definitely approve.

Chapter 18

Thankfully, the rest of my day was peaceful. Herc got his walk, and I got my time with Inspector Alan Grant. I was trying to decide if I wanted a chamomile or peppermint tea before bed when my cell phone pinged. A text.

I drew it out of my robe's pocket and peeked warily at the screen. With all of the hoopla going on lately, getting a message at this time of the day wasn't likely to be pleasant.

It was, though. In fact, it was extra-special, super-duper, fabulously pleasant.

Smiling, I read it once and then again for the sheer joy of it.

How about having dinner with me tomorrow evening? I'll get a babysitter for Max and Doc.

Absolutely! My finger pecked out the answer as fast as it could move, and I hit SEND before I could chicken out.

His response was quick as well, and it left me both breathless and ready to try out for the San Francisco Opera.

Then I'll see you at 7. My car is a dark blue Mercedes coupe, so don't call the cops when you see it in front of your house.

This quip left me smiling, and I sent back a smiley face in reply.

I looked at Herc, curled up in a ball of black-and-white fur, already snoring softly. He'd certainly know how to entertain himself without me around at seven tomorrow evening. When I would be out with Roger Smithson, retired dentist and one of the most charming men I had ever met.

I think I smiled even in my dreams that night.

* * * *

By the time I'd had my first cup of coffee the next morning, though, the day was already shaping up to be frenetic. Shortly after I'd gotten dressed and had fed Herc, Nora had presented herself on my doorstep with the newspaper tucked under one arm and a waxed-paper bakery bag dangling from her hand.

The expression on her face, however, was anything but sunny. In fact, she looked downright distraught. "Don't even bother with that 'good morning' nonsense, Sis."

She swept past me and into the house, kicking off her heels. That wasn't the best of signs since Nora was rarely without those ankle killers. Without them, she seemed almost, well, normal and not her usual invincible self.

I closed the door behind her. For once, she hadn't let herself in via that ridiculous lock pick. I followed her into the kitchen.

"Okay, I'll skip that part." I walked over to switch on the coffee maker. "Mind telling me what's up?"

She pointed to the newspaper on my kitchen table, the edges curled from the morning dampness. "Take a look at the front page, and then don't say I didn't warn you."

It took me all of a few seconds to see exactly what it was that had distracted my best friend. Plastered above the fold, front and center, a bold black headline proclaimed, POLICE MAKE ARREST IN MURDER OF LOCAL NEWS ANCHOR.

Next to the accompanying article sat a grainy photo of Shelby walking between Rachel's dad and another detective. Even with the poor quality, I could tell she was terrified.

"When did this happen?" I looked up from the paper, my head spinning from lack of coffee as well as the news. "I didn't hear anything last night."

The thought of last night made me pause, and I was tempted to share my good news. It would wait, though. First Shelby, then Roger.

"Apparently sometime early this morning. It was before the paper went to press, so I'm guessing about two, maybe three o'clock." She reached into the bakery bag and took out a bagel already split and smothered in cream cheese. She held it out. "Want half?"

I nodded and pushed a paper napkin across the table. I definitely needed sustenance to handle this latest blow. It would be difficult enough to think straight and formulate a rescue plan, and I wasn't the one who'd been arrested. If I've been routed out of bed at three in the morning and marched to the Portland Police Department between two detectives, I'd look terrified as well.

Poor Shelby.

"What can we do?" I dipped one finger in the cream cheese and popped it into my mouth, savoring the smooth taste. "Does she have a good lawyer?"

Nora stared at me, her bagel held halfway to her mouth. "You know, I've got no idea." She dropped the bagel and reached into her top for her cell phone. "I'm calling Louisa."

In less than five minutes, Nora had Louisa's promise that a lawyer would be on her way to the police station within the hour.

"And Louisa said this is one gal who'll tear a strip off of anyone who mistreats her clients. Said she's a real tiger in the courtroom as well." Nora took a bite of bagel and washed it down with a sip of coffee. "Whew, that's hot, Sis! Are you trying to melt my fillings?"

"It's freshly brewed coffee," I said mildly. "Were you expecting something cold?"

"Whatever." She wrinkled her nose at me and took another careful sip. "Well, we've handled one thing. Now what's our next step?"

"I wish I knew. I'm more concerned about why they'd arrest her just because she found the body." I took a sip of my own coffee, savoring the mild brew. "You'd think they'd be thanking her for reporting it."

"Well, there's that awful Instagram post." Nora nodded wisely, patting her chest where her cell phone was nestled. "They say there's no smoke without a fire, so maybe there was more going on between the two of them than that one post."

"Maybe. It's certainly possible, knowing how mean Babs could be. But . . ." I gave a half shrug. "I'm not sure. She has a good lawyer now, or will in the next little bit. There's not too much else we can do for her." I paused, thinking. "Of course, we can comb through the phone records Louisa brought over. There might be something in there we've overlooked."

"We've been over and over those things," Nora protested. "That's how we spotted the mayor, remember?"

"I know, I know." I leaned forward, speaking earnestly. "But maybe it's not so obvious. Maybe it's someone who's only called her once or twice."

"So how will that help? We can't just start calling folks and asking if they killed Babs Prescott."

I sat there for a moment, chewing my bottom lip as I thought.

"Hang on." I snapped my fingers. "I've got it. Let's see if we can match phone calls to broadcasts. You know, those 'in-depth stories' Babs did once a week? If we can figure out which phone calls were made after each story, we might find someone mad enough to kill."

"Like the one about the politician who was running a Social Security scam against senior citizens? Or the one that exposed an illegal dogfighting ring?"

I nodded eagerly. "Yes, exactly like that. There might have been something Babs talked about that really made a viewer mad enough to spit nails, as my granny would say."

"Well, it wouldn't hurt." Nora held out her coffee cup. "But first, a refill. I need more caffeine before I dive back into those phone records."

We settled down for a serious troll through Babs's phone records and the internet for the last few months of her "special in-depth reports." Herc was curled under the table, his warm body lying as close as he could to my slippered feet. Feeling him there reminded me of my upcoming date that evening. I wondered if Roger was really getting a sitter for the retrievers.

"Sis, you've been staring into space with a goofy smile for the last minute. What gives?"

I started, realizing I had indeed drifted into my own orbit. "Oh, nothing." My face heated, which gave me away, I couldn't resist smiling, and I knew my cheeks were pink.

"And I've got a tree house in my living room." Nora jabbed my arm with one finger. "C'mon, Sis. Spill it."

"Fine. If you must know, I've got a date tonight." There. I'd said it. Spilled the beans. Opened the barn door. There was no taking it back now.

"Oh. My. Word." Nora spoke each word as if it was its own sentence. "Are you serious?"

Her voice rose with each syllable, and Herc begin to stir restlessly. My face was getting warmer, and a damp patch spread under each arm. Fantastic. If I was this nervous just talking about it, how in the world would I act when the real thing was happening?

"Well, yes, I am serious. But that's not until this evening." I motioned to the pile of phone records strewn over the table. "Right now, we're trying to help Shelby."

"You're unbelievable, you know that?" Nora shook her head. "What are you wearing? And don't tell me it doesn't matter. Of course it does! We're talking serious dating material here, girlie!"

I shrugged, but my cheeks were getting hotter.

"We can do this another time." Nora tossed down her phone and turned to look at me with an appraising eye. "We need to get going if we're going to make it to the stores and the nail salon before your date."

I stared at her, my eyes widening in panic. Stores? Nail salon? "Absolutely nothing doing. He asked me out when I looked like this, and I'm not changing now."

"I'd be willing to bet he didn't see you yet this morning, sitting there in that old shirt and those disgraceful jeans." She wrinkled her nose as if she'd smelled something on the bottom of her shoe. "I'm telling you, Sis. No man wants a woman who looks like a model for Goodwill."

She looked so bothered at the thought that I had to laugh. "Nora, believe me when I say that Roger isn't that way. He's never once mentioned anything about my sandals or my hair or the way I dress."

Nora snorted contemptuously. "And what man would?" She paused a moment. "Well, okay, so my second husband had some sort of weird skirt fetish. And number five didn't like to see me in anything but pink." Her nose wrinkled again in disgust. "If I never see anything that color in my house again, it'll be too soon."

"I've seen you wear pink before. And you've got pink nail polish on right this minute."

Nora laughed delightedly, looking at her hands. "This, Sis, is what he would've called 'Jezebel pink.'" She shook her head as if she still couldn't believe she'd actually married a man who tried to dictate her wardrobe. "Anything but a sappy little girl color he hated. Makes me wonder if he had some sort of hang-up."

I shuddered at her words. I'd only met one of her husbands, in spite of our closeness, and it sounded like a good thing. Besides, she never seemed to stay married long enough or to choose someone who wanted to meet any of her friends.

Nora continued to stare at me appraisingly. "Well, if you're not going to let me take you shopping, at least let me take you to my hairdresser. You need to have someone show you how to fix up that bird's nest you've got there."

"Nothing doing." I thought about the disastrous perm she'd had last year. "You shouldn't talk, anyway. Your own hair is barely recovering."

She shrugged with a chagrined smile. "True. So, we choose another salon. This is Portland, not the back forty of some Podunk town."

"No thanks. And I mean it. Thanks, but no thanks." I reached up to touch my hair, mentally seeing the graying strands I'd pinned up that morning. "If Roger doesn't like me the way I am, then, well, he just doesn't." It was my turn to lift a shoulder. "I've managed fine without a man so far."

"You're a marvel among women. I could tell you some stories that would curl your hair. Wouldn't you like to have some of your own?"

"What, curly hair?" I teased. "Don't be silly, Nora." I picked up another handful of papers and waved them at her. "Let's focus on getting Shelby out of trouble before we make some for me, okay?"

"Fine." She began to click through the internet once more. "But don't say I didn't warn you."

We spent the next couple of hours searching for something that might indicate a connection between Babs's telecasts and upset callers. The longer we looked, though, the less optimistic I was about finding any such link.

Around noon, I pushed away from the table, groaning aloud as I gave my lower back a twist to relieve some of the stiffness from prolonged sitting. Glancing across at Nora, I saw she was paging through something that looked suspiciously like an online gossip magazine.

"See anything interesting?"

She looked at me, a guilty expression on her face. "Just the usual. You know, who's dating who—"

"Whom," I correctly her automatically.

"Fine. Whom's dating whom—" She looked at me with an impish smile. "Was that more like it, Miss Grammar?"

I ignored her. Instead, I started gathering up the scattered pages of Babs's phone records, stacking them into a neat pile.

"Are we quitting?" Nora set down her phone and lifted both arms above her head in a catlike stretch. "I sure could use some coffee."

"And I could use a nap." I stood and gave my back a final twist. "You're welcome to snooze on the sofa."

She looked at me as if I'd just asked her to recite Hamlet's soliloquy. "A nap? Why would I need a nap?"

"Because you're tired? That's usually why I take one."

She grunted. "And that's because you're turning into an old lady." She stood and stretched and gave a wide yawn. "Okay, maybe a rest sounds good right now."

"Yep," I grinned. "That's because you're turning into an old lady."

I was still chuckling when I closed the door behind her.

I awoke refreshed, Herc stretched out beside my bed, softly snoring. He was such a good dog and got along with other dogs without any problems. That was a good thing, especially since the man I was interested in had two of them.

I ate a late lunch, careful not to get too full. If Roger was taking me to dinner, I wanted to be able to enjoy the food as well as the company. If I had a pet peeve, it was a woman who picked at her food in front of a man and then gobbled everything in sight once she was alone. Never let it be said that Gwen Franklin was that type of woman.

Of course, I didn't want to appear gluttonous either. How did Nora manage to get around this conundrum? Staring at myself in the bathroom mirror as I brushed my teeth, I hoped I'd be able to enjoy the evening. Dating seemed like a chore, in my opinion. Maybe if I thought of it as an evening with a good friend, I'd be able to relax. With that cheery thought, I set about getting ready for my evening with Roger.

* * * *

Roger was right on time, his car drawing up to the curb at precisely seven. I hesitated a moment with on hand on the doorknob. Should I wait for him to ring the doorbell? Walk out to the car on my own? Let him come in and see Herc for a few minutes before we left?

I was still pondering these questions when a light tap sounded by my ear, causing me to jump and hit my elbow against the metal doorknob. Rubbing the offended joint, I opened the door.

"Good evening." Roger smiled at me, sending my heart soaring up into my throat. "Do you mind if I come in for a sec?"

"Not at all." I stepped back from the doorway, catching a whiff of something that reminded me of patchouli as he walked past. "Would you like something to drink?"

"That would be nice." He shrugged out of his sports coat and hung it on the back of the armchair. "Anything warm would be fine."

Thank goodness for that. I didn't keep alcohol in the house, except an old bottle of cooking sherry that probably needed to be tossed. Coffee and tea, though, I had aplenty. Pushing the button on my Keurig to heat the water, I looked over my shoulder at my date. No, not my date. My friend. I needed to eliminate that "d word" if this evening was going to be successful.

"Would you prefer a flavored coffee or one that isn't?"

He looked up from patting Herc and smiled. "Unflavored is fine. I'm not too picky."

I hid a smile as I busied myself preparing two cups of my favorite Ethiopian blend. If only Nora could hear that. There was one man on this planet that wasn't picky. Of course, my inner voice chimed in, he's taking *you* out to dinner. Did that mean he wasn't picky about his choice of dinner companions as well? I decided to overlook that thought.

By the time we'd had our coffee and chatted about the dogs, the weather, and the latest Portland news, I was feeling as relaxed as I'd ever be. In fact, I was probably more at ease with Roger than I ever was during a classroom visit by my principal.

* * * *

A chilly breeze blew in from the Willamette as Roger and I left the car and walked toward the small Italian restaurant's entrance. I was glad I'd added another layer to my ensemble. Who said denim shirts were out of style?

Mama Mia's Trattoria, housed in a historic downtown building, was abuzz with dinner conversation. I'd eaten here once or twice before, and my stomach was beginning to rumble out a greeting to the various aromas that met my nose.

Roger, one hand holding my newly bruised elbow, guided me behind the hostess as she led us to a table near the back of the restaurant.

"Would this be all right?" Our hostess appeared as young as Rachel and Addie, and I caught myself examining her face closely for signs of recognition.

I'd love to have one evening out without running into a former student, especially since I was out with a date. A friend.

A man.

So far so good, though, and I slipped into the chair Roger held for me with a feeling of satisfaction. No goofy Brent, no hormone-addled Nora, no problems.

No such luck.

Chapter 19

I'd taken one bite of my caprese salad when the skin on the back of my neck began to prickle. It didn't take me long to understand why.

"Fancy meeting your two here," said the cause of my discomfort. "Marcus, grab that waitress and get another chair."

"I'd be careful with my wording if I were you." I spoke automatically when I saw the broad grin on Marcus's face as he trotted off. My mind, though, was whirling as it tried to comprehend the stuff of nightmares. My best friend and her man had just crashed my very first date with Roger. I sincerely hoped there was a good reason behind the intrusion, not just uncontrollable curiosity. Of course, it might have been a coincidence. And pigs might fly.

Roger seemed to be taking it all in stride, however. He clearly enjoyed Marcus's company, and Nora, if I was being honest, knew how to keep a conversation going. I, on the other hand, had slipped back into my role of observer rather than participant.

I should have offered to bake a frozen pizza at home.

Over a dessert of cannoli and cappuccinos, Roger asked me about my family. Nora had already told several hilarious stories about our earlier years as friends, which had us all laughing, and now Roger put the spotlight squarely on me.

I gave a self-conscious laugh. "There isn't much to tell, really."

Nora began to protest. "You had a much more interesting family than I did, Sis. I am an only child. You have four brothers."

"And are you the oldest?" Roger asked.

"Yes," I said, "I am the oldest."

"And I think her parents had her first so they'd have a built-in babysitter and housekeeper," added Nora. "Made me glad I am an only child."

"So, you were the oldest of five," Roger, smiled. "I have it the other way. I am the youngest of four."

Marcus, who'd been concentrating on his cannoli, looked up. "So am I. *And* I am the only son." He shook his head. "It was pure hell, growing up with three older sisters. I swear they lived to torment me."

Roger laughed as he raised one hand to flag down our waitress. "More coffee? Cannoli?" When the next round had been taken care of, he said, "You and me both, pal. My oldest sister, Rena, loved to dress me up as a little girl and braid my hair."

The idea of Roger in a frilly dress and bows was amusing. He turned to me. "So, what did you do to your brothers? Put makeup on them? Teach them ballet?"

The idea of my bratty brothers sitting still long enough to have makeup applied was amusing.

"No, nothing like that. They were constantly getting into things and places they shouldn't be, and somehow, it was always my fault."

"That's probably why she's never been married or had kids," chimed in Nora, a wicked twinkle in her eyes. "I, on the other hand, had no idea just how rotten men could be."

"Oh, come on," protested Marcus. "I think I'm a pretty good specimen."

Before this side conversation could descend into a Nora-esque embarrassment, I said, "How about your parents, Roger. Did they spoil you?"

His cheeks reddened. "Maybe just a bit." He shrugged, taking a sip of coffee. "Being the youngest and the only boy made some things easier."

"Not my parents." Nora was clearly finished antagonizing Marcus for the moment. "They made me 'stand on my own two feet,' as my mom liked to say."

We fell silent for a moment as we drank the cappuccinos. I liked the flavor of the creamy coffee, not sweet and not bitter. Would it be too difficult to make this at home?

"I wonder," began Roger, "if boys are more 'spoiled,' to use your word, Gwen. Do girls ever get treated that way?"

Marcus gave a short laugh. "In my clan, the girls are treated like royalty. The guys are expected to work their butts off and take care of them."

"Sounds promising," murmured Nora into her cappuccino.

"I know I wasn't," I said. "But it doesn't bother me."

"It did back then." Nora looked across at me, froth from the coffee decorating her upper lip.

I decided to ignore her comment until I heard what else she had to say.

"Remember that time when those brats made a blanket fort in the living room and knocked over your grandpa?"

I laughed, thinking about it, and motioned for her to wipe her mouth.

"Knocked over your grandpa? Was he hurt?" Roger's voice was concerned, making me laugh harder.

"No, he wasn't hurt," I managed to say. "It was his urn." I stopped to wipe my eyes, thinking about that day and the expressions on my brothers' faces as they stood, mouths agape, staring in horror at the pile of ashes strewn over our mom's best quilt.

"I was spending the afternoon with her just to give her some female company. You should have seen them trying to scrape Grandpa off the floor before their parents got back from the airport with Granny." Nora chuckled and I smiled, remembering the look on my granny's face when she saw her late hubby being vacuumed up and replaced in his urn.

How I'd escaped getting the blame for that little escapade still amazed me.

"I just read an article about a mom who tracked down the kids who were bullying her son." Marcus pressed one finger into the crumbs left on his dessert plate. "She actually went to their school and threatened them. And recorded it on her phone as well, which might not have been the smartest move."

"Some parents are like that," I thought about some of the characters I'd met over the years. "One student in particular was a holy terror, and how he got into my class, I wasn't sure." I shook my head as I told them about the time he'd filled the keyhole on my desk with superglue. "And he denied it, even when the principal found the superglue tube in his backpack."

"What'd his parents do? If he'd been mine, I woulda hit 'im where the good Lord split 'im," Marcus said.

"Not his mom," I said. "She was mad, all right, but at me for taking him to the principal and at the principal for searching his backpack."

"Some parents just can't see the truth in front of their noses." Roger drained the last of his coffee, setting the small cup on the saucer with a tiny clink. "I might have been treated a little special, but I would have never gotten away with something like that, I can tell you that right now."

"We always hear about how solid a mother's love is." I lifted my cappuccino to my lips but didn't drink. "It makes it sound as though it's the strongest force in the world."

"Unfortunately, it can be blind as well. That student you had is a prime example."

I nodded at Marcus's comment. A memory began to stir in the back of my mind, a quote from a novel or play or poem about a mother's love being a terrible thing. Or maybe it was a beautiful thing. Either way, it could be a consuming thing.

I didn't have long to dwell on this rather depressing thought. Roger suggested a walk around the courthouse square, a recently renovated area in downtown Portland.

"It's getting cold." Nora pulled the edges of a short leather jacket around her more firmly. "Maybe I should break out the furs."

"Or wear thicker clothes," I suggested, giving her a jab with my non-bruised elbow. "I know just the place to find them, too."

"Not on your life, Sis. You won't catch me shopping there." Nora affected an expression of repulsion as she gave my denim shirt a tug. "Don't tell me. You found this there."

"Indeed I did." I gave a half twirl, holding out the edges of my new-to-me shirt in a mock catwalk pose. "You know what they say, everything old is new again."

"And where is this place?" Roger looked from Nora to me, a quizzical expression on his face. "I might want to check it out. I happen to like vintage."

"Vintage?" crowed Nora. "It's more like closet rejects."

"I happen to like shopping there. You never know what you'll find." I glanced at Roger, a teasing tone in my voice. "It's called Goodwill, and I'm a well-known customer there."

"Then I have an idea." Roger draped an arm over my shoulders, drawing me closer.

Marcus, after one look, slung his own arm about Nora's waist. Whatever he whispered in her ear made her giggle, and I watched them as they walked ahead of us, a two-headed shape in the dark.

"So, what's the idea?" I asked, more from something to say rather than curiosity. This whole dating game was brand-new territory to me.

"Why don't we make a morning of it and hit the local Goodwill? We might even find a fur coat for you." His arm squeezed me just a little tighter, and I looked up into his eyes.

Was he teasing me? My shoulders stiffened.

"And, no, I'm not teasing, Gwen." Fabulous. Now he was a mind reader as well.

The heat was beginning to work its way across my face.

"I honestly would love to spend more time with you, and doing something you enjoy would be a great place to begin."

"That I enjoy?" I know I sounded astonished, but, in all honesty, I was. When had anyone ever said that to me?

"Absolutely." Another squeeze. "Now we'd better catch up with those two or they might disappear on us."

* * * *

I wasn't sure when the thought began to percolate. I'd already been asleep for what seemed like hours, but a peek at my bedside clock told me it had only been a few minutes. I lay back on my pillow, staring at the ceiling. The trees were moving in the wind, a nightly gift from the river, and their branches made weird patterns across the room.

Another pattern was forming in my mind, though, and the more I thought about it, the more excited I became. I reached for my cell phone, eager to share my ideas with Nora, then hesitated. Judging by the way she and Marcus had said good night to Roger and me, their own evening was only beginning. I didn't want to interrupt them or hear about what I'd interrupted. I turned over my pillow and gave it one punch for good measure, resettling the filling into a more comfortable shape. My idea could wait until morning.

In spite of Shelby's arrest, I managed a solid eight hours snuggled under the comforter, my ever-vigilant—not—dog sleeping on the floor. My only hope was a burglar who would trip over him in the dark.

* * * *

Showered, dressed, and caffeinated, I headed out for Nora's. Herc had a full water bowl inside as well as out and his choice of napping spots, so I didn't worry about him. What I was worrying about, though, was Roger. Was he still feeling as upbeat about me this morning as he appeared to be last night?

It did no good to worry about it. What will be will be, as Doris Day had sung all those years ago, and I believed her. What was the exact phrase? *Que sera sera*?

The words were still spinning round and round in my mind as I punched the elevator's UP button in Nora's building. If I didn't switch songs soon, it would wear out a path in my brain. Maybe a few verses of Handel's "Messiah" would do the trick.

Nora answered the door quickly, almost as if she'd been looking for me. The round red spots of anger on her cheeks, though, indicated it was someone else she'd been expecting.

"Quit that caterwauling and get in here." She stepped back from the open door and waited for me to get inside before slamming and double-locking it. "There. That should keep the creep out."

I slipped out of my Birkenstocks and padded over to my favorite spot on one of the overstuffed sofas.

"Marcus?"

"Who else?" she growled. Throwing herself onto the other end of the sofa, she crossed her arms and glared at the floor. "I should have known it was just the Italian music and not me."

I stared at her, trying to understand her cryptic remark. "Music? What do you mean?"

She transferred her glare from the carpet to me. "All those schmalzty songs last night at Mama Mia's. Dean Martin, Frank Sinatra. I thought it was my magnetic self that turned him on, not those two-bit crooners."

"They're not two-bit crooners. Wasn't Dean Martin called 'The King of Cool'? And Frankie—well, there aren't enough adjectives in the world to describe his—"

"Oh, yeah, yeah. Stick up for two guys you never even met." She sounded childish, but I knew there was no stopping her once she'd decided to take this route. "The guy *I* know is the one I'm talking about."

I couldn't resist teasing her. "Oh, so I should stick up for him instead?" I smiled at her to show I was kidding.

She gave me one last glare and then leaned her head back against the cushions, eyes shut. "Men can be real jerks, you know that? I put the blame squarely on their moms."

"That's not fair." I stopped. I'd come over here to share my thoughts from last night, and this was the perfect segue. "Speaking of moms, I've got an idea."

"What? You wanna find his mom and tell her what an idiot of a son she raised?"

"No," I sighed a bit. Bringing her down from her high horse might take a while. Of course, I could always just knock her off and be done with it. Turning so I faced her squarely, I told her my idea.

For once, the maneuver worked beautifully.

"You've got to be kidding me, Sis."

"No, it's no joke." I started to stand and then paused. "You want some coffee before I tell you the entire idea?"

She waved off the suggestion. "I want to hear this first and then we can fill up on coffee. Sounds like we might need it."

"All right, I was thinking about the evening and the things we were discussing. Something had clicked in my head at the restaurant, and the more I thought about it, the more convinced I was I'd hit on a possible answer." I stopped and gathered my thoughts, careful not to leave out one bit. "It was when Roger said something about being spoiled as the only boy. I started wondering if parents, especially moms, tend to favor their sons over their daughters."

Nora snorted in amusement. "I think Freud had a term for that, Sis."

I shook my head. "Not *that* kind of favor, you goofball. I mean a real, honest to goodness, I'll die for you type of love."

Nora stared at me for a moment, and I could see the wheels beginning to turn. "Are you talking about moms that defend their kids against anyone and everything? Like the one Marcus talked about?"

"Yes. Exactly that. So, here's what I'm thinking. What if Tim really did kill Babs? Would his mom throw up a smokescreen for him, maybe even hide the evidence?"

Nora slapped both hands on her legs. "Absolutely, Sis! Remember how that woman went on and on at the shelter dinner? She talked more about Tim and how wonderful he was than she did about her time volunteering." She shuddered. "Kinda made me think twice."

We sat in silence for a few minutes. I'd come up with the motive, but how would we be able to prove it?

In one of those eerie, sister-like moments, Nora reached over and grabbed my hand. "You know what I think? I think we need to pay Mrs. Lafoe a call, don't you?"

I couldn't have said it better.

* * * *

The Uber driver obligingly took us through a Dutch Bros drive-thru for coffee. I chose a cold brew, and Nora ordered her White Zombie. When she offered to order one for our driver, a wizened old man who I suspected was sitting on a pillow in order to see over the wheel, he just smiled and patted his jacket pocket.

"I've got my own brew right here, girlie." He craned his neck around and gave us a sly wink. "A man's gotta have his secrets from his wife."

I crossed my fingers and toes that the "brew" was coffee and not some other drink.

We arrived safely, however. The house was imposing, set back from the road in a curtain of large trees. A curved driveway made of bricks snaked its way from the road to the side of the house, and the garage door stood open. Hopefully, that meant someone was home.

"We're not getting any younger." Nora started up the drive, a female Moses strolling confidently through the Red Sea.

I hesitated and then followed her, not wanting to be seen lurking like some crazed stalker.

"I don't see the front door," I murmured at her shoulder. "Do you think it's through there?" I pointed to an iron gate that stood ajar, fronds of lush ferns poking through the decorative bars. "Maybe that's an atrium or whatever it's called."

Nora shrugged. "Maybe. Wait here, and I'll peek."

I stood at the gate and waited nervously, peering over my shoulder for someone who'd kick me out for trespassing. There was nothing but a heavy silence, though, and when Nora poked her head around the wall, the movement made me jump.

"Something got you spooked?" She grinned. "Follow me, Sis. The door's standing wide open."

"Don't you think we should wait for someone to answer first?"

Nora, I knew, would see the open door as an invitation to walk on in, and I was right. With a sigh, I followed my intrepid leader into the quiet house. If we got caught, I could always say I was her caretaker.

The doorway we'd come through didn't appear to be the main entrance. Just off the entryway, a pair of hallways stretched out on either side, their wooden floors a shiny testament to someone's meticulous housekeeping. If this house was any hint, however, I'd guess it wasn't Mrs. Lafoe's efforts.

Nora paused for a moment, one finger tapping her bottom lip. "What's your poison, Sis? Left or right?"

"How about neither." I looked around for someone who'd either kick us out or call the police. "I don't think we should be in here without an invitation, Nora."

She laughed. "Wasn't the door open? I call that an invite." She gestured over her shoulder. "I'm going to go left. You can take the other side."

"No way," I said firmly. "Where you go, I go." *And we can be tried together for breaking and entering.*

"Cool," she grinned. "All for one and one for all, just like the movie."

"It was a book first." I couldn't resist correcting her.

She saucily wiggled her hips in response.

The corridor Nora had chosen to follow was wide and surprisingly light. Windows high up on the walls provided more than enough illumination, and whoever had decorated the house had chosen the "less is more" look. It was certainly different from my crowded little house, but to each his own. Besides, my decorating scheme had most likely cost a hundredth of the one for this place.

"Oh, nice." Nora stood at an arched doorway, looking around with approval. "I could see me in something like this. *Alone.*"

She disappeared into the room, and I followed her, not wanting to be caught without her. It looked like a living room of sorts, but it was so far back in the house, it couldn't have been the main one. I glanced appraisingly around the room, thinking. Maybe it was what they called a "sitting room," a space for more intimate visits or when the house's occupants wanted to be alone.

"I think this is as good as any place to start looking." Nora stood in the center of the room, casting a critical gaze on the various pieces of furniture and décor. "You take that side, Sis. I'll work my way around toward you."

"What are we looking for?" I stood with my hands on my hips, watching as she lifted cushions and opened drawers. "I'm not sure what kind of evidence there might be, if any."

She stopped in mid-trawl, staring at me. "Of course there'll be evidence. A woman was killed, right?"

"But not, I don't know, the traditional way. Didn't she have some sort of reaction to something? Or maybe it was poison." Although it had only happened recently, the murder seemed as though it had occurred long ago. Trying to recall the details took some effort.

Nora gave a laugh, and I looked around fearfully, hoping no one had heard her. "Traditional as in those books you like to read? That kind of traditional?"

"Maybe."

I wasn't going to get into a discussion of literature with her here, of all places. The mention of "those books" made me think about Miss Marple and the times she'd been caught snooping around someone's house. Hopefully, I wouldn't get caught, but if I did, I sincerely hoped the person doing the catching wouldn't be holding a gun. It was one thing to read about it and another entirely to experience it, and I knew which one I preferred.

"Well, come on then. Stop daydreaming and help look." With a sniff in my direction, Nora turned back to the carved desk that sat under one window.

I began to work my way around the room as Nora had suggested, pausing to examine the contents of a small cedar box on a shelf. It reminded me of the cedar chest—though it was much larger, of course—that my granny had kept at the foot of her bed. It was filled with piles of carefully folded linens and wrapped silver spoons, and she'd laughed when I'd asked her about it, calling it her "hopeless chest."

"My parents, your great-grands, gave this to me on my sixteenth birthday. I guess it was to help me get things organized for the big day, but I never added anything to it." She'd bent over and lifted out an embroidered table runner, turning it over so I could see the neat stitching on the underside. "My mother did all these for me, and I think my sisters added to it as well. I was more interested in caring for the horses we kept than accumulating senseless items."

I was letting these memories run through my mind as I automatically sifted through the jumble of things the box held. Nothing in there that might point to a killer, and I was just moving on to the next thing when something caught my eye.

You know those crazy moments when you couldn't believe what you were seeing? When things felt more fiction than fact? I was having one of those moments right then, and I could hardly bring myself to speak in case I'd made a mistake. Carefully picking up the item I'd found, I carried it over for Nora to examine.

The look on her face told me I'd hit the jackpot, won the lottery, found the gold at the end of the rainbow. I'd found the murder weapon.

Chapter 20

"Well, well, well." An amused voice came from behind me, and I swung around, Babs's missing EpiPen still in my hand, its patient name and dosage label still intact. "Looking for something, are we?"

"Yep." Nora sounded much braver than I was feeling, her tone as hard as the lump that had formed in my stomach. "And it looks like we found it."

Leticia Lafoe, green eyes narrowed and the edges of her mouth curled in the most feline of smiles, walked into the room and shut the door behind her with a firm click. The knot in my stomach lurched upward, sending my heartrate rocketing. Not good for the ol' ticker, especially when combined with high blood pressure.

Glancing sideways at Nora, I was relieved to see she still appeared in control of herself. The last thing I needed was for my best friend to faint or, even worse, drop dead of shock. Of course, she'd dealt with more of that type of situation than most folks would even dream about, thanks to the extensive litany of exes. Shocking Nora would take something more than mere murder.

Leticia looked almost disappointed at our combined responses. I suppose she'd been counting on a big reaction, one that might give her time to either escape with the evidence or—and here I gulped—time to do away with the witnesses.

As in me. And Nora. A quick sideways glance at Nora's tightly folded lips told me she'd already considered that thought. Maybe she'd already come up with a plan as well. I, the teacher who'd always bragged about her organization skills, had absolutely zilch.

I waved the EpiPen at her, one eyebrow lifted in question. "Care to explain?"

"That woman." Leticia snorted derisively, tossing her head like a wild colt. "She thought she was so clever, blackmailing my son as if he was some common criminal." Another snort. "*She* was the criminal. And before you ask, yes, I made sure she'd never live to spread such a malicious story about Tim."

Nora and I exchanged looks, and I gave her a small nod to go ahead. If we kept the woman talking, we might be able to get out of here alive.

"So, what could've been so bad? Surely you're not talking about the 'pay to pass' scheme, right? Didn't the school clear Tim of that nonsense?" Nora managed to inject incredulity into her voice, as if even thinking Leticia's precious son would ever be involved in something that sordid would be crazy. I wanted to applaud her Oscar-worthy acting.

"No, not that old issue." Leticia batted Nora's suggestion away as if it had been a troublesome fly. "She claimed Tim had acted, well, inappropriately with some of his students, if you can believe that." She drew herself up, indignation clear in every inch of her body. "I told her we'd raised him better than that, but she only laughed and told me she had proof."

Rachel. Had she told someone as flamboyant as Babs? Surely not. It had to be someone else. Knowing Tim and his self-assured manner, he'd probably done this to several young women and assumed he could get away with it. The very thought made my blood boil. I abhorred the idea of a person in a trusted position, such as an educator, stooping to such low behavior, and I said so to his mother.

"As if those girls could ever actually have a relationship with my son." Leticia's tone was spiteful, and only a warning glance from Nora stopped me from slapping the unpleasant expression from Leticia's face. "They were lucky he even knew their names, much less paid any attention to them."

What a twisted mind she had. Somehow she'd taken her son's unwanted advances on his students and reshaped them into something she could handle. No wonder she wanted to stop Babs from spilling the rather unsavory beans to the press.

"So, how'd he do it?" I tried to keep my tone casual, afraid the fear I was feeling would show through.

I didn't need to worry, though. Leticia was so full of herself she was ready to brag to an audience.

"*Tim*? You think my son did this?" She gave a laugh that sounded straight from a haunted house.

I exchanged worried glances with Nora. Had we gotten it all wrong? Mrs. Lafoe, though, kept talking as if I'd answered her question.

"Well, you know I had an interview with her just before the press conference." She preened, actually reaching up to pat her hair like an old-time pin-up girl. "I asked to borrow her lipstick, told her I wanted to look good for the camera. She laughed but gave it to me. I went to the bathroom, pretending to be embarrassed, and added a dash of peanut oil to the lipstick." She shrugged, a pleased expression in her eyes. "Easy peasy. I gave it back to her, managing to knock over her bag at the same time. When she was picking it all up, I snagged the EpiPen." She moved her shoulders in another shrug, her tone as satisfied as her expression. "Done deal. All I had to do was wait for her to use the lipstick, preferably without me around."

The door opened again, and Leticia turned to see who had entered, a fond look crossing her triangular face. "Tim, darling, you're just in time."

I groaned inwardly as my former peer entered the room.

He looked directly at me. "You have no idea what a pleasure it is to see you here, Miss Franklin. Or can I call you Gwen? I know how you hate anything, shall we say, so formal."

He dropped his gaze to my rather worn jeans and scuffed Birkenstocks, one eyebrow raised in mock surprise. A smirk very like his mother's curved his mouth, and I watched as they exchanged amused glances.

"Absolutely not! She's Miss Franklin to you both, and I'd suggest you remember that."

The three of us swiveled our heads in Nora's direction, and I was both touched by her display of loyalty and afraid she might have gone too far. After all, we were alone with two raving lunatics—there could be no other explanation—and neither of us was suited for combat of any type. Even if we were, I doubted very much the EpiPen I was still holding could do much in the way of defense.

And then I thought about Nora's shoes and my earlier comments about how dangerous they could be on the wrong feet. Or, and this was a stroke of true Miss Marple-like genius, in the right hands.

In one of those rare mind-melding moments, Nora and I locked gazes. I let my eyelashes flicker downward toward her heels in the merest of movements, and she responded. In one swift action, she reached down and grabbed her stilettos from her feet, tossing one to me. I snagged it in midair, holding the heel outward as I closed in on an open-mouthed Tim.

* * * *

When it was all over and the Portland Police Department and paramedics had departed with two very unhappy and battered Lafoes, we laughed shakily and agreed we must have looked and sounded like a pair of banshees, each with a designer high heel raised above her head, charging straight at the frozen mother and son.

Suffice it to say a sharp heel could do a lot of damage. The look on the officer's face when he'd bagged the shoes as evidence was definitely one for the books.

"You know, you two are getting quite the reputation for being in the wrong place at the right time." Shelby, one hand curled around a steaming mug of chocolate, grinned across my kitchen table at the two of us.

We'd come back to my place in order for me to change my top: it had a few unsavory Tim stains on it, and I wanted to get it soaking in cold water before they set.

Nora flashed a smile at Shelby, but I only nodded somewhat soberly, sipping my own hot drink.

"Oh, don't let it get to you, Miss Franklin. I mean really! How many old—oops, I mean *mature*—ladies can say they've helped the police catch a killer?"

"Mrs. Goldstein and I have no intention of making this a habit, I can promise you that." I spoke with a conviction I didn't feel. There was something in Shelby's comment that had made me feel, what? More alive? Needed? It was too bad someone had to die, of course, but still . . .

"Earth to Gwen!" Nora snapped her fingers in my direction, and I gave a small start, managing to slop a bit of hot chocolate over the rim of the mug onto my newly donned clean shirt. "Rachel just texted and said we need to get down to the station this afternoon to make our official statement. I guess her dad told her to tell us. Wonder why he couldn't do that himself?" She glanced at her cell phone and frowned. "And Junior wants to know if we want him to drive us there."

"Junior?" Shelby looked from Nora to me with a quizzical expression.

"Brent Mayfair." I shook my head emphatically. "And tell the boy absolutely not. I want to arrive there in one piece, thank you very much."

"That bad, huh?" Shelby's smile was amused. "I'd be happy to take you two. I mean, you *did* help get the heat off me. Actually," she added with small laugh, "I'd have to say you saved my reputation. Thanks for everything, Miss Franklin. And you, too, Mrs. Goldstein." She leaned over and put an arm around my shoulders, giving me a quick squeeze.

Beneath the table, Herc brushed against me. How I'd managed to live without his companionship before, I had no idea. Of course, it was thanks to Herc that I'd met Roger. My cheeks heated as the image of his tall figure flashed into my mind.

Beside me, Nora tilted her head as she stared at me, both eyebrows lifted almost to her hairline. "What? Have someone else in mind for a lift to the PD?"

She dropped one eyelid in a suggestive wink, the false eyelashes sweeping against her rouged cheek. I rolled my eyes. There was no way I was going to let her tease me about Roger, at least not yet. That would come with time, but it was still too early.

Besides, once he found out about this little episode with the Lafoes, he might not be interested. Being involved in one murder might be seen as incidental. Being tangled in a second might be construed as a bad habit, to paraphrase the great playwright Oscar Wilde.

"No, not unless you do."

I stared pointedly at her and saw she was blushing too. I sighed to myself. Marcus, of course. That man was a bad penny in a plaid coat. What Nora needed was a dog, not another man. I gave Herc another fond rub behind his ears and stood.

"I don't know about you two, but I need a nap before facing anyone else today, police officer or not."

I washed my mug in the sink and headed over to the sofa, ready to sink down and close my eyes for a while. Shelby and Nora could see themselves out. Or not. I had plenty of room for them each to take a nap as well.

I'd just gotten completely comfortable, all the wiggles out and my muscles beginning to soften into a drowsy state, when the doorbell rang. I wanted to tell whoever it was to go away and come again in, say, ten years, after I was rested and ready to face people once more.

Before I could sit up and rearrange what was certainly a sleep-flattened hairdo, Nora went to the door and opened it with a cheerful greeting. "Come on in, Roger. Gwen's right in here."

Roger was here? *Now*? I tried to sit up, but my feet were entangled in the throw blanket I usually kept draped over the back of the sofa. I gave it a kick, getting one foot from underneath the soft morass and on the floor as Roger came around the corner of the entryway, Max and Doc close behind.

"Gwen, are you all right?" His voice and expression were both concerned, and an unexpected lump rose in my throat.

I decided to stay as I was before I fell off the sofa in an embarrassing heap. Unable to speak, I held out one hand.

"I came over as soon as Marcus called me." His hand closed gently around mine as he knelt in front of the sofa. "Were you hurt?" He ran his gaze over me in an assessing manner, and my heart leapt from its usual resting place to somewhere in my throat. Considering that crazy lump of emotion that was already there, it was getting rather crowded in that part of my anatomy.

"I'm fine." I wriggled my second foot free of the blanket and swung it down to rest beside the other. "It was only the–the . . ."

I gulped around the lump, trying to stop the tears beginning to gather in my eyes. It was only beginning to occur to me how close I'd come to a very definite end at the hands of a crazed woman.

Roger, bless his considerate heart, simply sat beside me and gently laid his arm across my shoulders. I swiped at my eyes self-consciously

"Want some coffee?" Nora walked in with a tray containing two mugs and my battered steel coffee carafe.

"That's kind of you." Roger smiled his thanks at her and then turned to look at me, one eyebrow lifted in question. "Gwen?"

I nodded, still unable to speak clearly. Maybe a hot drink would ease the pain of trying not to cry.

To my great irritation, my best friend settled herself into the armchair, curling her bare feet underneath her. Shelby was right behind her, Herc at her heels. So, this was going to be a group visit then. I could handle that. There would be plenty of time for me to have Roger all to myself in the future.

That last thought sent a wave of heat up my neck and into my cheeks.

Nora, a knowing look in her eyes, gave me a wink before turning to face Roger. "So, Marcus called you, did he?" Nora smiled at me over the rim of her own coffee mug. "Sounds like he's finally earning his keep, if you get my drift."

"Sounds like he's a good friend," I said firmly. "Why don't you call him and ask him to join us? And feel free to get hold of Rachel and Brent as well." I gave Nora my own wink. "Might as well have our own Poirot moment of sorts, right?"

My small house was soon crowded, but it was full of the ones I loved and was beginning to love, if I was honest with myself. Herc and Aggie ran back and forth happily from the living room to the kitchen and out the doggie door, while Max and Doc lay on the sofa between Roger and me, one head on each of our laps.

"Look what I got, Miss F." Brent held up a pink box full of Voodoo Doughnuts. "I thought you'd need some sugar to help you get over the, you know, the thing you did."

"You should've seen her," laughed Nora. She reached for a vanilla frosted Dirt Doughnut, the top covered with chunks of Oreo cookie. "I swear I had no idea she could do that with just a shoe." She held up the donut in a mock toast. "To Gwen, my best friend for life and the baddest woman I know."

"Here, here." Roger lifted the plain glazed donut he'd chosen, smiling at me over the two retrievers. "Here's to the end of another adventure and hope for a more peaceful future."

"Amen to that," muttered Marcus around a mouthful of chocolate donut. "I'm getting too old for this sort of thing."

"But not too old for some—"

I lifted both hands in the air. "And not another word, if you don't mind." I glanced around at Shelby, Rachel, and Brent, my eyebrows drawn together in a frown. "Little pitchers and all that other jazz."

Nora gave a nonchalant shrug. "I really don't know what you're talking about, Sis. I was just going to say Marcus isn't too old for some adventure of his own. If you know what I mean," she added quickly before I could stop her.

The young people exchanged furtive glances and then burst into laughter. Roger, to my horror, gave me a smile that sent a wave of—of *something* up and down my spine. Aggie and Herc, who'd just come back inside, yelped and headed for the backyard again. I wanted to follow them. Maybe I needed a Portland breeze to cool my face.

It wasn't quite the Poirot moment I had in mind, especially since none of us were suspects, but I did get to enjoy a wonderful time with some good friends. Only Louisa was missing, but she'd soon be back from an impromptu trip to the South Pacific. The case, as I'd come to think of it, had really taken its toll on her. She'd been a providential help, though, when we really needed it, and I looked forward to getting to know the "Lady of Portland" better.

Reaching over Max and Doc, I tapped Roger on the arm. There was the visit to the police station Nora and I needed to make, and I suddenly wanted him with me. Gone, it seemed, was the old Gwen Franklin, who was used to doing things for herself and by herself. It wasn't such a bad thing, either.

He set his coffee mug down and turned to look at me, those beautiful eyes surrounded by laugh wrinkles making me go weak at the knees. Leaning across the dogs, I planted a soft kiss on Roger's cheek, not caring who saw me.

"To a more peaceful future." I fought down the heat suffusing my face. "Unless you've got other plans?"

"Other plans?" His eyes twinkled as he leaned closer. "You'd better believe it."

And that, as Miss Marple would say with a contented smile, was that. I couldn't have agreed more.

Acknowledgments

There is not enough room to thank my mother for instilling the love of reading in me. Reading and writing go hand in hand, and without that foundation, I might not be writing these words today. So, thank you, Mama. And I miss you. I'd also like to give a shout-out to the world's best literary agent, Dawn Dowdle. What a gal! She holds high standards and insists that I measure up, and I'm grateful . . . even after she's read my efforts and made changes all over the place. And last but certainly not least, huge thanks to my dear friends Mary Paredes Karnes and Kate Young. Without their constant encouragement I'm not sure where my writing would be right now. Love you two!

If you enjoyed CAT'S MEOW
by
Dane McCaslin
Be sure not to miss the next book in the
The 2 Sisters Pet Valet Mysteries
PLAYING POSSUM
Turn the page for a quick peek at
PLAYING POSSUM
Enjoy!

Chapter 1

"What. The. Heck."

Nora Goldstein, my best friend, sat frozen in her living room, one manicured hand holding out a letter as if it had bitten her. We'd just arrived back at her apartment after a grueling hour spent chasing a runaway dog, and all I wanted to do was sit quietly without any drama. I liked running a business with Nora, I really did, but some days made me wish I'd stuck with my original plan of doing absolutely nothing following my early retirement from teaching.

Still, Two Sisters Pet Valet Services kept me in pocket money for those occasional shopping excursions to the local Goodwill, and now that my allergies were in check, spending time with animals kept my blood pressure down.

Except for days like today, of course.

Glancing now at Nora and the object she dangled from her fingers, I could see that *her* blood pressure was on the rise. Something had her slacks in a swivel, as my granny liked to say, although "slacks" was the furthest thing I could ever imagine on Nora.

Today she was dressed, as usual, in black yoga pants, a tight neon green top, and ankle-breaking stiletto heels. Compared to my faded denim capris and occasional skirts, billowy shirts, and comfy Birkenstocks, Nora looked like a tropical bird. The two of us couldn't have been any more different, and I liked to think that was the glue that had kept us together since our kindergarten days.

Watching her now as she sat staring at the letter, her eyes opened as wide as they could go, I knew that my wish for a drama-less afternoon was kaput.

"I guess you'd better tell me what's up before you blow a gasket." I struggled to sit up as I motioned to the letter. "Care to share, or should I read it to myself?"

"I'm not sure I believe what I'm seeing, Sis." She waved the letter in my direction. "You'd better read it and tell me what you think it says."

With a slight groan, I pushed myself up and shuffled over to where Nora sat, plopping down on the other end of the overstuffed sofa.

"I swear to goodness." I leaned down and rubbed my legs with both hands and wiggled my toes, wincing. "Not only are my dogs barking, my calves are mooing as well." I glanced at Nora, my mouth twisted in a grimace. "Take my advice and drop that maniac animal from our client list. I'm in no shape to chase that thing again, no matter how much his owner offers us."

"Already done." She leaned back against plump cushions and thrust the letter in my direction. "Read, please."

I opened it and carefully smoothed out the stationery with one hand, noting the address embossed at the top of the page. "Is this from your lawyer?"

Nora shook her head against the pillows. "Nope. It's from the lawyer that my ex used."

"Which ex?"

That wasn't a facetious question. Nora, bless her little romantic heart, had quite a collection of men who carried the label of "ex-husband." It was thanks to these exes and their various divorce settlements that she'd become a millionaire in her own right.

"Number three. The one I like to call the 'Bottomless Pitt.'"

"As in Hades?" I lifted one eyebrow in question. "That bottomless pit?"

"Of course, and the fact his last name is Pitt. And because he managed to hide more money than he admitted to having."

I looked back at the letter and quickly skimmed the information. The brief paragraph inserted between the greeting and the closing made my eyes widen, and I could see why Nora had reacted the way she did. Clearing my throat, I held the letter up and began to read aloud.

"'Dear Mrs. Pitt.'" I looked over at Nora. "Mrs. Pitt? When did you ever use that name?"

She chuckled. "I never did. I was always Nora Goldstein, just as I am now." She paused, head tilted. "Maybe that's why none of the marriages lasted."

I grunted, looking back at the letter. "Maybe it was because all five of them were absolute stinkers. Except possibly the Bottomless Pitt, it would seem. Why in the world did he appoint you as his executor? Had you seen him recently?"

"No, not since the divorce." She held up one hand, counting off silently on her fingers. "Let's see. It's been at least fourteen, fifteen years. I've seen his kids Merry and Martin more than I ever saw him."

"That's bizarre. Maybe he thought you were the most honest person in his life and could be trusted to handle this." I handed the letter back to her.

Nora gave a short laugh. "And that's a pretty sad commentary on his family, I'd say. Although," she gave a small hitch of one shoulder, "I might agree with him. Both of his offspring were absolutely despicable."

We sat silently for a few moments. I debated getting up and making coffee, but a twinge in my right leg changed my mind. Maybe I should give Brent a call. He'd be glad to come over and help. Actually, Brent would be glad to come over and escape his younger brother. I was about to make the suggestion when Nora abruptly stood and headed for the desk she kept in one corner of the living room. Tucked discreetly behind a folding Japanese screen, its shiny top held a state-of-the-art computer and printer.

I sat with my head leaning back against the cushions as I listened to Nora rummaging in the various desk drawers. What I really needed was a good, long soak in Epsom salts. Herc, my black-and-white rescue dog, would have to be contented to use the doggie door to leave the house to do his business.

I'd almost drifted off to sleep when the sound of a shot brought me straight up, my heart pounding as loudly as the bass drums in the high school marching band. Had someone broken in and targeted Nora?

"That rat. That unbelievable, absolutely despicable, downright irritating rat!"

Another loud bang told me exactly what had startled me. Nora was slamming desk drawers as loudly as she could.

"If you don't want your neighbors to think you're being attacked, I'd advise you to bring it down a notch or two."

My best friend marched from behind the screen, two bright spots of red on her cheeks.

"And to which rat are you referring? Marcus? The Bottomless Pitt?"

She glared at me as she shoved her cell phone into her top, which doubled as her carrying case, and kept marching past the sofa and down the hallway. A loud slam told me she'd gone into her room and closed the door.

Marcus Avery was Nora's on-again, off-again boyfriend, a private detective whose reputation as the local Lothario sometimes got him into hot water with her. I could never figure out why he was so attractive to the ladies, to be honest. His physique was on the rotund end of the scale, and his thinning hair topped a round face that had seen better days. Apparently, he had a charm that I couldn't detect. As long as he kept my friend happy, though, I was content to leave it at that.

My own taste in men tended to run toward retired dentists with laugh lines and a wonderful smile. Particularly one named Roger Smithson, owner of two aging golden retrievers named Max and Doc, and lately, I had to admit, of my heart. Just thinking about him gave my pulse a little jump, and I was grinning like a loon when Nora banged out of her room and stomped back to the sofa.

Giving me another glare, she barked, "What's got you so tickled? You think dealing with the Bottomless Pitt is funny?"

I came back to earth from the cloud on which I'd been floating, landing with a thud beside one very irate Nora. Something had put her panties into one king-sized twist. Maybe she'd spotted an unflattering review of Two Sisters Pet Valet on Yelp. Or maybe this last order from beyond the grave had her reliving the problems from her marriage to the occupier of said grave.

I stared back at her, my eyebrows riding near my hairline. "Funny? Apparently not."

Leaning over, I gently touched one arm. She was trembling, almost vibrating, under my hand, and I was instantly on guard. This wasn't like Nora, not at all. If I didn't get to the bottom of the issue soon, I was afraid she'd make herself sick.

"Nora?" I spoke quietly as I scooted closer, placing my arm around her thin shoulders. "You need to tell me what's wrong, okay?"

At first she sat there stiffly, acting as if she hadn't heard a word I'd said. I was tempted to shake her and make her talk, but I wasn't sure how she'd react in her present mood. Besides, we'd only had a handful of real disagreements over our decades of friendship, and I didn't want to chance one now.

Finally, she gave a deep sigh and leaned back against me. The crisis, as my role model Miss Marple would say, had passed. She'd tell me in her own time.

"Hey, you." I gave her shoulders a little squeeze and stood. "I'm going to get us some coffee, okay? Then we can talk about this."

She nodded but said nothing. I got the coffee made in record time and carried the steaming mugs back into the living room. Handing her one, I took the other and reseated myself on the other end of the sofa.

"I'm not well-versed in the law and wills and that sort of stuff." I took a cautious sip of coffee and winced. It was still too hot to drink, but the aroma of the smooth Ethiopian blend was delicious. "Do you have to abide by your ex's request?"

Nora gave a half-hearted shrug. "I'm pretty sure it's binding, especially since he used a lawyer." She took a small drink of coffee. "Knowing him like I do, that man didn't leave any loose ends. And that's not what's bothering me, if that's what you're getting at."

"Ah." I looked at her, scrutinizing her face for any hint of what had made her so angry. When none was forthcoming, I decided to change tack. Whether she liked it or not, I'd get it out of her eventually. "If I were you, I'd make an appointment with the lawyer and get the scoop on what your role really is." I kept my tone neutral, still observing her closely.

"Oh, believe you me, I intend to do just that." Nora's lips were a firm line of annoyance. "I wouldn't put it past him to get in one last dig, you know? He never got over the settlement I got after our divorce." She gave a short, unamused laugh. "What a piece of work."

I gave her an uneasy look. She was beginning to sound cynical, something that wasn't like Nora. She could be sarcastic, certainly, but cynicism wasn't in her style book.

"What? Do I have something on my face?" Nora attempted a smile, but I wasn't fooled.

I hadn't been best friends with her for as long as I had to not be able to know when something was bothering her.

"You make that appointment and I'll go with you." I lifted my coffee mug in a salute. "One for all and all for one, right?"

She snorted. "Yep, that's us, for sure. The Two Musketeers."

I was glad to hear her sense of humor beginning to resurrect itself. "Then let's get this show on the road." I glanced at my cell phone. "It's early enough to cancel tomorrow morning's pet-sitting assignments. You can let the office know we can be there first thing tomorrow."

"No need." Nora's tone became brisk, businesslike. "Between Brent and Rachel, they can handle the jobs."

"If you say so." I frowned slightly as I mentally counted off the jobs. "I think we might need to hire another dog walker and free up Rachel to take on more of the pet-sitting assignments."

"Have anyone in mind?" Nora gave me a mischievous grin. "Maybe a certain gent who happens to like dogs?"

I wanted to stick out my tongue. Instead, I lifted my chin haughtily. "I don't know what you're talking about."

"And the Bottomless Pitt was the sweetest man on the face of this earth." Nora shook her head in wry amusement. "You call Roger and ask if he'll help us out. I'll get busy calling this lawyer."

Talking on the phone was never my favorite thing, and the advent of texting in place of actually speaking to a faceless voice had made my life easier. I never minded a face-to-face exchange, but there was something inherently awkward about carrying on a conversation with someone I couldn't see.

Still, texting Roger instead of calling him seemed somehow discourteous, as if he wasn't important enough for a call. I opened my contact list and found his name.

He answered on the first ring, and his cheerful voice made me smile. "Gwen! How nice to hear from you."

I heard the muted sounds of a television in the background.

He went on. "How are you today? Anything new and exciting?"

"Not unless you call getting a letter from an ex-husband exciting."

There was a momentary silence from his end of the line. "An ex-husband, you said? I thought you'd never been married."

I chuckled, imagining the expression on his face as he tried to figure this out. "Not *my* ex. One of Nora's." At this, my best friend turned to stare at me, one eyebrow lifted. I waggled mine in return. "Apparently one of them made her the executor of his will, and now she's got to talk to the lawyer. I said I'd go with her."

"Aha. That makes more sense." The sound of canned laughter rose in the background. "Give me a sec, would you? I need to shut this thing off."

"Sounds like you're watching 'All in a Day's Work.' Those candid camera type shows can get really silly."

"Indeed they can." There was silence as he clicked off the television. "Now, where were we?"

"I was calling to see if you could lend a hand tomorrow with the pet business." I shifted around on the couch, trying to find a more comfortable way to sit that didn't make my legs ache more. "Rachel and Brent will be here, of course, but with Nora and me at the lawyer's office, I'm afraid they won't be able to handle it all."

"Not a problem," Roger said instantly. "I'd be happy to walk a few dogs for you."

"Oh, that's great." I gave Nora a thumbs-up. "I'm sure there'll only be one, maybe two at the most."

"Fine. What time would you like me to be there? I'm assuming I'll start off at Nora's place, right?"

I paused, trying to think through the list of appointments. "Hang on a moment, Roger. I need to check before I give you the wrong information."

Nora was leaning against her desk, polished fingernails tapping an impatient staccato on its shiny surface. "They've got me on hold, if you can believe it. *And* I'm stuck listening to some God-awful pop song that sounds like a cat getting its tail pulled." She shook her head in disgust. "What was wrong with good ol' elevator music, I ask you? At least I didn't have to hear 'ooh ooh baby baby' over and over."

I distractedly waved her complaints away. "Listen, Roger said he'll be glad to help tomorrow. I just need to know if he should come over here in the morning or go straight to the client's house."

"Whatever you think." Nora's continuous fingernail tapping was getting on my nerves. "It might be easier to send him a text with the client's information. Everything's already open on my iPad." She pointed with her chin to the desk where the tablet lay. "The list for tomorrow is right there on the first page." Her fingers paused in mid-tap as she listened to something on the other end of the line. "And it's about time too. Do you have any idea how appalling your hold music is?"

I shook my head, smiling to myself as I grabbed the iPad from her desk. A sassy Nora was a normal Nora. And if that lawyer had any sense about him, he'd better be ready with all barrels locked and loaded, or at least with some answers.

My job would be to get answers from Nora, including what it was that had suddenly set her off. Was the Ghost of Rotten Husbands Past about to make a visit? If so, it had better be warned: no one messed with my best friend, and I'd do everything in my power to see they didn't, no matter if they were dead or alive.

About the Author

Dane McCaslin, *USA Today* bestselling author of the Proverbial Crime mystery series, is a lifelong writer whose love of mysteries was formed early in life. At age eight, she discovered Agatha Christie—much to her mother's dismay—and began devouring any and all books she could find that featured murder and mayhem. After retiring from her career as a high school and community college English teacher, Dane now devotes her newly found freedom to writing mystery novels . . . and reading for pleasure.

Printed in the United States
by Baker & Taylor Publisher Services